Those
in Peril

A Novel
by
John Frain

Front Cover Illustration:
Detail from "Holocaust off the Coast of America"
Oil painting by the marine artist John Hamilton, 1985.
Reproduced by kind permission of Christine Cox on behalf of Mrs B Hamilton
Photograph © Christine Rigby, 2005.

First Published 2005 jointly by Countyvise Limited, 14 Appin Road, Birkenhead, Wirral CH41 9HH in conjunction with author Dr. J. P. A. Frain.

Copyright © 2005 John Frain

The right of John Frain to be identified as the author of this work has been asserted by him in accordance with the Copyright, Design and Patents Act 1988.

British Library Cataloguing in Publication Data.
A catalogue record for this book is available from the British Library.

Please note: From 1st January 2007 ISBNs will contain 13 numbers these numbers will be the same as the present number printed below the barcode (ie. starting 978). Countyvise is showing both existing (10 digit) and future (13 digit) ISBNs on the Title page verso. Please continue to use the 10 figure number until 31st December 2006.

ISBN 1 901231 58 5   ISBN 987 1 901231 58 8

Eternal Father, strong to save,
whose arm doth bind the restless wave,
who bidd'st the mighty ocean deep,
its own appointed limits keep:
O hear us when we cry to thee
For those in peril on the sea.

W. Whiting (1825 – 78)

Detail from Merchant Navy Memorial at Pier Head, Liverpool.
© Christine Rigby 2005.

DEAR READER,
BEFORE YOU BEGIN THE STORY...
MAY I DETAIN YOU FOR A FEW MINUTES? I WOULD
GREATLY APPRECIATE YOUR ATTENTION.

I wrote this novel for three reasons:

(i)   to draw attention to the sacrifice made by merchant seamen during the Battle of the Atlantic, 1939 – 1945;

(ii) to illustrate that, in spite of these sacrifices, these men were treated with indifference and even hostility by some sections of a nation they had helped to save; and

(iii) to pay homage to the courage and steadfastness of the wives, mothers and families involved, for they contributed significantly to our final success.

This novel is a work of fiction set in a factual framework. Now, what does this mean exactly? Simply this....(i) the technical and historical details of the Battle itself, the convoy system, the Merseyside "blitz", the locations in which the story takes place etc., are all based on solid fact; but that (ii) woven within this framework is a fictional story peopled by fictional characters.

Here I must add the important disclaimer that since this is a work of fiction, any resemblance to real organisations, past or present, or actual persons, living or dead, is completely unintended and wholly coincidental. That said, however, almost all the specific incidents in the story, including those pertaining to the treatment of merchant seamen, are based on fact.

Thank you for reading what is, in effect, the author's preface. No part of a book is as intimate as the preface.

In it, the author emerges from his anonymity and speaks to his reader person-to-person. However, it is part of the folk lore that the author's preface is rarely read so I have adopted this informal approach hoping it will help me put some important points to you.

Just one other thing – you will see from the Acknowledgements section that many people have helped me in my efforts to tell you a realistic and, I hope, interesting story. In thanking them sincerely I must add that the responsibility for any errors is mine and mine alone.

John Frain
Liverpool, 2005

Acknowledgements

I would like to thank the many people who gave me encouragement and assistance during the preparation of "Those in Peril".

Captain Colin Lee, Master Mariner; Canon Bob Evans, previously Port Chaplain at Cardiff and Liverpool; Lieutenant Commander Brian Murphy R.N.; Captain Christopher Ryden, M.N.; Father Benedict Webb O.S.B. former naval surgeon, and Stuart Wood, Mersey river pilot and broadcaster, all gave me excellent specialist advice without which the novel would have been deficient. Colin Lee, on whom no call for assistance ever proved fruitless, also supplied the drawings for each chapter.

When the original short story, on which the novel is based, was broadcast in 8 abridged episodes, the "team" at B.B.C. Radio Merseyside were wonderfully supportive. Caroline Adams oversaw the production of the project with understanding and real commitment; Jimmy McCracken read each episode with passion and skill, emerging as a superb "Kevin Donnelly"; Roger Phillips, Presenter, was a fine "anchor man" encouraging interest in the projected novel in very many ways. I should also mention Angela Heslop, and again, Jimmy McCracken, for both of them encouraged my early attempts at writing fiction by producing short stories of mine.

Isabel Ferguson, Therese de Rouffignac, Rene Wheatcroft, Neil Verdin, Ivy MacDonald and Lisa Morris provided a great deal of background information on both the Merseyside area and the district of Toxteth in earlier times. Isabel was also a tireless helper in the quarrying of data from archival and other sources. Here I must mention the excellent help of Kevin Roach and his colleagues at the Liverpool Record Office and that of the staff at the Archive Section of the Merseyside Maritime Museum.

Mr John Taylor, Orthopaedic Specialist and Dr John P.J. Frain gave careful attention to, and advice on, the medical aspects of the novel.

Ruth Frain deserves a special mention and my deepest thanks. From the "ideas stage" she has been a tower of strength, shepherding both the short story and the novel through its various drafts and offering much valuable advice on the development and marketing of the project.

Pauline Carter, Paula and John Laird, Jean Lee, Martin Lynch, Anne Frain, Dr Anna Frain, Peter Frain, Father David Morland OSB and Eveline Paulson have all taken a keen interest in my efforts to write fiction and have offered their encouragement and support. John Davies, editor of "Clayfield", my volume of short stories due for publication soon, deserves grateful mention under this heading. Finally, a word on Christine Rigby, photographer to the project... "superb" will do.

"Authorship of any sort is a fantastic indulgence of the ego. It is as well, no doubt, to reflect on how much one owes to others."

J.K. Galbraith,
The Affluent Society.

Introduction

1.   This is a story with the Battle of the Atlantic, in World War Two, as its background. Although a work of fiction almost all its incidents are based on fact.

2.   The Battle was the longest of the War. It began a few hours after the War started and lasted for nearly six years.

3.   Britain's merchant seamen were unarmed civilians. On every voyage they faced death and mutilation in order to bring in the food, oil and war materials without which the nation would have been defeated and overrun. In this regard, Winston Churchill said that the only factor which gave him cause for lasting concern was the U-boat menace. He added that although many gallant actions and unbelievable feats of endurance are matters of record, "the deeds of those who perished will never be known."

4.   When the Battle ended, Britain had lost 2,426 ships and 29,180 of her merchant seamen. In relation to the total number involved this loss of life was of greater proportion than occurred in any of the armed services. To this figure must be added the hundreds who were wounded or maimed for life.

5.   The North Atlantic is wracked by violent storms. Its turbulence is unceasing and its cold winds chill mariners to the bone. It was the second great enemy the skill and bravery of the Merchant Navy had to face and overcome.

6.   There was a one-in-three chance of going to a cold, unmarked grave yet no single seaman ever refused to sail. It seems unbelievable then that, at the end of the War, in the general thanksgiving and recognition of heroism, the magnificent dedication of our merchant seamen went largely unremarked. Apart from the dedicated War memorials (for example in Liverpool and London), very few of Britain's other memorials mention any of them.

Contents

Dedication

This novel is dedicated to all the
merchant seamen who gave their
lives during the Battle of the Atlantic
(1939-1945), and to their wives and families.

Chapter One

The Injury

C-r-a-c-k! No knowledge of anatomy was needed...it was a bone breaking. Players and spectators winced. A second ago the air had been bursting with the yellings and urgings of opposing supporters. Now there was silence.

This was broken when Sam Hilditch, Toxteth Celtic's trainer and general factotum, was helping the injured player, Kevin Donnelly, from the pitch. A brawny man with florid features shouldered his way through the spectators and strode forward. He thrust his face into Donnelly's:

"Serves you bloody well right!"

The trainer put out his arm to protect his player:
"Mo......don't be a divvy......the lad's hurt!"
Mo(ses) Jolliffe muttered malignantly then returned to the group of spectators where he had been holding court. He tried to take up his denigration of Donnelly, but now his companions shifted uneasily or looked away.

A man acting as the unofficial referee came over to Hilditch and the injured player:
"How's it look?"
Hilditch had removed Donnelly's left boot and shin-pad. As the youth gasped and twisted, he eased off the sock and pointed to the area around the ankle. It was already swollen significantly....
"I think it's broken".
"Sounded like it," said the referee, who patted the player on the shoulder then straightened up:
"What d'you want to do? There's twenty five minutes to go. As it's only a friendly, if you don't want to carry on with ten men, we can abandon it".

It was an afternoon at the beginning of August 1940. The rules of soccer did not yet permit substitutes for injured players hence the referee's oblique reference to the handicap of playing with ten men.
"I'll just have a word with our captain," said Hilditch. The Celtic captain, Martin Tynan, glanced quickly around his team for a reaction and said: "We'll play on."

It was a courageous decision. The Toxteth men were already 3-0 down to Woolton M.O. The Woolton team was made up of clerks and junior officials employed by the Liverpool Corporation and other Governmental institutions in the City. These "municipal officers", hence the title Woolton M.O., were more popularly known as the "Wolves". The nickname derived from the fact that the old village was originally a farmstead belonging to Wulf, a Scandinavian, who gave his name to the previous Roman settlement. It was a happy coincidence that "Wolves" was a title of some significance in football circles.

The "Wolves" had always played second fiddle to a Toxteth team which, in the schools' leagues, then in the amateur leagues, had swept all before it. Now in this pre-season "warm-up", the "Wolves", with grim satisfaction, were turning the tables on Celtic.

However, Kevin Donnelly's injury, though basically self-inflicted, seemed to take the fire out of the rest of the game. The "Wolves" played it at a sedate pace adding only one more goal to their total. The first sign of the altered atmosphere was when one of the "Wolves" had gone to a group of his own supporters, retrieved his army greatcoat, and sprinted down to where Donnelly sat in pain and bitter disconsolation.

"Put this 'round you mate", said the Woolton player, a soldier on embarkation leave.

Kevin was embarrassed:

"I'll be O.K."

"No, go on.....it'll keep you warm 'till they get you back to change."

Without waiting for an answer he draped the greatcoat around Kevin's shoulders and tucked him into it.

As the soldier sprinted back, a girl who had been watching the match from the far side of the pitch began to walk anxiously around the touchlines towards Donnelly.

"What have you done, Kev?" she asked as she arrived.

Though he recognised the girl's voice he did not look up:

"What's it look like?"

The girl sighed:

"Don't be an apeth. I was only askin'."

In a more civil tone, he said:

"I've sprained it".

"No........Sammy says it's broken!", she insisted. His bad manners returned:

"I've sprained it!"

She was determined not to take offence, and after a minute or so, suggested she might help him make the short journey back to the changing rooms in the Dingle Vale School. The pitch was at the rear of the School. The teams were using it because it was one of the few pitches that had not been dug up for Britain's wartime campaign to grow more of its own food. He did not react to her idea so they watched the match in silence.

As Kevin sat there, twisting and turning to get relief from his pain, Sam Hilditch stepped back from his touchline exhortations of Celtic and rummaged in a battered leather bag. He drew out an Army issue water bottle, its khaki flannel covering and leather strapwork still in place.

"Get some o' that down yer," he prompted.

The youth took the bottle, but in disgust spat out what he was about to swallow.

"Hey!", said Hilditch, furiously: "I made that up that from my own tea ration – two ounces a week – an' you're wastin' it!"

"It's foul," said Kevin, unrepentant, picking the tea leaves from his lips and tongue.

The girl glanced at Kevin with bewilderment and anger:

"Barm pot," she murmured.

Her name was Kathleen Gallagher. She was a seventeen year-old from Toxteth, with a mass of auburn hair and the freckles to go with it. She was pretty, as the wolf whistles marking her progress around the touchlines had attested. She had deep feelings for Kevin Donnelly and could not remember when it had been otherwise.

As she glanced at him again her resentment softened.

Recently things had gone badly for him. In March, his father's ship had been torpedoed. A lifeboat had been found, but all its occupants, including Joe Donnelly, were dead. In June, the professional football club where he had been apprenticed told him it would not be "retaining his registration", code for "we don't think you'll ever make the grade".

She knew him better than he realised. He was not as surly and indifferent as he had recently appeared – and he ought not to have played in this game. His mind had been elsewhere. She knew how he played at his best. Today there had been no sign of it. She would try again to dispel his gloom,

"Don't be upset, Kevin," she said soothingly,.... "specially not by this load o'sconeheads," indicating Mo Jolliffe and his crowd. Then for reassurance she added:

"You've just had an off-day. That's all. I'll bet Dixie Dean has off days."

Her ruse failed, for Kevin's disdain deepened:

"Kathie.....what do you know about football? Don't talk like a ha'penny book. Look....." He was pointing to the pitch, but before he could say more she cut in:

"P'raps I don't know much – 'cept what a misery you are!"

To the jeers of the Jolliffe cohort she stormed away.

Donnelly had been about to point out the player who had devastated the Celtic defence. With only minutes to go, here he was still, with his swerves, dummies, dribbling and perfect passes. Everyone watched in wonder. The youth's name was Laurie Mather. Kevin had been around professional footballers for three years. He had seen them in practice matches and first-team games – the "stars" and the journeymen. Yet he had seen nothing to match the strength, skill, speed and polish of this inside-right on this pitch today. From the first whistle his display was proving to be a bewilderingly clever masterpiece.

Kevin recalled all that had happened before and during the match. There had been the usual banter when the teams were changing. Good naturedly, the Woolton contingent were reminded that Celtic were the inevitable winners in all they undertook and the "Wolves" were the inevitable runners-up.

"An' you're going to be up the cooey this time an' all," grinned Martin Tynan, Toxteth's centre-half.

The Woolton secretary, an affable man at all times, smiled more broadly than ever:

"Ah......but we've got a secret weapon!"

He pointed to a young chap putting on his kit. The player was just below average height and his face was slender. However, his shoulders were remarkably broad and his arms and thighs were hefty. Uncomfortable at being singled out, he smiled weakly and turned away to put on his boots. Martin Tynan would not be put off:

"Ah' whadda you do for a livin', besides bein' a secret weapon?"

The lad was embarrassed.

"I'm a trainee accountant with the Customs service," he answered quietly.

To the general mirth Tynan retorted:

"Well you'll need a head for figures, 'cos we're gonna bairst your ball today, wack."

Tynan's forecast was grossly wrong. This became clear in the very first minutes of the game. And no Celtic player was filled with more foreboding than Kevin Donnelly. He was Toxteth's left half-back ("left midfield" in today's terminology). One of his tasks was to stifle the efforts of inside-right Mather, the "secret weapon".

These days a player of Mather's guile and skill would play "in the hole behind the striker(s)." In the nineteen forties, five forwards played in line abreast. As well as being strikers in their own right, the right and left inside-forwards typically used their positional sense to find the open spaces where they could give and receive defence-splitting passes. This would not do for Laurie Mather, as he signalled when the game had barely started for, receiving the ball, he made directly for his "marker", Kevin Donnelly. Kevin, nonplussed, moved forward to dispossess him.

With sublime assurance, Mather brought the ball up to him, arched his body in one direction and as the Celtic man was committing himself to a tackle, swayed in the other direction and moved off at speed.

"Missed 'im, Donnelly!" jeered Mo Jolliffe, whose companions were much amused.

In the meantime, Mather had pushed a delightfully judged pass between two "Celtic" defenders. The Woolton left winger came streaking in towards it. With an enormous effort, Martin Tynan just reached the ball before him and clattered it to safety over his own crossbar.

Toxteth Celtic's past success had been based on solid, near-impregnable, defence. Sam Hilditch, an ex-professional who had scouted for more than one of England's top clubs, had schooled his defenders.... half-backs, full-backs and goalkeeper, to function as a cohesive unit. Now, thanks to inside-right Mather, their system was in shreds. His technique of bringing the ball to opponents then body swerving out of sight was pulling Toxteth's players so badly out of position the team was becoming ragged and disorganised.

In spite of his experience as an apprentice-professional Kevin was unable to cope with Mather's wiles. For one thing Mather varied his stride so subtly it was impossible to keep pace with him stride for stride. At times Kevin would react a split second too late to a shortened stride and discover that Mather had changed direction, gone behind him, and was now cutting in towards goal at a different angle.

"Missed 'im again, Donnelly," Mo Jolliffe would yell, though the merriment of his hangers-on was now more subdued, as Celtic seemed booked for a drubbing.

Another problem the "secret weapon" gave Celtic stemmed from his variations in pace. Occasionally he would make for their goal at three-quarter pace, lure Kevin into coming abreast of him, then accelerate at full stretch. As Kevin lunged after him in order to get in his tackle Mather would suddenly reduce his pace or stop altogether. This meant that Kevin had either tackled fresh air or gone charging on into no-man's-land. On every occasion when Mather left the Toxteth boy mesmerised the call would go up:

"Missed 'im again, Donnelly!"

By this time Celtic's supporters were feeling that Jolliffe's baiting had become unreasonable and damaging to their team's confidence. When one of them called:

"Either support the team Mo, or bag off!", there were cheers for the caller.

Despite the valiant efforts of Martin Tynan and others it became obvious that sooner or later the "Celtic" goal must succumb. Inevitably it did so, thanks to magnificent orchestration by Laurie Mather. In the thirty-fifth minute a Woolton half-back pushed the ball forward to him. More sublime technique as he gathered it and pivoted in a single silken movement.

This time he made for the right wing with Donnelly pounding after him. Kevin came up to his left shoulder and stayed neck and neck with him so as to force him towards the corner flag. This might then cut out the prospect of Mather lofting the ball into Celtic's goalmouth. Within two feet of the flag, Mather suddenly stopped, dragged back the ball with the toe of his right boot, twisted around with lighting speed, looked up and with his left foot floated a beautiful cross in the path of the "Wolves" centre forward who obliging battered it into Celtic's net without breaking his stride. Before the Woolton supporters erupted everyone was stunned by an exhibition of such balance, speed and skill they could barely believe what they had witnessed.

Mather had a decisive hand in two more Woolton goals and the game's second half was twenty minutes old when Kevin Donnelly became badly injured. Still tormented by the Woolton player's artistry and the constant barracking of Mo Jolliffe he went into a despairing tackle again a fraction too late. As he lost his balance his foot slithered on soft earth and he felt his left leg curving beneath him. He came down on top of it. The fearsome sound of breaking bone was heard and he was subsequently assisted from the pitch.

Dispirited, their morale in tatters, the Celtic players were immensely relieved to hear the final whistle. Secretly they were surprised to have escaped with defeat by a four goal margin only. Disconsolately, and helping Kevin Donnelly, they set out on a silent walk back to the changing rooms. When almost there they were joined by Mo Jolliffe who thrust his face forward again, this time towards trainer Sam Hilditch. The Celtic players began exchanging hostile words with Jolliffe, but Hilditch waved them on towards the School.

"See to Kevin," he said and then tensely, he turned to face Jolliffe:

"Well?"

"I take it our Tommy'll be in the team next week.... like he shudda bin this week......?"

Hilditch was on the verge of violence:

"Mo, you're a 'ard-faced get to come asking me questions after your carry-on today!"

"My lad shouldn't uv bin dropped! When Donnelly tried to turn pro you were glad of Tommy then! He's helped you win cups and championships for three years. Then as soon as that reject comes back, you drop him!"

"I pick what I think's the best team. Your Tommy understood that. 'e didn't get a cob on about it."

"Best team?.......best team?.......why d'yer think you've bin dumped four nothing? Donnelly's a cack-handed camel!"

"You did your bit to get us beat, didn't you Mo? You didn't come to support us. You come to start a barney. The way you got after Kevin was a disgrace. If his injury's a bad 'un, you've had a hand in it. An' remember this – he didn't pick the team, I did!"

"My lad's a better player than 'im, We've got better players than 'im in our back entry."

Hilditch pointed towards the hobbling Kevin Donnelly:

"Well, I'll tell you summat – I'll never lose faith in that lad. If he gets over this injury, he could be another Frankie Soo. You'll see."

Hilditch was a native of Prescot. He had watched the development of Hong Yi ("Frankie") Soo first as a brilliant schoolboy player then as a superb force in the Prescot Cables team which played in the Cheshire County League. Soo had signed for Stoke City, then a top-flight club, in 1933. With his performances at left half he had thrilled the Stoke supporters and was destined to follow the young Stanley Matthews into the England team.

In every movement of Kevin Donnelly, Sam Hilditch could see Frankie Soo. He would never change his opinion of Donnelly's promise.

"Look – forget the abbadabba – will Tommy be playin' next week or not?" Jolliffe demanded.

"I'm not goin' to discuss that with you, Mo. I'll see who's fit next week then I'll pick our best team."

This did not satisfy Jolliffe:

"If Donnelly's so good, why wasn't he signed up as a professional?

"It's a long story. The club nabbed him quick enough... then did nothing with 'im. They're a first-team club. No idea how to bring youngsters on. I've told you – Kevin can still make it."

"Tommy's always done 'is wack for you – he's never let you down."

"I know that Mo an' if I think Tommy should play, he'll play. What with lads getting' called up, an' injuries, I don't know what the team'll be until match day."

Jolliffe looked doubtful and before he strode off could not resist adding:

"You'll do no good with this manky lot – 'cept in a beer belly and tattoos league!"

When Hilditch reached the school he found Kevin Donnelly being helped to change by the others. He pointed to the injured leg:

"How is it now?"

"Sore, but it should go down when I've rested."

"It needs lookin' at!........I'll come to the Southern with yer...."

"No! no!," Kevin protested. "If it's no better in the morning I'll see about it."

"Kevin....you can't take chances......think about your future!"

"It's only a sprain, Sam....."

"It's bust, Kev..... they could 'ear it over at the tram sheds."

This was Martin Tynan and since the tram sheds were at the junction of Aigburth Road and Ullet Road some distance away, this had to rank as one of his better bon mots.

"It'll be O.K."

"It's bloody broken!" bawled Hilditch, exasperated.

"If it is, I'll see to it!"

Hilditch clenched his hands and paced the Dingle Vale dressing room, a cloakroom full of narrow benches and small clothes pegs.

"How're you goin' to get home?"

"I'll rest my duff leg on the pedal and push the bike along with my other foot."

The barrage of protests was of no avail: as soon as Kevin had gathered his kit he stuffed it into a carrier bag and departed. Trainer and players rushed to the School entrance to see him go,

To lessen Sam's concern, one of the players said: "He looks steady enough."

"I wish his father was around," Sam sighed, "he wouldn't let him mess about with that leg."

It was Martin Tynan's turn to calm the situation:

"P'raps it's as well to leave 'im on his own. He's got ter get today's match out of 'is system."

By now Kevin had crossed Dingle Lane and was pushing his bicycle wearily up Dingle Mount. Halfway up the slope he had to rest – to catch his breath and ease his aching ankle. At the top of the Mount he turned left into South Hill Road and freewheeled carefully down its broad back into Cockburn Street. When he reached its junction with Beresford Road he was about to turn down towards his home when he saw his mother kneeling on the pavement before the front door. As he peered at his mother, Kathleen Gallagher, the girl with the auburn hair, stepped back into a doorway so as not to be noticed. She had followed him from Dingle Vale to assure herself he could make the journey.

Kevin continued watching his mother for an

instant. She had cleaned the doorstep and now rubbed it energetically with a wetted donkeystone. Next the resulting ochre coloured paste would be smoothed over to give the step a clean, cared-for finish. War or no war, "stepstoning" was important and could not be neglected. To complete the ritual Kevin then knew that she would clean the bricks above the step to the left and right of the door. The patina on the bricks was testament to the years of attention they had received from Liz Donnelly's steaming floor-cloth.

Toxteth folk spoke of her respectfully as a "clean woman." Cleanliness was one of her distinguishing characteristics, in truth her obsession. This was why her sons' surplices were always the cleanest on the altar, why their linen was always the whitest in the classroom, why every vase and figurine was purged of every hiding speck of dust and why the massive Victorian cast-iron fireplace had been black-leaded so gleamingly it had the commanding presence of a Wurlitzer organ.

Sadly, another of her characteristics was the inability to give or receive affection, at least in the usual sense. Kevin had noticed this whenever his father was departing for sea-service. His proferred kisses were rapidly turned away onto her cheek and, seemingly, she received them with impatience. Her way of loving his father was to ensure that his shirts were ironed immaculately, that every garment he put on had been assiduously "aired off" and that she slipped him a shilling when his lack of fortune would otherwise have deprived him of male company.

Her son knew that if she spotted his injury now there would be no tender concern, no laying on of hands. Instead she would scold him without pause for getting injured and plague him to see a doctor. He remembered well enough how she would make him feel ashamed when he caught a cold – but would then trudge the streets, whatever the weather, to find him the appropriate remedy.

One other thing was clear: in spite of her implacable exterior, the loss of his father had broken her heart. So she missed Vincent, her soldier son, profoundly and had now fallen back on him, her other son, not only for the comfort and support of his presence, but to give her life purpose. Knowing all this, and in this luckless period of his own life, Kevin knew that he could not endure the burst of recrimination news of his injury would bring. So he resolved to conceal it and bear the pain until it had abated.

Instead of going home immediately he turned his bicycle around, pushed it the short distance to the top of Gosford Street, then freewheeled cautiously down its significant slope. This brought him on to Grafton Street from where he could look out over the Brunswick Dock and the river in solitary contemplation of his injury and the mortifying failure of his hopes for a career in professional soccer. When he was sufficiently composed he would return home. In the meantime, Kathleen Gallagher, unobserved, continued watching.

Back at Dingle Vale the teams had changed and departed. Sam Hilditch and the Woolton Secretary were leaving. Hilditch had discovered the latter's name was Russell Fishlock. With the relaxed informality of the Merseysider he said:

"Well done, Russ....you murdered us today."

"I told you we had a secret weapon," smiled Fishlock.

"He was mustard alright. I s'pose the professional clubs know about him.....(?)"

"One or two have been sniffing 'round, but frankly he's not that bothered. He's set on being an accountant."

"Well, you'll be hard to beat with 'im in the side,"

"Unfortunately, that won't happen. He's just had his call-up papers – due at Catterick on Monday."

The two shook hands and as they parted the Woolton man said:

"I'm sorry about your lad."

"Yeah well.........it was a wild tackle.   Kevin was somewhere else today....but that's takin' nothin' away from young Mather."

Then they went their separate ways.

Nearby the orange glow of a Mersey sunset was pushing its edges onto the pitch.   Over the touchlines a solitary seabird wheeled and swooped.   It rested momentarily in one of the goalmouths, but after some fruitless rooting among the stud-marks it soared away.

The pitch was now deserted, a little desolate even. There was nothing to mark the magnificent display that had occurred there, though Toxteth would talk of it for years to come – until the young had tired of the tale told by the old, that is.

Chapter Two

Path to the Atlantic

That settled it – he would go to sea. All day Kevin had wandered aimlessly, on trams, off trams, angry and bitter. Despite his injured ankle he had walked a lot too – down Ranelagh Street, into the City Centre, back to Toxteth – all to ease his anger.

Now it was evening and he was close to home. He looked down...across Brunswick Dock to the river. The Mersey glowed as the sun set. Its sunsets were always fascinating but tonight he was more interested in the crumpled card he held. When the letter-box had clattered he knew his grade-card had arrived. It must say "A.1". Instead it stated he was unfit for military service.

During the call-up medical he was asked to walk across a room. He thought he had heard the doctor murmur "oh dear". His left ankle was examined but there was no comment. The rest of it went well so he felt soon he would join his brother Vincent in the King's Regiment. Now that wouldn't happen.

He felt shame as much as anger. Friends and relatives were off to the war but he would have to skulk around skirting the whispering. And they would whisper: some with pity, others with contempt.

When the appalling news had arrived, Kevin's thoughts had turned, instinctively, to his father, whose wise words and sympathetic smiles would have done much to ease his anguish. As when the football club had rejected him, he had an overwhelming desire to be in touch with his father, some way. So today, when he had stepped down from the tram at the Lewis's building, he had retraced one of the walks he and his brother had made with him. More than once between sailings, Joe Donnelly had taken the schoolboys down Ranelagh Street, along Hanover Street, into Paradise Street and Canning Place, returning by way of Park Lane and Jamaica Street, across Parliament Street then, the last leg, along Grafton Street to home.

Today, as his walk progressed, Kevin had noted again the buildings and their features which his father had pointed out with such pride. First, the Mersey Mission to Seamen building at the corner of Paradise Street, with its rich ornamentation of terracotta and coloured bricks. He had said this was where sailors had a warm, comfortable place to sleep, eat and read and where they would be encouraged to save rather than squander their money.

Next into Canning Place. The Sailors' Home was nearby. With its superb turrets at each corner it had been built in the style of great country houses. The grandeur of this building had made a great impression on the boys and their father was keen to draw their attention to the ornamental work at its front entrance. Above the doors was a finely modelled replica of the great Liver Bird and around it the stuff of sea and ships – trophies, medallions, ropework, capstans and pulley blocks – all richly detailed in the stone.

And the Home had an even greater surprise for them because its interior was built like the interior of a ship – with the accommodation for the sailors leading off a great gallery on each floor. Kevin also had a personal memory of their visit. They had been introduced to Danny Killen, an old shipmate of their father's. Kevin recalled how the seaman had sat on the edge of his bed, white haired and tired now, but with bright eyes and a keen brain. He had asked the two of them about their schooling and their favourite subjects. When Kevin had said "Writing and Composition," old Danny had said "Well, I've got something for you." His gift was a Swan fountain pen which Kevin still treasured. His father had said: "it must have cost him at least two pounds."

Finally Kevin stood before the Custom House. Joe Donnelly had explained it was built after the manner of a great Greek temple. He had said that in 1823 it had been constructed as the largest building in the town. There was little or no ornamentation on its façade: the very scale of it provided its majesty and dignity.

On his way home he thought a great deal about his father's scholarship. He had gone to sea with little schooling yet he used such words as "pediment", "portico", "atrium", and "classical" with an obvious understanding of their meaning. Kevin knew that neighbours and shipmates said that he had "read every book in the Library." Nor did they say this dismissively, as if he were a "doley" striving to fill in his day, but respectfully, recognising him as a tireless self-educator. He had left his sons standards to aim for.

Nearing the end of his journey, Kevin narrowly escaped further injury. He had emerged from the Toxteth end of Jamaica Street and, preoccupied with pain and fatigue, had almost stepped into the path of a lorry ascending Parliament Street from the Docks. Before gaining the pavement on the far side of the street he had avoided by a hair's breadth another lorry which was going down to the Docks. The experience held fast his attention so that a minute later when he stubbed his foot on the edge of a Grafton Street paving stone he could not prevent his headlong fall to the ground at the entrance to Toxteth Brewery.

A dray horse leaving the Brewery had reared in fright and though Kevin covered his head for safety he could see the sparks and hear the clatter as iron horseshoes slammed down onto granite setts.

"W...h...o...a!......whoa!.....whoa!",
yelled the drayman, pulling at the flying reins with his great arms to control the animal.

When the commotion had subsided and the dray was nestling by the kerb, the drayman looked around angrily:

"Binhead! You bin on de bevee?!"

Kevin's heart sank. It was Mo Jolliffe, who had barracked him so venomously at the Celtic v. "Wolves" match. The burly Jolliffe at first looked scornfully at Kevin then recognised him and took in his painful predicament:

"Wassupp?", he asked.

"Nothing. I'll be O.K. I just caught my foot on the paving stone."

"Yer nearly wasn't O.K. Yer nearly finished up under the 'oss!"

Kevin looked up at Jolliffe, embarrassed. "I'm sorry," was all he could manage. He began to walk on.

"Hey!....'old on! Where yer off to?", asked the drayman, taking in the youth's obvious discomfort. Kevin pointed along Grafton Street:

"Home."

"Well, 'op up 'ere. I'm goin' that road."

He extended his arm down to Kevin. As he took Jolliffe's massive hand he noticed the man seemed to have no wrist, his thick forearm extending without pause into the great hand. Donnelly was a broad shouldered, sturdy lad but the drayman had no difficulty in yanking him up onto the seat beside him effortlessly and at great speed. Then he made a clicking noise, let the horse feel the smack of the reins on his back and they started forward.

"'s that leg still bothering yer?", Jolliffe enquired.

"Well, a bit."

"'ave yer seen the doc?"

"I think it's getting better."

"Doesn't luk like it!"

Kevin was anxious not to pursue the matter.

"How's Tommy?", he asked.

"Ooh fine! Bin called up! He's at Oswestry. He says Western Command 'ave a good football team, with plenty of professionals ter pick from. They play league clubs! If Tommy gets a game with 'em 'e'll be laffin'."

The news that yet another of his circle had been called to the colours depressed Kevin even further and he said little else until the drayman set him down.

"Yer'd betta get that leg seen to, d'yer 'ear?!" counselled Jolliffe.

Kevin nodded and muttered his thanks. With a click of his tongue and a flap of the reins, Mo went on his way.

Because he was now limping badly Kevin decided

against going home immediately so he picked his way carefully down Gosford Street and settled into his favourite spot in Grafton Street where he could look out over the river and ponder. Mo Jolliffe had been quite friendly in his rough-tough way. It mirrored the attitude of many in Toxteth, especially the children, for he had become something of a local hero. The incident had occurred just a few days ago following an air raid in which houses had been demolished nearby on Wellington Road. The following morning he had visited the site and, despite the protests of an air raid warden, had infiltrated himself into a group of civil defence workers peering into the destruction. Kevin had seen Sam Hilditch, the Toxteth trainer, among the group and approached him.

"Better not come here, Kevin – the whole lot's likely to come down."

"Then why are you standing here?,"

"We heard summat – think there might be somebody in there."

"Where?"

Kevin followed Sam's pointing finger. As he peered into the shambles of what had been a dwelling he could see a heap of rubble beneath the remains of a chimney breast. Arched over it at a precarious angle was a row of floor joists supporting the tongued and grooved timbering of a bedroom floor.

"Well, if somebody gets under that flooring – takes the weight – you could find out what's under the rubble."

Taking his own advice, Kevin picked his way over bricks, plaster, doors, window frames and broken furniture. As he settled his broad frame under the joists of the hanging bedroom floor, police officers and civil defence workers were yelling at him to come back from the dereliction. Only Sam Hilditch knew Kevin's nature: he would not heed the warnings. Accordingly Sam went forward and began to move the rubble where the sounds had been heard. In seconds he was joined by others.

The episode had no happy ending for although they brought out a youth of Kevin's own age, he was dead. This took nothing away from Donnelly's frightening display of courage and the streets of Toxteth rapidly became full of it. The best barometer of public opinion was the attitude of the area's children. Since his injury, and with the chirpy cruelty of all children, they had begun to call him "Hoppy Donnelly" or "Peg leg Pete." Now all that had vanished and they lavished on him the adulation hitherto reserved for other real heroes, such as the crews of His Majesty's ships "Ajax", "Exeter" and "Achilles" which had done for the "Graf Spee" and for the fictional heroes to be found in their comic papers, principally "Rockfist Rogan, R.A.F."

Even the angry Police Inspector who had reprimanded him when he had emerged from the demolition could not resist slapping him on the back as he slunk away. Only his mother was seemingly unimpressed:

"You haven't got the sense you were born with!", was her observation. If she was proud of him, she was determined to conceal it.

So here was Kevin alone with his thoughts on the railed off escarpment of Grafton Street where he could look down over the river. The improved attitude of Mo Jolliffe had triggered his reverie – even he had seemingly heard about the incident on Wellington Road. Anger had fuelled Kevin's impulse to dive into the bombed-out dwelling. He felt the war was certainly "hotting up". Liverpool had not yet been blitzed on the scale of London and Coventry but it was not being overlooked. As he gazed down on the Brunswick Dock he recalled that on the seventeenth of August it had been hit with high explosives, as had the North Coburg and the South Queen's Docks. In early

September the Anglican Cathedral had been damaged
and what had once been a set of superb windows had
been reduced to glittering trash. Even the wonderful
Custom House had been hit by both high explosives and
incendiaries at the end of the month and today he had
seen for himself that the damage there was serious.

On the seventeenth of September the Rootes Aircraft
Factory at Speke had been hit by high explosives and on
the following night there had been heavy damage through
the whole of the City, including the railway line at nearby
St. Michael's Station.

And the atmosphere had changed, for people knew
there was worse to come. The view was expressed that
now France had "gone", Jerry was that much closer to
Liverpool – Merseyside was well within the range of the
Luftwaffe. So there was a new climate. The chirpiness,
the togetherness and the "business as usual" bravado
were still there but underscored by apprehension, anger
– and expectancy.

The next moment, momentarily, his thoughts were
interrupted by the insistence of the sunset. The soft glow
of the river now took on a fiery intensity and the sky itself
became a kaleidoscope of yellows, oranges, golds, greys
and blues. He had seen only one kaleidoscope to rival the
sunsets – that once when the sun had burst through and
projected a colour feast onto the walls of St. Malachy's
Church. That had been nearly as good.

The river itself was packed with shipping. On the far
shore, cargo boats were standing off Ellesmere Port and
Birkenhead. In the middle distance vessels were bustling
down to Garston, making the most of the evening tide. He
looked down at a vast spread of vessels, fixing the types as
his father had taught him – merchantmen and passenger
liners, salvage vessels, dredgers, hoppers, luggage tenders
and the ferries of course. Crammed together they made a

floating roadway from shore to shore.

The buildings in the King's and Albert Docks obscured his view of the Pier Head but he knew that around it would be another mass of river and ocean going traffic. So important to the world was Liverpool, his father said, that after many a voyage home they had had to wait at the harbour bar for three weeks before a berth became free.

He looked down again at his left ankle. It had let him down – well, it and his own obstinacy. Because he could not bear more bad news, he had limped about for weeks hoping, then persuading himself it was only sprained. He had applied comfry, hot and cold compresses, every other household remedy and endured the constant tirades of his mother. Now he knew it was more than a sprain – serious enough, in fact, to keep him out of the Army, at a time when it meant so much to him for his own sake, his father's sake and his City's sake, to take an active part in the war.

So sport had rejected him and the Army had rejected him. Well, he thought about it and it didn't matter. He would join the Merchant Navy and when he was master of his own ship people would see he was no bad penny. And one day he would marry Celia Molloy and they would live in one of the big houses in Fulwood or Grassendale.

His thoughts clicked onto Celia, as they often did. Dark haired and rosy cheeked she had been his sweetheart since childhood. Certainly, that is how he saw it. They met at infants' school then moved to junior mixed school together. One day he found her crying. Some boys had been teasing her and were about to run away with her lunch-box. He had waded into them and retrieved it. Hearing of this, Miss Regan, the headmistress, had said:

"Kevin Donnelly, it will be your duty to look after Celia. Remember this is a strange place to her."

After that he saw himself as her companion and protector. Often, it was arranged that they were milk monitors together and Kevin would walk her home to the big house on Princes Avenue beyond the busy Park Road. Their propinquity increased his tenderness and it was a great blow when he learned she was leaving his care to go to a private school. Yet he decided that all wasn't lost....he would see her each week at church.

He knew where the Molloys' pew was located so on the Sunday after she had gone to her new school he sat behind her pew. He was overjoyed when her family came in and she waved to him. Her father, Mr Francis Molloy, a prosperous ships' chandler, noted this and was hardly pleased.

"Hadn't you better join the rest of the school, young man?" he asked. Holding Kevin by the arm he then took him to the other side of the church and spoke earnestly to Miss Regan who pointed out to Kevin where he must sit in the future. The blushing boy was embarrassed and angry.

Since then he had seen Celia just once, soon after her fourteenth birthday. Accompanied by her elder sister, Ursula, she had been riding a new bicycle. As Kevin watched she lost her balance and fell. Her white silk dress was dirtied and torn. She was bleeding at the elbows and knees. He ran to her but was assured by Ursula there was nothing he could do, they must get home quickly. They then discovered that the front wheel of Celia's bicycle wouldn't revolve.

"It's O.K., Celia," Kevin said confidently, "one of the shoes is bent and the brake block is jamming your wheel. I can soon fix it."

He ran to where his own bicycle lay on the pavement and rummaged in his saddlebag. Using a spanner as a lever he eased the shoe and the block away from the wheel until it spun freely.

"Thank you, Kevin," smiled Celia and waited for him to speak. No words would come. He could only nod.

"We must go, Celia," said the older girl imperiously. As they went, Ursula looked back and said "thank you" making it sound more of a rebuke than a gesture of gratitude.

Now, on this mild Autumn evening, four years later, Kevin suddenly stirred himself. He must go home and face up to telling his mother of his decision to go to sea. Certainly, it would not be easy.

The reaction was in line with his forecast. A tearful Liz Donnelly protested and argued. He pointed out that had he passed the medical he would have had to leave home anyway. This only increased her opposition. So didn't he see that it was all for the best? At least he would be safe and could do important work here at home – on the docks, even in a munitions factory. And anyway, how did he know he'd be passed fit for the Merchant Navy?

Kevin sighed:

"Mother, the Government doesn't tell us everything – but they can't hide the facts – twenty ships a week are being sunk. If we don't get more food in and stuff to fight the war, it's just a matter of time for us. And as far as the medical's concerned, they're desperate for crews. If you're breathing, you're in."

She continued to plead but he would not be shaken. He was young, the country was in a "bad way" and he had to "do his bit."

The following morning his mother's tears had subsided but she was silent. Then, at the end of a dull wartime breakfast, she said:

"If you're adamant, you should find out more about it, then decide. Tom Gallagher wants to talk to you."

'Chippy' Gallagher was their next-door neighbour. He

had been a ship's carpenter for nearly fifty years, hence his nickname. The boy grinned secretly. His mother had run true to form. Whenever his father had wanted to go back to sea, when his brother had announced he would volunteer for the Army and when he, himself, had wanted to be a professional footballer she had tried to overwhelm each proposal with a mass of arguments. Then she had suddenly subsided, even suggesting how each of them might cautiously progress his idea. She had obviously arranged the meeting with "Chippy" Gallagher. It was as though she had to have her say but having said it, and knowing her menfolk, she would develop a philosophy and co-operate with the inevitable.

Half an hour later Kevin knocked at the Gallagher's door. His mother's intonation had suggested their neighbour would hardly say encouraging things about the lot of a merchant seaman. Well, he would see.

Behind the door he heard a rush and some squealing. Then it was opened by Kathleen Gallagher, third of the four daughters in the family, the girl who had tried to help him at the time of his injury and who had followed him home so surreptitiously.

As she held open the door, struggling to check the youngest pair of the four Gallagher boys and smoothing down the mass of her auburn hair, Kevin noted how pretty his young neighbour was becoming but he added the speedy rider that Celia Molloy was even prettier.

Kathleen was guarded at first as though anticipating more of his ill-humour. Then Liam, one of the boys, eluded her grasp and peeped from behind her skirts, an imp of mischief. He looked like an elf peeping around a toadstool. Kevin smiled at him, remembering that he and three other Gallagher children had been evacuated to North Wales at the beginning of the war. Kevin remembered them setting off for Lime Street Station each with a pillow-slip containing a few belongings. When he asked his brother Vincent why the pillow-slips he had said dourly "because poor folk haven't got suitcases and they haven't got suitcases because they never go on holiday." At all events, the children were back in Beresford Road within six weeks there being no effective remedy for their homesickness.

When Kevin smiled, Kathleen relaxed and responded with a smile. He noticed her white, even teeth.

"Hi Kevin.....come to see Dad?"

"Please...if he's in"

".....course. Come through."

She followed him down the hallway and chanced a delicate question:

"How's your leg?"

"So so."

"You ought to get it seen to, Kevin."

"Seemingly," he answered, polite but dejected.

He went into the living room. Gallagher was sitting in a rocking chair by the fire. He was a tiny man and as he rocked, his feet left the floor by a significant distance. He was carving a wooden boat. It was well advanced so its intricate detail was already admirable. The man looked up:

"Hallo, lad," he nodded.

"'morning, Mr Gallagher," Kevin answered and then, pointing to the boat, he said:

"That looks good."

"It's for the little un's birthday."

He nodded towards Bernard, the child at his feet, who was gazing at his intended possession with pride.

"Chippy" laid the boat to one side then brushed some slivers of wood from his lap onto the newspaper lying open on the floor.

"Well, sit yer down," he gestured.

When the boy was settled Gallagher looked at him:

"Your Ma tells us you want to go into the Merchant Navy."

Kevin nodded:

"Why?"

"Well....I want to do my bit I suppose....and I'm not fit enough for the Army."

The man laughed:

"If you're not fit enough for the Army, you won't be fit for sea service."

He leaned forward.

"You look fit enough. What about all the football you play?"

"That's the problem. I've crocked my ankle."

"Well can't that be put right? You've bin limpin' around for ages. Have you seen a doctor?"

"...suppose I'll have to."

The little man shook his head. He thought for a second:

"Why d'you want to go to sea all of a sudden?"

"I erm.....I want to do my bit."

"Hasn't your family done its bit?.....your father was lost at sea and your Vin is in the King's..."

"That's not my bit...I can't hide behind them."

The carpenter sighed:

"Do you know what the Merchant Navy's like?"

Kevin shrugged:

"Same as any other job I suppose."

"No lad....I've had a lifetime of it and I can tell yer.... it's the hardest, cruellest job in the world."

"Why?"

"It's maulin' work. An' while yer doin it you're always wet and always hungry."

He went on, gathering momentum:

"Now yer've got two enemies....first there's Jerry with his torpedoes an' shells. North Atlantic's crawlin'

with U-boats. On the surface they can do over 17 knots...
that's faster than most of our escorts. Submerged they
can do over 7 ½ knots....more than some o' the old coal
burning tramps in our convoys do on the surface. They're
murderous them U-boats. They can come at you from
thousands o' miles away an' as well as their torpedoes
they've got an 88 millimetre deck gun an' anti-aircraft
cannons. That 88's a vile weapon. Some of our ships,
even 7000 tonners an' that've bin sunk by gunfire so's
Jerry can save his torpedoes. An' remember this, now
France has packed in, Jerry doesn't have ter get into
the Western Ocean by the long road. He can come out o'
French ports as well. An' the Royal Navy can't watch both
ends, can it?"

Gallagher stopped to rake the fire and put more coal
onto its dulling bed. Kevin watched, intense:

"What about our escorts, Mr Gallagher? I've seen
them on the films."

"Too few and too small, very often. A lot of escort
work's done by corvettes, ours or Canadian. They'll do
15 knots top whack an' all they've got's a 4 inch gun an'
a few depth charges. If you're lucky you might get one or
two escortin' a convoy of 40 or more merchantmen....if
you're very lucky you might get a destroyer. I've sailed in
convoy when our only escort was an A.M.C."

"A.M.C?"

"Armed Merchant Cruiser. They take a passenger
ship, strengthen its structure so they can put a gun on
it out o' the Ark an' give the ship a fancy name – Armed
Merchant Cruiser. AMCs are being asked to do the
impossible....sink U-boats and take on Surface Raiders.
Yet yer see the kind o' blokes we've got in 'em....like them
on the "Rawlpindi."

Kevin looked blank, so "Chippy" continued:

"She took on "Scharnhorst" 'n "Gneisenau", German

warships. "Rawlpindi" was still firin' when she sank. Captain Kennedy and 270 men were lost, many of 'em ex-merchant seamen. An' talkin' of Captains, what about Captain Stubbs?"

"Who's he?"

"Stubbs of the "Doric Star"! He comes from Grassendale, along the road. Lives just up from the river."

"What happened?"

"The Graf Spee, yer know, the German pocket-battleship, fired at her. He started transmittin' he was under attack. The Jerries told 'im to stop. He took no notice. The Royal Navy got his message and the Graf Spee's at the bottom of the South Atlantic."

Kevin smiled and shook his head. "Chippy" leaned forward:

"Yeah...an' there's a lot o' seamen like him out there, unny you never hear about 'em."

The door opened suddenly. Kathleen came in with a tea tray. She smiled:

"You two still at it?"

"If he wants ter know about life at sea, we haven't started yet."

She touched Gallagher's shoulder:

"An' you're the one to tell him , aren't you Dad?"

She winked at Kevin. Her father made as if to throw a slipper at her but she was too quick for him and closed the door rapidly behind her.

The boy leaned forward:

"You said there were two enemies....?"

"Yes....the other's the sea, especially the North Atlantic, which is where you'd be. The place is cursed..... hateful and bitter cold. In Winter it's always violent. When one gale's over another one comes. In Summer it moderates but it's not much better. An' all the time from one horizon to th' other the sky's as grey as lead. It's purgatory, lad. An' I'll tell you summat else, if you get torpedoed an' there's a force 9 gale on, you've no chance of survival."

"Chippy" paused at this point and looked steadily at Kevin who sensed he was about to make a telling comment:

"Have yer 'eard of the 'Vardulia'?"

The youth could only shake his head.

"Donaldson Line. Six thousand tonner – loaded with coal an' general cargo. A few years back she foundered out there. All hands gone."

For a few seconds Kevin was thoughtful. Then he looked up:

"I'd still like to have a go at it."

"Why?"

"If nobody does the job, we'll lose the war, won't we?"

The man's little hand grasped the poker and he gave the fire further attention.

"Well it's your life," he sighed. "I promised your Ma I'd talk to you about it. I didn't say I'd talk you out of it."

They looked at each other.

"Have you thought who you'd like to sail with?"

The youth was puzzled:

"How do you mean?"

"The line....the shippin' company."

Donnelly shrugged

"Dunno...any line...one's as good as another, I suppose."

Gallagher looked disdainful:

"You're wrong there. If your father was here he'd tell you. Some ships are 'ell 'oles. The quarters and mattresses are filthy. The food's lousy an' there isn't much of it. You eat your grub standin' up and like as not you'll find cockroaches runnin' over it. There's no such thing as a cold room. They keep the food from goin' rotten by stockin' up with ice. Usually there's no runnin' water so you've got to keep yourself clean usin' the pump on the well-deck. When you're off watch the only way to keep warm very often is to sneak into the galley an', if you can find room, stand by the cook's fires."

"It sounds grim."

"Well you've got to know what you're getting' yourself into."

The carpenter again gave the youth a long steady look. Then he wagged his finger:

"An' don't forget – the ship's company, the Master an' the Mates make a lot o' difference to life at sea. I've bin on some ships where the crews were treated like dirt – nobody gave a tuppenny damn about 'em. But at the other end of the scale you've got the Blue Funnel Line - Holt's. Now they're considerate and think that if they do their best for the crews, the crews'll repay 'em, with loyalty and efficiency. In peace time, Holt's carry their own insurance and 'ave ships built to their own standards, very, very strong – well in excess of what Lloyds' want for their classifications. So don't think one line's as good as another – it's not true."

Kevin nodded but said nothing so "Chippy" pointed to a framed picture of a ship hanging on the wall at the far side of the room:

"I never got to work for Holt's, but that's the best line I've sailed with an' the best ship!"

"Chippy" jumped off his chair and went towards the picture, Kevin followed. He took in the lines of the ship on the colour photograph. The vessel looked sleek and modern. It was painted with a red finish coat at the base of its hull. The major part of the hull was jet black but from the upper edge of this was a broad white band about three feet in width which extended to deck level. The ship's upperworks and most of its funnel were also painted white, with a band of black atop the funnel. This livery emphasised the trim appearance of the ship.

The caption on the picture read" "Wirral Peninsular Line." Beneath it was a small facsimile of the "house flag". This bore the letters "WPL" superimposed onto the flag's background which was divided diagonally into black and white. Below the ship another caption read:

"M.V. Willaston; built Cammell Laird, Birkenhead. Registered Liverpool, 1935; 5,000 tons."

At the bottom of the picture these details were added: "Company fleet: M.V. Willaston; Neston; Puddington; Burton; Thornton; Mollington."

"She looks smart," said Kevin. "I see she was built in Birkenhead."

"Yeah," smiled "Chippy", with pride. "We know summat about buildin' ships 'round 'ere. Like the "Clement"."

Again Kevin looked uncertain so Gallagher came to his assistance:

"The "Clement" – Booth Line - built at Cammell Lairds. She was that tough the "Graf Spee" had a helluva time trying to sink her. Langsdorff 'ad to try everythin' 'fore she went under!" The little man stroked his chin:

"Have you seen the docks on the other side of the river?"

"No."

"Well – we'll go over there if you like. This great port isn't just Liverpool, y'know."

Now "Chippy" was in full spate, nodding towards the "Willaston" he added: "Yeah – she's smart, they're all smart. The "Willaston"'s the flag ship. I've sailed on her and the "Burton" – East Africa, South Africa, the Red Sea – that's where WPL's trade was before the war. They're all 5,000 tonners, all built a few years back an' all diesel-powered."

"Does that make a difference?"

"I should say so. U-boats can spot smoke from a coal-burning ship 50 miles away. An' yer diesel is a faster vessel anyroad."

He tapped the phoptograph:

"If you're goin' to sea, I'd like to see you in summat like this."

Then he faced Kevin:

"Remember – anything that can float is being pushed into convoys now. We're in dire straits. Some o' the coal-burners can't keep station even in a slow convoy. An' if your ship's a straggler, Jerry'll pick it off. Go to sea if you have to – but go in summat decent, lad, where you've at least got a chance."

He tapped the picture:

"WPL's got some of the handiest, best-kept ships sailin' out o' the Mersey."

Kevin shook his hand:

"Thanks a lot, Mr Gallagher. You've been a big help."

"That's alright. I'm only doin' what your father would a' done, lad. Now if you want to know anythin' else, come back. But think about it before you do anythin', d'you hear?"

"Sure.....and thanks again."

As he was leaving, Kathleen and her mother appeared.

"You off then?" asked the girl, her disappointment evident.

"Yes – thanks very much for the tea. Your dad's been really helpful."

"Mm....when he starts about ships he never stops," said Mary Gallagher.

"There's a dance in the school tomorrow night.

Would you like to go, Kevin?" asked Kathleen, somewhat guardedly.

"Oh no, thanks."

"One or two of the lads you knew at school'll be there...they're either on leave or on the point of going...." His face dropped. She'd said the wrong thing.

"I couldn't very well dance with a gammy foot," he murmured.

"No...." said Kathleen, embarrassed.

"You get that foot seen to!" Mary Gallagher barked.

He nodded to them both and closed the door behind him. Now to face his mother. He was quite clear about what he would say. And if "Chippy" was supposed to have put him off, he oughtn't to have told him about the "Rawlpindi", the "Doric Star" and, of course, the "Willaston". What's more he'd go with "Chippy" over to the Birkenhead side of the river. He felt enthused.....he wanted to know all there was to know.

Chapter Three

The Troubled Goodbye

Now it was October and every day it became clearer that in this war, Liverpool was a front-line city. A week or so ago, the Wapping, King's, Queen's, Coburg and Brunswick Docks had been extensively damaged by air attack. No fewer than thirteen warehouses and their contents had been laid waste. The Admiralty store in Canning Place had been demolished. The magnificent Dock Board and Cunard Buildings had been damaged by high explosives dropped in Brunswick Street. Even a Council School in Banks Road, Garston had not escaped the enemy's attention.

These "incidents", as they were euphemistically

called, fuelled Kevin Donnelly's determination to get into the war. The City and its people, so important to his father and now to him, were hurting. Lives and livelihoods were being maliciously wrecked. How could he, strong and able, hide behind a trifling injury, when others, his father included, had already given their lives in defence of Britain? No, his mind was made up.

So, throughout the following week, he tried to make it clear to his mother that if the Merchant Navy could find a place for him he was ready. It was an uneasy, tiring time for them both, which understates the situation significantly. Liz Donnelly began by upbraiding him for his obstinacy. Yet, she asked, was this any surprise? Hadn't he always been stubborn?

His schoolmasters had been certain that staying on at school would have ensured his future but no.... he wanted to become a professional footballer. Well, oughtn't he to have become apprenticed to some trade, to help him later on? No....all he wanted was a football apprenticeship. Result?.....he was eighteen years of age, without a job and without prospects.

"Chippy" Gallagher had already told him what mauling, badly paid work it was at sea. Now it was more dangerous than ever.

"Apart from your Dad, just think of the men from around these streets that've already been killed," she exclaimed.

"And remember what your Dad said – 'oh they want us now alright, but when the war's over, we'll be back on the scrap heap'!"

To lend force to her next point she walked over to him and looked into his face:

"Have you thought about the future at all? Just a few years back, from what your Dad told us, sixty thousand merchant seamen were on the streets looking for work

- not six thousand, sixty thousand! With a lot of officers, master mariners some of 'em, having to sign on as able seamen."

Kevin thought he had some answers here:

"Chippy' says it all depends what Line you're with – he says some Shipping Lines are quite good. An' as for the future – unless we get more men at sea, there'll be no kind of future for any of us."

"Hmph!", was her response and she always managed to give quite superb emphasis to this seemingly innocuous expression. Then she returned to the attack: why was he in his present predicament? A blind man could see – he was too stubborn to visit a doctor about his ankle, which was obviously serious otherwise it wouldn't have kept him out of the Forces.

In the end, however, her tears, recriminations, arguments and pleadings made no difference. So, exhausted, on the morning he set off for the General Shipping Office in Corn Hill, she followed him to their front door. Wiping her eyes once again, she said:

"You're bringing your pigs to a nice market – you'll see!"

It was an aphorism she conferred on any situation beyond hope or redemption.

It took another week for him to obtain the appropriate documentation: an i.d. card, a licence and the necessary clearance from the seamen's trade union. Then, within a day or so, he was called to the Shipping Pool at the Pier Head for a medical examination.

The doctor dispensed with preliminaries, concentrating on the injured ankle. After asking about the when and how of the accident he handled the ankle carefully. His eyebrows came together in consternation:

"Have you seen your own doctor or visited the hospital with this?"

"No. I thought a sprain cleared up in time."

"It isn't a sprain. It's broken.....or was broken," the doctor snapped.

"How do you mean, doctor?"

"It's knitted again, and badly. You need attention or you'll have that limp for the rest of your life."

It took a few seconds for Kevin to digest this. Then he heard himself say:

"I still want to go to sea."

The doctor sighed:

"Then you've got more courage than common sense."

He appeared not to hear the youth's further pleading but finally he said:

"If the convoys weren't desperate for crews I wouldn't even discuss this. Do you know what the job's like? Have you any idea what you'd be getting into?"

"Yes," said Donnelly, with such conviction the doctor did not pursue this line. Then he considered:

"Look, if you'll agree I'll fix an appointment with an orthopaedic specialist for you. As things are, that will take a few weeks. In the meantime I'll clear you for sea service, but for one voyage and one only. Then....whether you go back to sea or not.... you'll keep the appointment with the specialist.....clear?"

Elated, Kevin nodded....even one voyage would be better than sitting around while others got on with the war.

"Whichever Line takes you on will probably ask you to sign a waiver so no responsibility falls on them for any accident you might have because of your ankle. O.K.?"

Again Kevin nodded.

An hour later he was back in Beresford Road reporting all this to "Chippy" Gallagher. The little man smiled and whispered:

"The Willaston's due out shortly. I'll have a word with

Hugh Riley."

"Is he the Captain?"

"No, the donkey man," laughed "Chippy"

"Donkey man?"

"Yeah....well, motor man he's called on a diesel-powered vessel. On a steam-ship he's a donkey-man. He looks after the donkey engine."

"What's that?"

"It's not the main engine. It's an ancillary engine – for the fire pumps, generators, ventilation and the lights. You'll get the hang of all that. Anyroad, Hughie was my mate. He'll sort summat, you'll see."

Kevin nodded uncertainly.

As he was leaving the Gallaghers he bumped into Kathleen. Impulsively he gave her his news and noticed how fearful she looked. Plaintively she said:

"You'd better be careful. Ooh Kevin......ships are getting sunk all the time."

He grinned.

"They won't bother with me, Kath. I'm only the can-lad."

She threaded her arm through his. He was embarrassed but did nothing. Perking up a little she said:

"Listen, would you like to go to the pictures with me?"

He was uncertain.

"When?"

"Thursday night?"

"Mm......I think that would be O.K."

"Well don't look so happy about it, misery."

He laughed. She squeezed his arm and then, as she turned towards her front door, released it. Looking back, she said:

"Meet me outside the main entrance to Lime Street Station. By the North Western Hotel – this side. Six o'clock and don't be late. The shilling seats are hopeless after half-past and it's John Mills."

As the door closed behind her he acknowledged that since she had begun working at the Water Street head office of a banking chain her appearance had improved. Previously the name "Kath Gallagher" had conjured up the image of a girl in ill-fitting clothes sometime owned by her elder sisters. He recalled when once he had looked askance at her turn-out she had countered unabashed: "You know how it is in our place Kev, first up, best dressed."

Still, she had irritated him just now. She was likeable, of course, but she had manoeuvred him quite brazenly into this "date". Pushy females had no appeal for him. Worse, he now felt disloyal to Celia Molloy, whom he had cared about since childhood and hoped to marry one day.

He completed the remaining arrangements to sail for WPL Ltd, under the Wirral Peninsular Flag, during the following day, Tuesday. At the offices of the Line in Tithebarn Street he met Mr Ian Dunlop, the First Mate of the M.V. "Willaston" and immediately liked this smart, quietly spoken, relaxed Scot who asked shrewd questions, waited patiently for the answers and smiled his genuine interest. Donnelly agreed to sign on as a deck boy for a single voyage on a WPL vessel to be designated. He also signed the waiver relating to his damaged ankle as the doctor at the Shipping Pool had forecast.

Forty eight hours later a letter arrived at Beresford Road. It instructed him to report to the Huskisson Dock at 08.00 hours on the following Tuesday, five days hence. Immediately, he resolved to share his news with Celia Molloy. True, he had not seen her for some time but he was sure it would make no difference. She would be pleased to see him again and after their friendship was re-established they would reach an understanding. If he was to be away at sea for long periods this was important. He would ask her to wait until he had earned enough to marry her. It was going to be a tall order for both of them so the sooner he went to see her the better.

He braced himself, showed the letter to his mother, then tried to stem her tears with repeated assurances he would look after himself. When "Chippy" Gallagher saw the letter he grinned, then whispering lest the Germans overheard, he said:

"This'll be the "Willaston"! I knew Hughie Riley wouldn't let us down. An' if George Stephens is still the Master you couldn't be sailin' under a better bloke."

"I met an officer of the Line......named Dunlop. He set me on. He was very friendly."

"Well there y'are y'see. I told yer they were a tidy outfit. Yer on de pig's back, lad."

Gallagher then began to busy himself. Presently he returned to the sitting room with what looked like a small mattress. He held it up:

"'ere. Yer can 'ave this. It's seen better days....but at least all the sea water's dried out of it now."

"What is it?"

"It's your bed. You 'ave ter supply one."

"What?!"

"You provide de bed. An' stop cribbin'....th' officers are worse off....as well as findin' their own beddin', towels and soap, they've got to buy a uniform, a sextant an' even nautical tables fer navigatin' the ship!....an' a few years back, a Third Mate was paid £10 a month."

He shook his head at Donnelly:

"Yer goin' inter a different world now. You'll see. 'ere!....take it."

As Kevin struggled with the mattress, a memory formed. Yes....funny it hadn't struck him before....but his father had done this too. The bulky bundle he had shouldered out of the house was something to sleep on.... who would've believed it?

He spent the remainder of the day at a timber yard in Grafton Street to earn a few shillings for the cinema visit with Kathleen Gallagher. When he reached Lime Street that evening his back ached, his arms ached and, most decidedly, his ankle ached. He forced himself to walk as normally as possible when they made for the cinema in London Road but his discomfort did not escape her:

"It is worrying. You've got to see a doctor," she insisted.

This time there was no scolding, only concern. He supposed he was glad on both counts. In the cinema she slid her arm across to him and locked it into his. His irritation with her returned. A nice girl didn't behave like this. Then he fell asleep.

Returning home, as they turned out of London Road to face St. George's Plateau the wind tore into them. For Kevin, the monumental splendour of St. George's Hall blocked out all sensation of the wind's buffeting. He was remembering some of the many things his father had said about the Hall, of how its "massive power and originality" had come about through the adaptation of "classical architectural ideas" in an inspired way. Joe Donnelly had said that on his long sea journeys images of the City would enter his mind's eye and they always contained the Liver Building and the sixteen Corinthian columns of the St. George's Hall great portico. He had remarked that Queen Victoria had deemed the Hall as "worthy of Ancient Athens." He had talked of......

"Hey! Goss-eye!....the tram!," Kathleen was yelling. They had to run for it, much to Kevin's renewed discomfort.

On the journey home, her disappointment was

clear:

"A great boy-friend you are. I might as well have gone to the pictures on my own."

Again her presumption aggravated him.

"I'm not your boy-friend, Kathleen," he told her quietly, then he apologised for going to sleep.

"I'll bet that ankle has been keeping you awake," she suggested.

He didn't respond.

At her doorstep, impulsively, she kissed him on the cheek. Now he was not irritated because he sensed her sympathy and was moved by this. She thanked him for the cinema visit, whispered "Look after yourself," and was gone. As she disappeared he thought:

"She's had a miserable time really, and it's all my fault."

Friday found him buoyant. Pain and anxiety had slipped away, for this was the day he would visit Celia Molloy. He took some time planning what he would say. He brought his shoes to their brightest shine, having washed and shaved fastidiously. Then he pressed and brushed his only suit most carefully. He hesitated at first but presently asked his mother whether he could borrow the cufflinks which had belonged to his father. Liz, who had been watching him carefully, nodded but said nothing. Finally, with the remnants of his brother's Brylcreem, he brought his hair into perfect order. Yet, after all that, it was well into the afternoon before he felt brave enough to make for the imposing residence of the Molloys on Princes Avenue.

He went through the front gate without qualm but hesitated on the path to the heavy entrance door feeling intimidated by the magnificence of its stone architrave and the balustradings to the first floor windows. He swallowed with awe, as he had when a schoolboy. Then, mind made up, he rapped on the door with the heavy knocker. He winced as the sound thundered through the house. Only then did he see the bell-push.

"First mistake," he gulped, clenching his hands nervously. They were clammy. When the door opened, a beautifully dressed, middle-aged, rather stout woman looked at him doubtfully. This was Mrs Dympna Molloy, Celia's mother. He had been expecting to see one of the two maids he remembered. It crossed his mind they were probably on "war work" before he smiled and said:

"Hallo, Mrs Molloy."

She hesitated, thought, then asked:

"Yes?"

"I was wondering if I could see Celia, please?"

She frowned:

"What about?"

Obviously she did not recognise him so quickly he began to explain:

"Well......well.....you see, we were at school together and I'm going away....so I came to say goodbye and ....."

"She's just about to leave....but I'll see," said the mother, her expression verging on disdain. Before turning away, she gestured that he should stay where he was. After a long few minutes he could hear muted talking in the hall beyond the door. Then Celia Molloy appeared. The pretty girl he remembered had become a beautiful woman. He gulped with reverential wonder. It was her quizzical look which brought him to earth.

"Hallo, Celia," he gasped.

She smiled, guardedly, but didn't speak.

"It's Kevin.......Kevin Donnelly........from school........ remember?"

Her memory stirred but she was anxious not to affirm it. At last, she said:

"Oh yes. How are you?"

Her question was not rooted in real interest, but this was lost on Kevin. A new silence descended and it was becoming awkward.

"I know it's a long time since we were at school. I used to bring you home across Park Road. It was always busy. Then a little while back I helped you with your bike. Do you remember now?"

To catch her reluctant nod of agreement he would have had to have been very perceptive. She was still silent and his confidence was ebbing away. This led him to make a futile gesture: his palms were sweating and he rubbed them down the front of his suit. Astounded by his own action, he looked and felt completely servile. Despite his self- disgust he forced himself to continue:

"Anyway, I was hoping we might see each other again.....sometime. I called to tell you I'm going away for a while.....and......"

"Where?"

Suddenly she had discovered her tongue.

"Oh...to sea. I'm going to sea. As an apprentice.... well....a deck boy, like,....at first."

Her face hardened:

"That's not much of a job!"

Noting his hurt she managed enough good manners to add:

"Still, you've got to start somewhere."

Knowing she had made things worse her unease increased. How could she bring his call to a finish, she wondered. Then she sighed almost visibly for the door opened wide and Mr Francis Molloy appeared with some emphasis. Ignoring Kevin he turned to his daughter:

"You'd better get a move on if you're going to that tea-dance. It's quarter to four."

Kevin noticed a young fair-haired R.A.F. officer standing behind Molloy. Above his left breast-pocket were pilot's wings.

"Yes...yes, alright," smirked Celia trying hard to conceal her relief.

"Well, good luck then......Kevin. I hope all goes well for you. I must go now. Goodbye."

She favoured him with a synthetic smile.

"Goodbye, Celia," he said to the door which was now closing rapidly. Miserable and angry, he walked back along the path towards the gate. They had closed the great oak door in his face. In fact, this had been in his favour – it protected him from the giggling going on behind it.

His meeting with her had been disastrous. He was furious with himself for letting it go so badly wrong. Remembering her beauty only intensified his self-reproach. And why had he wiped his hand on his suit? Had he really done that? Certainly he had, for there was no disputing the slavishness that had wracked him standing before her.

Her father had no time for him, that was clear. Well, too bad, because he had no intention of abandoning his interest in her. Once she came to know him again, realised the depth of his feelings for her and began to share his ambitions, it would all work out. He was at the lowest pitch of humiliation and misery but did not intend to languish there: she was too great a prize.

In spite of this resolve, however, the hurt he felt gave him no rest in the days that followed. He became curt with everyone, especially his mother, the handiest victim. She had to endure the vituperation he was unable to direct at the Molloys. He realised how unbearable he had become when, finally, Liz Donnelly said sadly:

"I think the sooner you go to sea the better."

On the day he joined the "Willaston" he rose early. So did his mother. They breakfasted in silence. At the beginning of the month the Luftwaffe had attacked the East Toxteth Dock with incendiaries. This had further deepened his depression. What right had they to do these things? Well now at least he was getting a chance to hit back.

When he was leaving, his mother followed him to the door. They faced each other, embarrassed. Uncertain, he stepped out onto the pavement. She followed him. Her agony was plain and impulsively he took her into his arms. He was shocked for he could feel her trembling in her fear and desperation. "Watch what you're doing," she choked. Now he realised fully what his leaving meant to her. He had to break away, before he changed his mind.

"I love you, Ma....don't worry," he whispered. Then he strode up the slope of Beresford Road. At the corner of Cockburn Street he looked back and waved. She was wiping her eyes but waved back vigorously. Gagging with emotion he turned the corner. It was good that their parting had been a loving one for they were never to see each other again.

Chapter Four

The Leaving of Liverpool

His journey on the Liverpool Overhead Railway, to join the M.V. "Willaston", began at Toxteth Station. With his bedding and other possessions he was not too welcome on the crowded morning train. However, with some contrivance, and many apologies, he finally found a seat and wedged his belongings between his knees. Luckily he was on the side of the carriage nearest the river which gave him a magnificent view of the dock system and the forest of hulls, upperworks and masts stretched out below.

His first journey on the "Docker's Umbrella", as it was affectionately termed, had been with Vincent and his father. Having just learned to read, he remembered bursting with pride as he had repeated the message on the poster by the ticket office:

"Round trip of 13 miles
to see
the Finest Docks in the World
and the
Giant Ocean Liners.
1st Class 1/-
3rd Class 9d.
The first overhead electric railway
In the World."

His reward was a toffee apple. A real apple, that is, covered with a cap of melted toffee. Vincent got one too, for his hours of work helping him through his story books. Then Kevin recalled every detail of that day.

His jaw tightened as he looked down on the East Toxteth Dock which he knew had been attacked by incendiary bombs just a few nights ago. Then the stations began to appear – Brunswick, Wapping, Custom House. As they went through James Street he saw what appeared to be a large passenger liner anchored midway between the Liverpool and Birkenhead shores and knew instinctively this was a troopship.

They reached Pier Head, the busiest station on the line and he relaxed comfortably as many passengers left the train which next moved off to the Princes Dock station. His thoughts turned again to the questions his father set them about the Overhead Railway: "next three stations after Canada, going north?" (Brocklebank, Langton, Alexandra) "next three stations after Sandon, going south?" (Nelson, Clarence, Princes). "When was the line opened?" (1893) –"first one to answer gets a penny."

Then he recalled today's parting from his mother. He had always resented her belligerent concern but this morning he had understood fully the depth of her love for him. Even now, under his fingers, he could feel her trembling. He also understood fully, for the first time, the depth of his love for her. But he must for now keep thoughts of her out of his mind lest he might leap from the train and return to Toxteth.

The journey over, he stood in the chill air at the gate of the Huskisson Dock. He was admitted to the Dock office where his papers were checked. The berth of the "Willaston" was indicated to him. He set off towards her and frowned – the smart black and white paintwork in "Chippy's" picture had gone. She was painted grey overall. Then, with a curious sense of relief he saw that all the other vessels in the Dock were grey painted. It was O.K., he was making for the "Willaston" alright and he guessed correctly that the grey paint was wartime livery.

"Oi, lad!"

The loud call came from behind him. He turned. Despite the distance he had come he saw that the lodge keeper from the Dock office was beckoning. Kevin's ankle began to ache as he reached the man, who jerked his thumb towards the Dock wall:

"Your girl's out there. Wants to see you."

The youth's heart battered his rib cage. So!.....he knew it!.....Celia hadn't meant to rebuff him! It had been awkward for her, seeing him again after such a long time....that was all. Forgetting his ankle now, he raced back through the Dock gates, smiling expectantly.

Standing in the road was Kathleen Gallagher. He could not conceal his disappointment: a quiet "oh" was all he managed to say. She was hurt and bewildered:

"Well, don't look so happy about it!"

He hated himself for having upset her but could only wonder what to say. In order to mask her feelings she became matter of fact:

"I didn't know you were sailing from this far up. I'll be late for work. Listen......I thought I'd come to see you off and wish you all the best."

"It's good of you Kath, but I'm sure it'll all work out O.K."

"Yeah, well – you take care – d'you hear?"

He noticed the tiny points of light in her eyes, her unshed tears. She held out her hand:

"I want you to have this. It'll keep you safe"

He looked down, at a St. Christopher medal.

"Oh....thanks," was as much as he could manage.

A silence, then she kissed him on the cheek and embarrassed by her own emotion she turned away and ran back along Regent Road.

"Come back safe," she managed to call over her shoulder.

He limped through the Dock office and made for the "Willaston" again, bewildered. Why were things so complicated?

Boarding the vessel was easy enough. Getting anyone to notice him was harder, in all the rush and bustle. Then out of the activity a smiling youth emerged:

"Hi ya. You Kevin Donnelly?"

When Kevin nodded, the smile broadened:

"I'm Billy, Billy Elkin. We're muckers."

Kevin was uncertain.

"You'll be werkin with me," Elkin explained.

Now a broad-shouldered, uniformed man of medium height was coming towards them. He looked tough and his rasping voice confirmed the impression:

"You Donnelly?"

"Yes...."

"Yes, what?"

Kevin thought quickly:

"Yes....sir."

The man looked him up and down, considering:
"That ankle of yours....saw you limping aboard. Sure
you can cope?"

"Yes, sir."

Kevin had tried to answer with assurance though
the pace of the work going on around him made him less
certain.

"Hm. I see Elkin's introduced himself. He'll show you
where to stow your gear. Then report back here. We'll be
sailing before long and there's still plenty to do. So look
sharp!"

In spite of this rather dusty introduction to seaboard
life, Donnelly was excited to hear they would soon be
under way. He followed the deck boy, trying to hide his
limp.

"Was that the captain?" he asked in a whisper.

Billy laughed:

"No.....that's Martin Swain, Third Mate. "Swain the
Swine", we call him. He fancies himself a bit, but he's
O.K. Except we're supposed to work to Dave Porter, the
Bosun's Mate, who leaves you to get on with things....
but Swain keeps dippin' his oar in....so we never know if
we're comin' or goin'."

When they reached the crew's quarters Billy noticed
the dejection on Kevin's face as he tried to infiltrate himself
into the tiny space where he would live and sleep.

"It's a bit pokey but that's more space than you'd
get in the Royal Navy," Elkin said cheerily. "Though
their food's better," he added in a quieter voice. Then he
became enthused again:

"An' we're right next to the galley see!"

He steered Kevin to an open door nearby, nodding to a
young Chinese seaman busying himself with cooking
pots and the galley fire.

"You can always nip in here for a warm," Elkin

confided.

"Can you do that?"

"I should cocoa. Well, whenever you can like. When you get a force eight gale up your jumper you'll be glad of this place."

Kevin nodded. He remembered Chippy Gallagher's advice that, off watch, the best way to keep warm was to get to the galley fire.

Billy was beginning to enjoy his role of mentor:

"Harry Merritt, the cook's, a bit of a misery but he won't say anything as long as you don't leave the door open. Tai Lok's the assistant cook...you saw him. He's jonnick, he'll make you a drink as soon as your head's round the door."

Then Billy became confidential:

"Just don't let the "Swine" see you in here, off watch or not. O.K.?"

Kevin nodded, as knowingly as he could.

When they returned amidships, the Third Mate told him that, for now, he was to assist Elkin in whatever he was doing. As Donnelly worked he became conscious of being watched. Unobtrusively, he glanced towards the foot of the companion-way leading to the bridge. Standing there were a tall, uniformed man and an elegant elderly gentleman wearing a Homburg hat. When he caught their stares he looked away quickly. Had he been within earshot he would have heard himself being discussed:

"I noticed that young fellow limping, Mr Stephens. Who is he?"

"A lad signed on for the voyage. Mr Dunlop says he has some sports injury or other."

"Will he be able to manage?"

"I think so, sir. We're indemnified for any accident due to his problem. Actually, he's the son of a man I've sailed with – chap called Donnelly- good man. Unfortunately, he died in a sinking just after the war started."

"And this boy has decided to have a go himself, eh? Well....it says a lot for his pluck. Let me know how he gets on will you?

"Yes, Mr Miles."

Later, when the men had moved on Kevin learned from Billy that the tall man was Captain George Stephens, master of the "Willaston" and the elegant older man "in the Anthony Eden hat" was Mr Miles Edmonds, one of the joint owners of the Wirral Peninsular Line. Billy added:

"He's a nice bloke. Comes down to visit every one of his ships before they sail. Yer won't find many owners doin' that, mate."

In the next few hours Kevin found himself at the edge of the ritual involved in getting the "Willaston" completely prepared for the voyage and moving her out of the Huskisson Dock and into the Mersey. It was a ritual with its own language, not all of which he understood and it moved to a climax when the pilot came on board. Then the orders came crisply: "Everybody at stations?"; "engines on standby"; "tugs fore and aft made fast"; "let go headrope"; "let go backspring", "dead slow ahead". He saw the tugs take the strain, assist the "Willaston" to move stern first from the berth then swing about in the dock so that she went bow first through the locks and into the river where, in mid-stream, she dropped anchor.

At that moment, in Liverpool 8, Mary Gallagher was nodding towards the Donnelly house next door:

"You know, Tom, that poor soul's on her own. I think I'll ask her in for a cuppa tea."

Over the tea, Mary referred to her daughter's long trek to the Huskisson Dock to say farewell to Kevin:

"She was an hour late for work.....but she didn't drop into trouble. They're letting her make the time up."

Liz Donnelly nodded with relief:

"You know, it's amazing how your Kath clings to Kevin."

"She's been daft about him since they were nippers," piped in "Chippy". Before raising her teacup again, Liz smiled a small smile of gratification for she thought Kathleen "a lovely girl" but as she remembered the immense care her son had taken before his visit to Celia Molloy, the smile disappeared.

A few miles down the river, on the foredeck of the "Willaston", Kevin was enriching his labours with thoughts of Celia.

"Hey!....Donnelly!....don't stand there like a statue!......help get these mooring lines stowed away!" He looked up. This was a new voice....guttural, somewhat breathless. A thick-necked squat man confronted him. Later he learned that this was Dave Porter, the Bosun's Mate.

As Kevin bent to his task, Billy Elkin was grinning at him. Somehow this made up for Porter's ferocity. Before long they began to move down river towards the harbour bar. Passing the Langton and Alexandra Docks he was able to see the severe damage caused by high explosive bombs some nights earlier. He learned from the conversations of the other crew members that some dock sheds, the Harbour Master's house and four ships had taken the worst of the onslaught. Coming abreast of the Gladstone Dock his pulse quickened for this was where His Majesty's warships were berthed. Glimpsing the tightly massed destroyers and corvettes left him with the feeling that in this perilous sea war Britain had something at least with which to fight back.

Having helped Billy with the mooring lines they next lashed the ship's derricks into their crutches. As they moved into Liverpool Bay it felt distinctly more turbulent than in the river and presently they reduced speed.

"Why are we stopping?", Donnelly asked.

A voice behind him said:

"We're going to muster here with the rest of the convoy."

He turned to face a tall man, middle-aged, spare, with light wispy hair and a craggy face. The man smiled:

"You're Joe Donnelly's lad, right?"

Kevin realised who the questioner was:

"And you're Hugh Riley....the donkey man, sorry the motor man."

"That's alright. Diesel ship or not, a lot of old timers still call me the donkey man."

"Thanks for having a word with the Company for me"

"It's O.K. They didn't take much persuadin'. I've been watchin' you workin'. You look strong enough but they'll insist you get that foot o' yours put right afore they'll offer you an apprenticeship....if you're stayin' at sea that is. I was sorry to hear about your father. I knew him well y'know. Sailed with him all over the place. If you're anythin' like him, you'll do."

A young man was coming towards them. He seemed even younger than Billy and himself, Kevin thought.

"Mr Riley."

"Yes, Alan?"

"The lights are on the blink in the Old Man's cabin. He wonders if you could get the Third Engineer to take a look."

"Sure," said the motor man and went back along the deck.

The newcomer grinned:

"Hallo. You Kevin Donnelly?"

His grin was infectious. Kevin smiled and nodded. This relaxed, dark-haired lad who spoke in cultured tones seemed extremely friendly. He put out his hand to Kevin who, faintly embarrassed, shook it.

"I'm Alan Wilson, an apprentice with WPL. Like you, this is my first voyage with them. The Captain asked me to check you'd found your bunk O.K. and stowed your gear."

"Yes. Thanks."

"Mr Swain and Dave Porter will explain about your work."

"They've already put me right," said Donnelly with a wry expression.

Wilson noted it and laughed:

"Don't worry. They're not as tough as they seem. Anything I can help you with?"

Struck by a sudden thought, Kevin said:

"Yes. Where are we going?"

Alan Wilson laughed. Billy Elkin, within earshot, joined in. Then the amiable youth became more serious:

"We're going to Canada. We'll be coming back with a full cargo – war materials an' that. Now, when we've formed up into convoy, we'll be joined by our escorts. Today, we're sailing up to the Western Isles – you know – Barra, South Uist...?"

More with interest than certainty, Kevin nodded.

"Anyway, they're on the edge of the Atlantic and we'll be mustering there with a bigger convoy."

"Now then, Wilson! Don't keep these men loitering! They've got work to do!"

By now, the Third Mate's voice was unmistakable. He approached them briskly.

"Elkin!.....I told you to make sure the derricks were stowed and lashed...."

"They're done, sir," cut in Billy.

"And what about the hatch tarps and the wedges? Are they checked?"

"We were just goin' to....."

"Go and check them now! We'll soon be under way. I'll be back shortly and if they haven't been done you're in trouble. We're making for the Western Ocean, not Sefton Park lake! So get cracking!....and take him with you!", he bawled, motioning to Kevin.

As he watched the boy from Beresford Road limp away, the Third Mate was disdainful:

"Just look at that," he murmured to Wilson.....,"when it comes to crewing, we're nearly running on empty these days."

"I think he'll be O.K. really Mr. Swain and he's sturdy enough. I saw him handling the hatch tarpaulins. And he was just asking me about the voyage. I....."

"That's all well and good, but there's work to do and that includes you."

Then improving his tone, Swain continued:

"The Old Man wants me to take you through the ship's bag. We need to look at the manifest and check it with the cargo documents. The paper work can be a pain in the neck if you don't know what you're doing. He thinks you ought to get clued up on that side o' things, so let's go and have a shufti."

As they moved off, Swain became confidential:

"A word to the wise – it doesn't do to get too cosy with the crew. O.K?"

Without agreement or insolence Wilson smiled. He would learn all there was to learn, he would do all there was to do, but he would be his own man.

That evening, a small convoy, fourteen ships in all, escorted by a Flower-class corvette and an ancient sloop, made reasonable speed northward through the Irish Sea. The convoy was arranged in two columns. The "Willaston" was in the middle station of the seven ships in the port column. Donnelly's exhilaration at leaving Liverpool Bay had been marred by his first bout of seasickness but recovered now and off duty, he had come on deck keen to see what was going on.

Winter was arriving and he shivered in what old salts disapprovingly called "a lazy wind": one that went through you rather that 'round you. But his curiosity blotted out any discomfort as he peered through the night at the progress of the convoy. He noted how the escort vessels moved along the columns of the ships exhorting them, by Aldis lamp signals, to keep station. He was reminded of the busy sheep dogs seen on his cycling journeys to North Wales.

He stayed by the ship's rail. Gradually his mind became a blank backdrop. Out of it emerged the beautiful face of Celia Molloy. The wind's moaning gave force to the misery he still felt recalling their recent meeting.

"Feeling better?", said someone at his elbow. It was the motor man.

"Yes....thanks....Mr Riley," he replied, smoothing over his confusion.

"I was just watching the convoy. There's more to it than I realised."

"Oh aye. Lots o' snags in convoy work, even in port."

"How?"

"Well, you saw how long we were formin' up and getting' under way. That causes congestion. Then when the convoy sails its pegged back by the slowest ships and some convoys are a right rag-bag, I can tell you. Everything's bein' pressed into service, no matter how unsafe."

Then he pointed to the dark outlines of the ships around them:

"But the biggest problem is keepin' station, see? Aye."

The pointing finger circled around to the vessel dead

ahead of them:

"See her blue stern light? Well, the Old Man must keep us five cables length from it. An' in poor visibility she trails a fog buoy so we can take our station from that."

"Why?"

"Collision! If we run into one another, Jerry needn't send U-boats to sink us."

"Is it tricky, keeping station?"

"What?!....stands to sense. An' remember – we've had no peacetime practice for this. The Merchant Service has to learn as it goes along – an' the Royal Navy does."

Then he deemed it wise to enlarge his explanation:

"Your average Master's a loner. He's learned to look after his own ship, plot his own course and get every trip over as fast as he can. The owners expect that as well, or they'll lose money. So your captain isn't used to bein' herded 'round with a lot of others an' told what to do."

Kevin frowned:

"So why have convoys?"

"'cause it's safer. That's what they found out in the First World War."

Riley swept his arm around the convoy:

"If this lot tried to cross th' Atlantic on their own, it's even money they'd be sunk."

Just then the wind increased measurably, piercing their clothes with ease and driving them both below decks.

Later that night Donnelly was arguing with Elkin the merits of footballers and football clubs. They were joined by Harry Feltham, a giant of a man well over six feet in height with chest and shoulders in proportion. He was not yet known to Kevin.

"Watch out, the Navy's 'ere!" chimed Elkin.

Feltham was a jaunty Londoner with a fine-toned voice who was often to be heard singing the latest "hits", if only to himself. He feinted as if to grab Billy's throat. The lad from Bootle jerked his head away only to find himself held fast in a tight arm lock. He was not in the least put out by his predicament and alluding to Feltham's size asked chirpily:

"Where you bin?.....windin' the Liver clock?"

In a mock threatening voice, Feltham said:

"I shall ram you into my pop-gun, Frisby Dyke, an' blow you out to the fishes, if your manners don't improve."

When Billy was released, he said for Kevin's benefit:

"This is the DEMS wallah.....slummin' with the likes of us."

As the Toxteth youth still looked blank, Feltham explained that DEMS meant Defensively Armed Merchant Ships, that he was a DEMS gunner, a rating in the Royal Navy, who had been assigned to the "Willaston" to take charge of the 4 inch gun mounted aft and the machine gun on her bridge. Apart from operating the "4 inch" himself, he was also responsible for training up merchant seamen as additional gunners.

"You can come an' have a gander at the "4 inch" if you're interested," he said to Kevin and turning to Billy he grinned:

"Not you......cheeky sod!"

Kevin couldn't believe his luck and was thanking Feltham when Billy added:

"Stand well back 'case he blows the bloody thing up."

Their discussion on soccer was then resumed. Feltham would not agree with the eminence being allotted by the other two to the Everton and Liverpool clubs. He argued strongly for the cause of Arsenal F.C.

"So you support that lot, do you?" queried Elkin. Then, winking at Kevin he added sympathetically:

"Still, I've haird there are such toe-rags about."
Calmly, Feltham was shaking his head. He was not an Arsenal supporter.

"What's your team then?", persisted the lad from Bootle.

Swelling with pride, Feltham replied:

"Clapton Orient!"

"That's not a team, it's a tropical disease," observed Hugh Riley who was working his way through their small space. Even Feltham was contributing to the general laughter when Alan Wilson joined the group.

"Everything O.K.?", he asked Kevin.

"Yes, thanks. It was interesting – you explaining where we're off to."

"Anything else you want to know?"

"Well.....I was wondering what cargo we're carrying."

"Not much actually, considering she's a five thousand tonner with five holds. We're in ballast, mainly."

"What's that?"

"Material to weigh the ship down and steady her. It could be heavy solid stuff or water or both. If a gale hit us and we were riding too high in the water we could soon keel over. Usually it's cargo that puts the trim of the vessel right but there's not much to export right now from Britain. It's not so much what convoys take that's important, it's what they bring back."

"So we've got no cargo, apart from this ballast?"

"We have actually. More than most I should think. I've been looking at the manifest and the shipping docs. We've got a lot of expensive ceramics from Stoke, glassware from Stourbridge, Sheffield cutlery, worsted cloth and Harris tweed, carpets from Kidderminster. Oh, and we've got sixteen crates of one pint mugs for the Canadian Army.

What cargo we have is well below our carrying capacity but most of it is valuable - you'd have to work all your life to afford some of it. It's the scrapings up of what our factories made before they went on to war work apparently. Anything that'll earn us dollars."

Kevin was thoughtful. Up to now, when he had looked down at the Mersey all he knew was that the merchant ships came and went. Now the importance of the service was becoming clear. And he supposed the world of work had its first fascination for any novice but to him sea service was especially intriguing. The weather was foul and so was some of the language but he could put up with both.....they were part of the job.

Alan Wilson continued talking but in quieter tones:

"Most of the ships in the Atlantic convoy will be going direct to Halifax. When we're on the other side, we'll be peeling off with some other ships that have exports and putting into Boston first. Then we'll go up the coast to Halifax to take on our return cargo and form up into another convoy."

Kevin tried to conceal it but he was bursting with anticipation. He could not wait for the adventure to begin.

Chapter Five

Outward Bound

At first light on the following morning, Donnelly felt himself being nudged into consciousness. It was Billy Elkin:

"Come on Kev. Board of Trade sports in thirty minutes!"

"What?"

"Boat drill.........has to be done within twenty four hours of sailin'."

"What's boat drill?"

"We muster by the lifeboat – the port station for us – in life-jackets. Well, come on!....... jump to!"

Donnelly wasn't sure about the life jacket. He watched

Billy putting his on then produced what he thought was a passable imitation. Elkin shook his head:

"What a barm cake you are, Toxteth. You look like a bag o' muck tied in the middle. Come 'ere!"

Minutes later he surveyed his handiwork then sighed with some emphasis:

"Makin' a Merchant Jack out o' you's goin' be all uphill, mate. Bet there's unny me that's diddy enough to try it."

They both laughed.

Kevin noted they were checked off from a muster list. He also learned there was a list of the ship's full complement on display outside the crew mess room. Looking at it when the drill was over, and concentrating on the jobs rather than the names he learned that the Willaston's crew comprised: the Master; the First, Second and Third Mates; a Radio Officer (Marconi); one DEMS gunner; a Chief Engineer plus his Second, Third and Fourth Engineers; one Deck Apprentice/Cadet; two Deck Boys; a Chief Steward and Second Steward plus seven members of the Engine Room Crew and eight members of the Deck Crew. He totalled this to thirty men in all. Thirty men hopeful of pitting their skills and nerve against the ocean and the enemy, then coming through with the job done.

In the days that followed everything transpired as Alan Wilson had predicted. In all, sixty four merchant vessels assembled within sight of South Uist. Within thirty six hours, twenty two of these had sailed south. The "buzz" was that they were bound for West Africa en route to Cape Town. The other forty two vessels, including the "Willaston" were mustered into seven columns of six. The escort comprised the corvette and the sloop which had accompanied them from Liverpool Bay, together with two other corvettes.

These latter vessels had just undergone fast working-up in anti-submarine warfare and sea training of their crews. Then they had been newly commissioned as escorts. They had sailed from the training base at Tobermory Bay on the Isle of Mull. So, in the convoy setting out, many more than Kevin Donnelly were "new to the job." Four vessels, therefore, made up the escort group for this convoy. Later in the war six escorts would be the norm for a venture of this kind.

On a grey morning in early November the convoy sailed west. Soon after it was under way, a light but persistent drizzle descended. In the early days of its progress, aircraft of R.A.F. Coastal Command appeared from time to time. As the deck boys went about their duties, Elkin pointed them out:

"They'll cover us for the first four hundred miles. That's the limit of their range. The U-boats'll leave us alone while they're about. Then we're on our own, mate."

"All the way to Boston?"

"No, well, I don't know. Y'see if we were goin' straight to Halifax or St John's, the Canadian Air Force would cover us for the last four hundred miles. I don't know if we get air cover to Boston. America's neutral."

"So if a convoy's covered for the first and last four hundred mile stretches, Jerry's likely to pop up in between........is that it?"

"Right. The middle bit's called 'the black hole' and that's where he gets up to his tricks. You don't have to be good at sums to figure he's got plenty of space to clobber us when he's ready. That's why we have to zig-zag."

The boys continued working, each with his own thoughts.

The weather waited until the convoy was well into the Atlantic before it put in its most emphatic appearance yet. At first the winds only stiffened so that Donnelly wondered why lifelines were being rigged around the decks. In an hour or so the turbulence had increased and in a few more hours the seas were mountainous and the winds vile. As the convoy struggled to make any progress at all, the youth understood the reason for the lifelines.

When the gale was at its worst, Willy Merritt, the ship's cook, put his head into Kevin's bunk space. He held out a billy-can:

"First Mate wants this coffee, on the bridge."

With a look of disdain he put it down and disappeared. Kevin did not like Merritt. He had a sour face and a matching disposition. Possibly his off-handedness resulted from years of defending small portions and burnt offerings. Or perhaps periodic incursions of the sea, which put out his fires and ruined his creations, had something to do with it.

When Donnelly stepped out onto the deck, though not a fearful individual, he felt, quite clearly, his life was in danger. The gale tore at his face, his life-jacket, his legs. He fought for his breath. He clenched his teeth and step by slow step, made his way forward. The bubbling wet deck felt like ice beneath his feet. The vessel's superstructure, housing the galley, crew's quarters and bridge, was pierced by an alley-way. He was now crossing the end of this and reaching out to grasp the companion-way leading to the bridge.

As if on cue, an immense wave hit the "Willaston's" port side beam on. It heaved her into a thirty degree list to starboard. The sea burst its way across the vessel funnelling at tremendous speed through the alley-way. The billy-can was flung from Kevin's hand and he fell to the lurching deck. Only his left hand on the lifeline was saving him from being washed away.

Yelling with the agony of his effort he pushed his right hand through the raging water and grabbed the lifeline with it. However, while he hung on for his life the sea was determined to batter his grip loose and suck him down to its depths. Every last ounce of his strength was ebbing away. He knew he was weakening fatally and felt himself about to let go of the line.

This was when he felt an arm slip under his shoulders and he glimpsed another hand grasping the handrail of the companion-way. Now a body was lying across his own holding him fast against the surge of the sea. The mouth next to his ear was yelling: "Hang on, Kev!" It was Billy Elkin. The vessel was still being battered by the monstrous seas, which surged without ceasing through the alley-way. There was no sign of the "Willaston" righting itself and the boys hung together in mortal peril. They could not endure their struggle to breathe for much longer.

After a few more seconds of torture the "Willaston's" list began to decrease and Kevin felt a second pair of arms locking themselves around him.

"Can you get to your feet?" The coughing, wheezing nature of the urgent question signalled the latest helper was Dave Porter, the Bosun's Mate.

Donnelly stirred and struggled, but his feet could get no hold on the slippery deck. As the ship continued to take on wave after wave of water, the constriction imposed on it by the narrow alley-way compounded its force so that the three of them felt as if some massive fire hose was trying to wash them away.

"Help 'im get on his feet!" spluttered Porter to Billy Elkin "an' hold fast to the lifeline!"

In the next two minutes the huddled men had eased themselves back along the lifeline away from the end of the alley. Presently, they managed to reach the galley door, struggled to open it, then fell in a heap into the warm, steamy space of the galley itself.

The three tried to recover their breath. This was the hardest for the bosun's mate, who was still on his knees, his body jerking up and down with the effort. Merritt, the cook, gave them no help and glanced only at the galley floor where the trio had shaken as much of the North Atlantic as they could.

Still breathless, Porter turned on Kevin:

"What the......hell........were you doin' out there?"

"Taking coffee up to the bridge."

The Bosun's Mate glanced at Billy Elkin, exasperated:

"Aren't you supposed to be looking after him?"

His yelling rose above the thunder of the sea and the agonised rocking of the "Willaston".

"I didn't know he'd gone," Elkin protested.

"Where were you?"

Billy pointed:

"In the galley coal bunker, getting stuff out for the fires."

Porter turned again to Kevin:

"Who sent you out there?"

The boy was spared embarrassment when the cook, said sourly:

"I did."

"Have you no more sense? The lad can't walk properly never mind cross a deck in this weather!"

"How'm I to cope without help? The assistant cook's sick. There's only this pair to lend a hand."

He nodded towards Kevin:

"If he's not up to the job, he shouldn't be aboard."

Porter did not answer, but looked angrily at Kevin and Billy:

"I'm going to tell Martin Swain either to keep a closer

eye on you or let me do it, without interfering. You pair of silly buggers!"

Coughing again he left and as he did so more sea water burst through the open door as if to lend force to his remarks.

Some hours later the pair were trying to sleep in spite of the roaring winds and the battering waves. Kevin looked to the bunk above him:

"I'm sorry I got you into trouble, Billy."

"It's O.K., mate. It wasn't your fault. You've gotta go where you're sent."

Kevin knew that the lad above him had saved his life. He fumbled for appreciative words:

"Thanks for coming after me, anyway," was what he managed at last.

"It's O.K. ole custard," came the chirpy reply, then Billy began to laugh.

"What's funny?"

"Did you see ole Porter's face?......it was purple!"

Elkin then began to sing quietly. With a little effort, and despite the howling winds and the creaking protests of the "Willaston", his tune could be recognised as "Run, rabbit, run." Kevin thought one thing certain: whatever alarms were in store for them, they would be bearable with Billy for company.

A little later, Alan Wilson arrived. By now it had gone around the ship that Kevin had almost been swept away. Wilson had heard of it when he came off watch. He smiled, as usual, but was concerned:

"What have you been up to?"

"I nearly lost an argument with this weather. When the big waves hit us I thought we were a goner."

"Well.....these tubs'll take some battering."

Kevin was dispirited:

"How come you and Billy can get around in it and I

can't?"

"Your foot won't help much, will it? Anyway, it's moderating now so it'll be easier. That's how I've managed to get down here."

The lad from Liverpool 8 shook his head:

"I feel a liability to everybody. I've made a pig's ear of a lot I've been told to do....and other people put their lives in danger because I'm useless,"

"Look ...don't fash yourself......you'll get used to it. Get your foot put right and give yourself time. It's obvious you're as strong as anybody else round the deck and you'll be as capable, you'll see."

Kevin was hardly convinced:

"It just seems to come so naturally to you and Billy."

"No.....not naturally, we had to learn. Besides, I've been around boats since I could walk. My dad has a yacht. I've crewed for him.....been all around Britain. That's how I know about the Western Isles, you know, where we mustered? What happened wasn't your fault. You shouldn't have been sent out in weather like this."

Donnelly smiled a little. One day before long this cadet would make a fine officer, probably have his own ship.

"Listen," said Wilson, "I'm off for some kip. I'm on again next watch, but I've brought you a tot. Drink it, it'll warm you. And cheer up!"

He grinned again and left.

Kevin rubbed his throbbing ankle and drank down the rum. As it warmed him he felt better about things and lay back on his bunk. The force of the gale was still strong enough to heave the "Willaston" about, but he tried to close his mind to it. He was just drifting off to sleep when Hugh Riley appeared.

In his seemingly offhand way, he was concerned:

"How are things?"

"Fine. Just lost my footing, but I'm O.K. now, thanks to Billy here."

Kevin pointed upward to where his colleague was sleeping deeply.

"You shouldn't uv bin sent out," Riley growled. "I've told Merritt what I think on that score."

They talked on for a while then, after a small silence, Kevin said:

"To be honest, I never thought weather could be so terrifying."

This prompted the motor man to become quietly philosophical:

"Right now we've got no option, but to sail in this vile muck. Make no mistake, the North Atlantic's no friend to ships or sailors. It's never at rest.....always stirring itself up. With one depression coming so quick after another you get to think the weather's all depressions. You've to sail through thousands o' miles of menance. The sea'll bubble and boil and tear at everything and the sky's grey from one horizon to another. If it's not grey it's black. An' we've got to keep station in it while we're zig-zagging."

Steadily, he looked at Kevin then pointed towards the still-turbulent sea beyond the ship:

"U-boats are one thing, but that is your enemy as well. An' if you don't keep your wits about it, it'll have you."

Kevin looked at the motor man who pressed him:

"D'you hear?"

"Yes."

Riley looked at the boy again:

"O.K.?"

Kevin nodded. Riley smiled and left.

There was another storm before they reached the Mid-Ocean Meeting Point (M.O.M.P.) where escort duty for the convoy was taken over by a Canadian destroyer and two corvettes, with the original escort group due to return to Britain after it had located and joined a homeward bound convoy. At this stage rumours emerged across the outward bound convoy that it was being shadowed by a U-boat, but no attack materialised. The "Willaston"s master, George Stephens, found no cause for joy in this. As they stood together on the port wing of the bridge he confided to Ian Dunlop, the First Mate:

"Jerry's canny. If he attacks now, he knows that all he'll sink are empty bottoms. If he waits till we come back he'll get the cargoes as well as the ships."

They watched as the new escorts on the flanks of the convoy fell into the familiar role of beating up and down exhorting all vessels to keep station. Because some of the ships had seen better days they found it hard to maintain the eight knot speed set for the convoy. Perhaps the notion of being left as stragglers, with its high possibility of being attacked and sunk, lent force to their crews' efforts to flog every vestige of power from these old stagers.

As Stephens watched the activities of the escort he mused:

"We're favoured having that destroyer with us. Let's hope he stays with us when we divert to Boston. Otherwise, we'd be well set up for the visit of a surface raider. 'Sparks' has handed me a signal warning that the 'Admiral Scheer' may be about."

At that point, Kevin Donnelly brought coffee up to the bridge.

"Have you recovered from your soaking, young man? asked Stephens.

"Yes, thank you, sir," said the youth with all the assurance he could manage. As he left the bridge, Stephens turned to Dunlop:

"How's he coping?"

"Quite well. He's strong as a lion. I think if he decided he liked the life he could be useful to us."

"Mm, pity about that gammy leg."

"He's seeing a specialist when he gets back – he was medically cleared for this voyage on that proviso."

In that Autumn of 1940 the North Atlantic lived up to its benighted reputation, but despite the foul weather there was excitement and relief when, at last, planes of the Royal Canadian Air Force appeared out of the overcast to protect the main part of the convoy en route to Halifax. Almost immediately the R.C.A.F. appeared, the six vessels in the port wing column of the convoy, including the "Willaston", altered course for Boston accompanied by a single corvette. Intact, they entered its port on a still, starry night. Though exhausted, young Kevin Donnelly was also excited. "If only Celia were here," he thought. Yet it didn't matter: when he returned he would tell her all about it.

Chapter Six

Delight and Disaster

At first Kevin, having no money, or so he thought, resisted Billy's urgings to accompany him ashore. Then, a flicker of memory – what had his mother pushed into his jacket as he was leaving home? He pulled an envelope from his pocket. In it were five one-pound notes. Five pounds..... from the seemingly matter-of-fact woman who cared for him so much. Five pounds! How had she managed to save this? He was astounded.

Boston was a revelation. Billy told him he had "put in" there previously and he pretended to be blasé about the city's charms - but his own fascination was clear. After the hand-to-mouth existence of wartime Liverpool, the lights, the food on offer and the welcomes they received stunned them. What a strange life seamen lead, thought Kevin – out of hell and straight into heaven.

The boys were in a down-town bar where, Billy explained: "Your lot go out on de ale." By "your lot" he meant the families of the sometime Irish immigrants who were also such a feature of his own native city. Despite the history of Ireland's relations with the U.K. the boys were being warmly welcomed by the Bostonians when, quite quickly, they were joined by a smiling, friendly couple who introduced themselves as Bridie and Gerard Keating. Bridie (nee Tobin) was a third generation Irish American. Notwithstanding his Irish names, Gerard was originally a native-born Englishman. He had emigrated to the U.S.A. in the early nineteen thirties, become naturalised and was now a successful businessman in food distribution. When the boys introduced themselves the fact that Kevin's family name was Donnelly added more impetus to a fast-emerging friendship.

Bridie was anxious to know if they had eaten. She was assured that they were about to order but she swept this aside: they had to have "a home-cooked meal."

"She's a great cook," smiled "Gerry" Keating and asked:

"How soon are you due back on the boat?"

"No later than noon tomorrow."

"Right - then you can stay the night with us," put in Gerry. Bridie nodded vigorously. The boys smiled at each other, then at the Keatings and shrugged their agreement and thanks.

They were leaving the bar and bumped into Alan Wilson.

"Oh....," he said to the youngsters, smiling but a little disconcerted.... "you just leaving? I was trying to track you down..."

Gerry Keating sized up the situation instantly:

"A friend of yours, obviously,"

As they nodded, he smiled at Alan:

"We're just off to our place, care to come?"

Wilson read the enthusiasm in the eyes of his colleagues and said:

"Well....yes. If it's not inconvenient."

"Not a bit!", grinned Bridie, "the more the merrier."

Further introductions were quickly over and twenty minutes later the Keating limousine purred up the drive of a large house in a prosperous Boston suburb.

They were given a tour of the property while Bridie prepared the meal with great verve. For the youths, each minute revealed a new wonder. Keating was not to know that Billy and Kevin were seeing bathrooms and carpets for the first time. They were intrigued by the telephone, which Bridie employed intensively, even while she cooked. The refrigerator and the radiogram, with its capacity to take a stack of records and play them in sequence, had them spellbound. Even Alan Wilson, whose own house contained at least some of these wonders, was mightily impressed.

"It's just like in the pictures!", Billy declared forcefully.

"Pardon me?," said Gerry.

"Like it is on the films," Alan explained.

"Oh....the movies!", Gerry laughed, "you hear that, honey? .....they think this place should be in the movies!"

Later, after a sumptuous meal of many courses, and as the three were trying to express their deep gratitude, Gerry suddenly became serious. Quietly, and with some difficulty, he said:

"It's nothin'....an' the least we can do for the job you're doin'." He looked quickly at Bridie. She smiled encouragingly but he felt unable to say more.

They then talked into the small hours but even when the youths had gone to bed, the Keatings were reluctant to retire.

"The old place knocked their eyes out," grinned Gerry, remembering.

Bridie kneaded her neat little hands together anxiously:

"What must it be like to live over there? They tried hard not to bolt their food but poor Billy's stomach rumbled whenever he put a morsel to his mouth."

Gerry thought for a second:

"I think Alan's used to better things but the other two are dirt poor – an' they have to mix it with U-boats to make a livin'."

This increased Bridie's anxiety:

"Did you see the flimsy clothes they wore? An' the boy who limps – Kevin – his shoes look to be made from cardboard. An' how can they work in Winter without any warm clothes?"

"They're surely not dressed for the North Atlantic – 'cept maybe Alan," confided Gerard.

"Is it dangerous out there?", wondered Bridie.

"Dangerous! You kiddin' me? It's murder, an' these kids are only civilians!"

"Gerry!....we've gotta take 'em down town in the mornin' and get them new clothes."

Her husband smiled:

"Sure, honey. I thought you'd get 'round to somethin' like that."

This was how, at noon next day, the three youths stepped from the Keating limousine each sporting a thick, roll-necked, cable-patterned sweater. Kevin's pride in his new, sturdy twenty-five dollar boots was matched by that of Billy Elkin in his new moleskin trousers.

As they boarded the "Willaston", their minds were

closed to the fierce looks from Martin Swain and Dave Porter for they were concentrating on waving their goodbyes to the Keatings on the dock side. From the bridge two others were watching. Captain Stephens looked but said nothing and First Mate Dunlop merely smiled and shook his head. Billy Elkin was still smiling as he turned towards Martin Swain and this fuelled the man's wrath:

"Been enjoying yourself, have you? So you'll be set up for some hard work then, eh? We'll be under way in an hour so get changed and report back here pronto."
Billy disappeared with Kevin following. Alan Wilson made his way to the officers' quarters.

As the Keatings motored out of the port area, Gerard was smiling:

"I'm glad we met up with those kids. Made me feel younger. What are you thinking about, honey?"
Bridie didn't answer. Her attention was gripped by anxiety. In a futile gesture, she looked back towards the "Willaston's" berth but by now it was well out of sight.

That afternoon the M.V. "Willaston" set out for Canada, sailing well within what was described as the Pan American Neutrality Zone. During this leg of the journey, whenever off duty, Kevin made for the port rail of the vessel. He would think of home and, inevitably, would see the face of Celia Molloy and wonder what she was doing. Her deprecating comments about his job still hurt but they fired his ambition. He would succeed and that would make his hopes about her realistic. He thought of his mother and knew well enough what she would be doing – either praying for his safety or shining the already shining home for his return.

He hoped she was not worrying too much, but knew such hope was futile, she always worried too much. He wondered how she ever supported the burden of her worries. Still, what a tale he would have to tell her about

Boston and the Keatings. She would probably dismiss it as hopeless exaggeration but, in the end, he would convince her it was true.

Thinking of his mother led him back to Bridie Keating, for how like his own mother she was. The goodness of the woman and her concern for them had made them feel like her adopted children. And like every mother she had been reluctant to let them go. Perhaps for a little while they had made up for the children she did not have. He hoped so.

He watched the fairyland of lights that shone out from America's north east coast line. This also reinforced his memories of the Keatings and the fairyland they inhabited. U-boat crews surfacing near the coast to recharge their vessels' batteries would recall how clearly they had seen car headlights and breathed in the wondrous smell of the pine forests – an elixir after the stench in which they lived and worked when submerged. The lights would continue to shine even after the United States entered the war. They outlined coastal shipping beautifully in U-boat periscopes and were extinguished only after the bitter slaughter of ships and sailors.

After a short, intermediate voyage, the "Willaston" sailed past the City of Halifax, Nova Scotia and entered the superb Bedford Basin. Kevin was on deck as they made their way into it. He was so awestruck he paused in his work and went over to the ship's rail. Hugh Riley joined him. The motor man noted the boy's wonder at this superb natural harbour and the number of ships anchored within it.

"This is where the convoy forms up, as you can see."

"Yeah right. It's so calm in here."

"That's what makes it ideal: ten miles square, all deep water, sheltered from the gales and ice-free all the time."

Now the "Willaston" was picking her way through the other merchant ships.

"Thirty three of 'em," said Billy, completing his counting.

"Thirty four with us," added Riley, "and more to come."

Having negotiated the Basin the "Willaston" moved forward and began to take on cargo for the return to Britain. This included wheat and other precious foodstuffs, small arms and ammunition and additional strategic war material.

During the loading, Alan Wilson was everywhere, involved in everything, not walking when he could run. His enthusiasm was contagious so that Kevin began to enjoy the task, sharing Wilson's unspoken aspiration to deliver the vessel's riches to where they were so badly needed.

Donnelly was on the foredeck coiling a heavy rope as though it were a child's plaything. Alan grinned as he skipped by.

"Are we ready for the hatch covers?", Kevin yelled after him

"Practically," the apprentice called back "if we took on another bit of cargo we'd be over our marks!" Then he grinned again and was gone.

The loading over, Kevin straightened up. His back felt broken but this did not diminish his sense of accomplishment.

"What now?", he asked Billy Elkin.

"We wait for orders.....so's we can muster with the rest of the convoy."

As Billy looked across at his colleague, he saw his face was white. He knew the signs now. Kevin's foot was playing him up. Unobtrusively, he made his way over to him.

"Listen, mate.....yous bin graftin' away at this loadin'. If yer foot's playin' you up, skive off to the galley for a warm. If Tatty 'Ead comes I'll tell him yous gone to the 'eads."

"No...no...I'm O.K.," was the quick reply. It was true his ankle pain was intense but he was determined to do his stint. Enough had already happened to make him feel a passenger. Also, he had seen the amount of gruelling work his shipmates got through without complaint and it had shaped his own resolve: he would "skive off" to nowhere.

Over the next thirty six hours the "buzz" was that they would be sailing in a convoy of forty eight ships, some bound for Belfast, the majority for Liverpool. The convoy would group into eight columns each of six ships. The "Willaston" would take station as the fifth ship in the starboard outer column.

"Not the best of places," averred Hugh Riley, "an' what's worse we're sailin' on a Friday." According to sailor's superstitions the last fact was not good. To emphasise his disgust, Riley went to the ship's rail and spat into the harbour.

"What's the word on the escorts?", he asked the passing Martin Swain.

"To the M.O.M.P., one destroyer, a corvette, and an A.M.C., apparently."

Riley shook his head sadly as Swain was turning to the two deck boys.

"Elkins! Donnelly! There's loads to do yet! Get mobile!"

They busied themselves, and Billy glanced sidelong at Kevin:

"I feel like givin' 'im a Timpson – right where he sits down. Get mobile!....get mobile!....he's bin vaccinated with a bloody gramophone needle."

Friday came and at first light the convoy put out into the North Atlantic. In only the second hour of its progress, and as if to counteract the tranquillity of the anchorage it had just enjoyed, it ran four square into a massive easterly gale. This seemed intent on blocking any further incursion into the wild, mountainous seas now raging off Canada's coast.

Once again, masters and crews gave themselves up to the struggle to keep their vessels on station. Moreover, the banshee wailing of the storm and the impenetrable overcast meant that the planes of the Royal Canadian Air Force, which would normally have protected them for the first leg of the journey, could not now take to the air. All in all, the atmosphere within the convoy had become miserably apprehensive.

Moreover, B-Dienst, the German intelligence service, had already intercepted and decoded messages from the Commodore of the convoy to H.Q. Western Approaches in Liverpool. And so, even at this stage, the Germans knew a great deal about the size and composition of the convoy, its speed, its routeing and its escorts. They were astonished that only three escorts were being employed. The Allies were in a worse state than they had imagined.

Berlin acted swiftly on this information. The U-boat nearest the convoy was ordered to proceed towards it rapidly. It was to take up position to its rear and "shadowing" the merchantmen, transmit details of their progress. This would enable the team of Admiral Karl Donitz, head of the U-boat service, to direct a horde of his submarines towards them in due time.

Over the next few days, the gales eased somewhat but the seas were still angry enough to make zig-zagging, and the keeping of the "Willaston" on station, difficult and tiring. Captain Stephens peered through the gloom to locate the stern light of the vessel ahead. Hours of this were doing nothing for his disposition. He crossed from the port wing of the bridge to the voice pipe:

"Get some coffee up here and try not to fall down with it!", he rasped, then immediately regretted his comments, for the deck-boys were hardly responsible for the arduous situation.

Surer now of the where and how of his footfalls, Donnelly set out from the galley with the coffee. As he made his way quite competently along the deck the Flower-class corvette acting as one of the escorts came abreast of the "Willaston" then passed on. The sea was still heavy enough to make the little craft bob like a cork. Kevin had seen it, in its role of "whipper-in", hustle up and down on the flank of the convoy since it had left Halifax. He knew little yet of either the sea or seafarers, but enough to admire the skill and resolution of the escort vessels.

That night the men off-watch in the "Willaston" were laughing, joking and still reproving Harry Feltham for his support of Arsenal F.C. There were whistle and catcalls when he said:

"I shall always support 'em – us gunners have to stick together."

Then someone said to the giant Feltham:

"Come on, long stomach – give us one of yer exotic dances."

As the DEMS gunner went through a series of serpentine undulations his "audience" hooted its delight, until Third Mate Swain put his head into the space and yelled:

"Don't let's just tell Jerry we're here! Let's send him an invitation!"

Up to that point, Kevin had been thinking that if his shipmates were as scared as he was they hid it most effectively. Then as things quietened considerably they talked for the umpteenth time of the massive win on the football pools someone had once almost had, the long-odds winning racehorse someone had almost backed and the film someone had seen when last in port which, according to his wife had been so "lovely" she had "cried all through it."

Both deck boys were lying on their bunks:

"Bill – why did you go to sea?"

"Simple – ter ger away from the ole fella."

"Your dad?"

"Yeah"

"Don't you get on with him?"

Billy laughed –

"Yer know Kev – for a scouser – yer don't 'alf use posh blabber."

Then quietly, he said:

"He's a scally. Th 'unny peace we have is when e's in Joe Gerk's."

"Where's that?"

"Prison, appeth."

"He's been to prison?"

"Regla customer. He'll gerra carpet for bein' on the rob an' just after he's come out, pop goes the letter-box – anuther blue paper wid a duck on."

Kevin knew that the "blue paper" was a police summons. He guessed correctly that a "duck" was the Liver Bird, but he was still in need of guidance:

"What's a 'carpet'?"

"Three months. He's done two o'three o'them jus' lately so the Beak says next time they're goin' ter throw the key away. I bloody well hope so."

He was being "nosey", but Donnelly persisted:

"Why does he carry on robbing?"

"Ter get splosh - for drink an' gamblin' – then when 'e's lost it an' 'e's skinny 'e comes home an' knocks us about."

It was quiet for a while before Kevin sighed:

"I'm sorry, Bill. I really am."

Elkin tried to sound matter of fact:

"Yeah well – I done give a monkeys fer meself – I bin gerrin back handers off 'im since I was little – but I can't stand 'im biffin' me mam an' the little uns."

"What?"

"Oh, yeah. Course de owl gerl's a barm cake –'stead of puttin' 'is gear on the street, she waits on 'im 'and an' foot. Gets 'im shairts from Lee's an' decks us an' erself out from Paddy's Market. Anyroad, I've left 'em now."

Despite the encumbrance of his life-jacket, Kevin raised himself up on his elbow:

"What?"

"He wuz talkin' about me keepin' dixy for 'im while 'e turned this house over in Crosby."

"Dixy?"

"'case the scuffers come."

His companion understood now and Billy continued:

"I told him to get lost. There wuz a hell of a barney. It gor 'im nowhere so he went off on the slops, come back bladdered an' started pickin' on little Helen. – so I chinned 'im an' left. I'm in the Seamen's Mission an' me mam come down to see us. I told 'er I'm gonna make some crust outa this job an' the next time e's inside I'm takin' us away - fer good – so she'd berra make 'er mind up on that."

Kevin was bewildered:

"Where will you go?"

"Morecambe."

It sounded so incongruous and was said so decisively Donnelly had to stifle a laugh. After a pause for composure, he asked:

"Why Morecambe?"

"Me mam's gorra posh sister there. Keeps a hotel –

well, a bir of a boardin' 'ouse really but me Auntie calls it
a hotel – Bayview – which is right enough, from the attic
on a fine day. She 'asn't seen us for yairs. That's Uncle
Sidney's influence. He's all plus fours an' no breakfast
as well, an' he looks down on Bootle. They won't like us
turnin' up but they'll 'ave ter put up with it till we sort
ourselves out."

Then he heard Billy murmur:

"If we've got to sleep in our life-jackets they should
make these bunks with a bit more space. I'm wedged fast
in 'ere!"

Silently, Kevin agreed. Given the situation, the life jacket
was indispensable but trussed up in it, he found difficulty
in sleeping for more than a short stretch.

Not far away from the boys and coming closer by the
minute was another seaman who couldn't sleep. He was
Herr Kapitanleutnant Markus Holzbauer, Commander of
the type VII-C submarine which had been deployed to
shadow the "Willaston's" convoy pending the arrival of a
"wolf-pack" of other U-boats.

Holzbauer's vessel, like all VII-C U-boats, had been
designed with the primary aim of enclosing power plants,
batteries, trim tanks, ballast tanks, torpedo tubes,
torpedoes, cannon shells, anti-aircraft ammunition, the
sound room, control room, radio shack and all the other
technological paraphernalia within its 220 feet by 20
feet steel body. For its predatory missions, a crew of fifty
men with all their food, water, eating, sleeping and living
accommodation had then to be crammed into what space
was left.

The Commander's quarters, opposite the radio
shack and directly beyond the control room hatch, was
in no sense a closed room on the side of a passageway,
as provided for the captains of surface vessels. It was
nothing more than a bunk, two lockers and a writing

board. Privacy was allowed for by a green curtain.

The putrid air in the boat was one reason why Holzbauer slept badly and sometimes not at all. The "air" was a stench compounded of vomit, stale diesel oil, perspiration, human waste and mould – the mould that contaminated food, clothing and everything else it touched. The worst aspect of this foul atmosphere was that one became habituated to it. Only when submerging after a spell on the surface did they come to realise what a cesspit they inhabited.

The other reason why the Commander could not sleep tonight was anxiety. His wife's last letter was very worrying. The Telsner family had disappeared. No-one knew where they were. Enquiries to the authorities had revealed nothing, only a cold, cryptic response that they had been "moved East" and that the Telsner leather business had been closed. This meant that Holzbauer's own father, Ludwig, Secretary to the Telsner company, was now unemployed.

Constanze, wife of the Commander, had explained that because of their financial situation the family, though still in Hamburg, had been forced to give up their elegant, commodious flat near the Binnenalster Lake. They were now in the working-class district of Hammerbrook. Although he could read between her lines, the letter's tone was determinedly cheerful.

Though the house was old, she said it was large enough for his parents, Ludwig and Aloysia, to have their own accommodation. The little ones, Katja and Antonia, had their own bedrooms. The dining room was large – so they used it as a sitting room too. The parlour room made a good-sized drawing room and music room. Unfortunately, some of his parent's beautiful furniture had to be sacrificed but despite the tortuous move across the wartime city, they had managed to bring Constanze's piano with them.

Herr Probst, her voice coach, had reduced his fees so that she could continue to work with him. With the piano installed, Antonia, their four-year old was doing splendidly. Katje, their two-year old, was delighted to have the small dressing room off the main bedroom as her playroom. So she had quickly adjusted to her new surroundings – the move from the Binnenstalster forgotten. Finally, they all loved him dearly and wanted him home soon. Did he have any news on this?

Holzbauer tried to think but constructive thought was elusive. He was too stunned by other things in the letter. "The Authorities seemed most anxious to know whether we were related to the Telsners. They were only assured we were not when I pointed out who you were and what you were doing." It was clear to him that "the authorities" were the "Geheime Staatspolizei" ("Gestapo"), and were interested in the Telsners because they were Jewish.

Shlomo Telsner was a good man, a holy man. Markus remembered his father's words: "He has saved this family from the gutter." Markus also recalled how, when he was a nine-year old in 1923, democracy in Germany seemed to have failed. The constant street fights between the Communists and the right-wing Freikorps were still fresh in his memory. Also clear were the memories of the chaos of the worthless currency, the mass unemployment, the failure of the great banks, and the sight of folk setting off each day with a ration cheque and a spoon in their pocket in the hope of finding some kind of meal.

His father, Telsner and other businessmen believed that, in the end, the five and a half million unemployed would rally round either the Communists or Hitler's people, the N.S.D.A.P. ("Nazis"). You had to say the Nazis appeared to have "ordnung", some discipline at least, whereas the Communists were a by-word for chaos. No-one knew whether the Nazis were a good prospect for Germany, though with some bad sides or a decidedly bad prospect with some good sides.

Certainly the construction of the autobahnen, other public works and the militarisation to redress the iniquitous Versailles Treaty had "corrected" the worst of the unemployment. Though many were uncomfortable with the anschauung – the appeal to emotion rather than reason – order, authority, strong leadership – perhaps these were what was needed.

Yet once the N.S.D.A.P. were in power, the moves to a one-party state and the repressive measures against the Jews had made Holzbauer apprehensive. He had been on leave two years ago when on "Kristallnacht" Jewish synagogues, businesses and shops had been subjected to a wave of terror. A tearful Telsner had exclaimed:

"We 'stabbed this country in the back', what do they mean? Two of my brothers were killed in the last War and I was awarded the Iron Cross. My family settled in Bavaria six hundred years ago. I am an Israelite only in my religion. My Fatherland is Germany. Chancellor Hitler resents our success. He fails to understand that a minority can only feel secure when it is as good as the majority. The desire to excel is deep in Jewish culture. Until now we have felt safest in Germany believing it to be the most tolerant state in the whole of Europe. Perhaps our easy integration was taking place only in our own hearts and minds and not in those of the German people. Or maybe this is all down to the vile propaganda of that man Goebbels."

This then was Shlomo Telsner who, with his gifts and interest-free loans, had helped his father to delay the bankruptcy of his business and, when this did happen, had found him work in his own organisation, reduced though it was, first by the collapse of the economy and then by the war. Here was a man of discreet good works who had helped others in the community, Jewish and non-Jewish.

Holzbauer's own duty was clear: he was, and would continue to be, a naval officer loyal to the Fatherland in its prosecution of the war. Yet he could never forget that his place in the Naval Academy, hence his naval career, had been made possible by a gentle Jewish old man whose life was now in jeopardy. Such a prospect was no exaggeration. He remembered the comments attributed to Hermann Göring after "Kristallnacht":

"They should have killed more Jews and broken less glass."

Suddenly, in the U-boat, there were movements beyond the curtain. Holzbauer stuffed Constanze's letter into one of the lockers and swung his legs free of the bunk. He pulled back the curtain. Ensign Wetzel stood there, with Graefe, the radioman. Using the standard naval abbreviation for his Commander's full title, Wetzel spoke first:

"Herr Kaleun, we are in the vicinity of the convoy!"

Holzbauer nodded. The ensign went away swiftly. Graefe then produced a signal, just decoded. As the arrival of the other U-boats was now imminent, and since he was low on fuel and torpedoes, Holzbauer had asked for permission to attack without delay and then make for port. He noted with satisfaction that an immediate attack was sanctioned and he was subsequently to proceed to the Atlantic port of Lorient. He would even be spared the tortuous return to Kiel. What a difference the capitulation of France had made!

He bustled towards the control room. It flashed through his mind that he must have some soothing, reassuring words for Constanze when he returned. Then he banished the thought guiltily, for now he must concentrate.

Surrounded by the indicators, gauges and scales which controlled the position of the U-boat were Chief Engineer Gregor Kriebel and two hydroplane operators. The Commander made for the periscope shaft and gave the order to proceed to periscope depth. Kriebel watched the movement of the column of water in the Papenberg instrument. This indicated the rise and fall of the boat. The hydroplane operators were concentrating intensely. The expert setting of the planes was vital. If the periscope rose too high out of the water, their position could be disclosed to the enemy. If it plunged beneath the water at the strategic moment, the Commander would see nothing. Seconds ticked by then Kriebel exhaled: "Periscope cleared!"

Holzbauer was astonished – they were almost upon the convoy. The periscope was retracted. He ordered the U-boat to proceed into the convoy itself between its seventh and eighth columns on its starboard side. On this voyage, well to the south west of his present position, he had already accounted for two merchantmen. Two of his original fourteen torpedoes had failed, because of faulty detonators. Like many another captain at that stage, he had signalled his frustration to the Seekriegsleitung (German Naval Staff). So far there had been no improvement. He had used six torpedoes successfully on his two victims and two for an abortive attack on another vessel. So he had four torpedoes remaining and having already decided upon his primary target he moved stealthily towards her, having given the order to surface.

On the "Willaston", though thoughts of their peril never left their waking minds, the men off-watch continued their laughing, joking and general banter. They were completely unaware that, incredibly near to them, a two hundred and twenty foot metal monster, with a surface displacement of six hundred and sixty tons, was gliding past them to destroy its quarry.

Holzbauer tensed – there she was – unmistakable – her long foredeck, her tall bridge amidships, her other accommodation upper works right aft around her funnel. She was the tanker reported to him in the signal decrypt. Among the rag-bag of vessels in the convoy, she looked elegant and prosperous and stuffed with the pay-load the British needed most – oil. He flicked at an eyebrow as the beads of perspiration ran down into it and he began to compute the factors in his firing control solution. His mouth was dry as he began the sequence:

- present range and bearing of the target
- target's course and speed
- distance from U-boat to target
- speed of torpedo
- · computation of distance ahead of the target's present position the torpedo should be aimed at, so that the target sails into contact with it.

The U-boat closed to its appropriate firing position and the Holzbauer gave the order to fire. Ninety seconds later, "Clan Chieftain", the doomed tanker, was struck by two torpedoes. Crews on watch in nearby vessels were stupefied. A seemingly boundless ball of fire was surging skywards. Dusk became day as the tanker burst with a tremendous roaring and tearing. Tons of metal, fountains of flaming oil, corpses and body parts spewed forth into the biting, hateful cold of the Western Ocean. All those looking towards her gasped as the "Clan Chieftain's" hull disappeared into the black surge. She had died in two and a half minutes. And now the watchers were held fast by the terror of it - where next? who next?

When the tanker exploded Kevin had been struggling to sleep, hampered by his life jacket in the cramped bunk space. He burst from his quarters and ran towards the port rail of the "Willaston" trying to get as far for'ard as possible in the direction of the explosion. The vessel jerked violently under his feet. Showers of metal and burning wood were still crashing onto every part of its bridge and decks. He shrieked with agony as he tripped on a heavy spar and fell with his damaged ankle beneath him. He got to his feet and was starting forward again when someone stepped out of the chaos to block his path:

"No.....not this way, lad."

It was Hugh Riley who now tried to restrain the struggling youth.

"Hey, no!......," Kevin yelled as he twisted to break free, "...there are men in the water...look....we've got to help!"

Suddenly Riley let him go. The two of them fell and slithered to the port rail where they hung on grimly then slowly, painfully, regained their feet. For the rest of his life Donnelly would remember what happened next. On many a night he would wake, crying out at the memory of it. Dusk was now well advanced but in spite of this he could see the great pool of oil which had poured forth from the bowels of the tanker. In that viscous muck, which made his eyes smart despite its distance, at least a dozen men were visible. Some were dead but whole, others dead and mutilated beyond description. And some were still dying, crying in agony as the crude oil burned their lungs and they vomited a slop of blood, mucus and destroyed tissue.

Miraculously, two or three still had life left in them. They turned their terrified faces up towards the "Willaston". Lit by the lamps on their life-jackets their pleading, beseeching faces were clearly visible. One man with strength enough lifted up his arms in supplication, begging to be saved.

A group of the "Willaston" crew had congregated at the rail. Tugging at each of them in turn Kevin shouted: "We need lines!"

"No we don't!", called Riley, "we can't help."

"We can't leave them. We've got to save 'em!" bellowed Kevin. At this the motor man seized Donnelly. Angrily he pinned the boy's arms to his sides:

"Why don't you do what you're bloody well told?! Don't you know this is hard for all of us?.....more than we can stomach? The orders are to keep moving! We can't pick up survivors, that's the escort's job. If the convoy stops, Jerry'll have easy pickins'. Hundreds'll die."

The deck boy wrenched himself free from Riley's grasp and yelled:

"I don't care. It's murder if we leave 'em. What the hell can the escorts do?"

The tortured screaming and pleading still coming from the glutinous sea seemed to emphasise his question but even as he yelled the logic of what was being said to him made its way into his understanding.

They were leaving behind the beseeching, bobbing heads and Hugh Riley said to him softly:

"You've seen a tanker sunk, son. Now you'll never see anything worse."

In two or three more minutes the "Willaston" passed beyond the sea of fire marking the grave of the "Clan Chieftain". Donnelly fancied that an occasional cry of agony and terror still pierced the freezing night air. Crew members on the deck of the "Willaston" looked at each other with terror and stupefaction.

At that instant Herr Kapitanleutnant Markus Holzbauer was concluding a second firing control solution. He terminated the sequence by releasing his final torpedoes. Both missiles sped away towards the "Willaston".

Water, smoke and flame gushed into the night from the doomed freighter. Before Kevin, shielding his face, turned away from the blast and heat, he forced a glimpse at what the gusher was flinging aloft – wood from the "Willaston's" decks, steel and iron from the upperworks and the failing rag-doll bodies of men. He felt impelled to look again at the havoc and, incredibly, saw the bow of the ship rising vertically from the waves. Transfixed, unbelieving, he could only stand there. Even as secondary explosions began to rend the "Willaston" to fragments he could not move. Then – someone was tugging at him frantically. He could just hear a shrill, desperate Hugh Riley:

"Her back's broken!....she's goin' under!...get to the starboard lifeboat!"
Kevin pointed:

"We're supposed to muster at the port lifeboat!"
Exasperated, Riley bawled:

"It's smashed to bits! Now move!"
Still he did not respond, so Riley pushed him. They fell together and slithered into a crazy hollow in the deck. The youth had a fleeting recollection of a film scene – a shell crater on the Western Front. A soldier reaches it then, horrified, realises he has two smelling, swelling, blackening corpses for company. No corpses here, he thought, but that same figure of Death that had stalked the Somme was present now and close at hand.

He struggled to leave the slippery hollow and reached out towards a beam of wood lying on its rim. It was coated with oil. Each time he tried to lever himself up against it, his hands slithered off the beam and he fell back into the dip. Eventually when Riley had dragged him by his feet from the hollow, the exhausted motor man pointed towards the starboard lifeboat hanging from its davits a short distance away:

"Now – come on!,"

Kevin got to it on all fours.

At the davits, three or four men were cursing and struggling. The lifeboat was stuck fast. In their frenzy, the sailors pushed, heaved and jostled each other, finally chopping at it to free it from its supports. Without a word, Riley pushed Kevin violently. He fell into the boat and Riley tumbled in after him. Then, as the boat was swung out over the tormented sea, its forward fall snapped and it plunged bow first into the waves.

Miraculously, though it had shipped much water, the boat quickly righted itself. One or two men who had jumped clear of the broken ship were thrashing around it. Figures in the boat, including Donnelly and Riley, were now hauling them aboard. Martin Swain was trying frantically and as best he knew how, to manoeuvre the lifeboat away from the "Willaston" lest the suction as it sank took the lifeboat down with it.

The freighter was now two-thirds submerged. Making a bizarre "V" shape, only its bow and aft sections were visible. Paralysed with fear and rigid with piercing cold, the Toxteth lad could only gape as the remnants of his ship were disappearing. Suddenly, above the massive creaking and groaning from the remnants of the "Willaston" and the yelling of men in the water he could hear the voice he knew so well:

"Kevin!....Kev!......"

It was Billy Elkin. By now, and however inexpertly, Third Mate Swain had managed to bring the life-boat stern-on to the "Willaston" and some distance away from what little was left of her. As quickly as he could, Kevin stumbled towards the stern and peered out into the night. Yes.....it was him.....only a few yards away.....Billy's petrified face and extended arm. Kevin put out his own arms, yelling:

"Come on, Billy!....Come on!"

In an instant he was pushed roughly aside and someone dived into the water. The would-be rescuer was clearly a powerful swimmer and, ignoring his own danger, he submerged repeatedly to find the deck-boy before the sucking sea claimed him.

After some minutes, Riley and Donnelly shouted their relief in unison as the swimmer reappeared. It was difficult to see in the surging humps and hollows of the waves.....but yes!......he had his arm about someone who now appeared unconscious. As the swimmer inched his way towards the lifeboat, the motor man and the deck-boy felt every bit of his pain and exhaustion. Then Riley went over the side to help the pair in their last stretch. Willing hands pulled the three of them aboard.

Kevin knelt by the huddled mass. The exhausted rescuer and Hugh Riley were vomiting sea water and mucus into the pool shipped by the boat. When the rescuer looked up finally, Kevin saw it was Martin Swain.

The rescued man lay in the slopping water in the bottom of the boat. Hugh Riley bent towards him. Suddenly the old seaman straightened:

"He's breathin'!"

Rapidly he tore off his own reefing-jacket and helped Swain to lift the body out of the shipped water. Riley then draped his jacket over it. Donnelly leaned over, relieved that his shipmate was still alive. He rocked on his heels against the movement of the boat. His mouth opened. It wasn't Billy Elkin. Alan Wilson it was who had been snatched from the sea.

"Where's Billy?", he asked dazedly.

Quietly, Riley said: "Looks like he's gone, lad."

"But he can't have gone!....he was there!....just there!"

The youngster was pointing. In more insistent tones, Riley repeated that Billy was gone.

All was silent now, save for the tireless sea and the bobbing boat. As Donnelly just stood there dumbfounded, someone else who had swum towards the boat out of the night was being hauled in. It was the First Mate, Ian Dunlop. The atmosphere in the boat seemed to lighten as the soft-spoken Scot landed among them. He was an experienced man who would take charge, they knew that.

Dunlop wiped the water from his face and hair but as he took in his surroundings he became immediately concerned at the water shipped by the boat.

"Get bailing......bail out fast," he urged.

The others found bailers and fell to the task frantically but in his stupor Kevin still did nothing other than brace himself against the side-to-side rocking of the boat. Then a familiar voice bawled:

"Get bailin'!"

It was Dave Porter, the Bosun's Mate. The youth looked at the soaked, stubby figure, just making out the wispy hair matted across his face. Porter was opening and closing his hands in anger and frustration. Kevin wanted to smash the face he looked at but then, as if the wilful, fatuous action would give him some power over a situation that overwhelmed him, he did something for which he immediately felt stupid and ashamed – he began to scoop water out of the boat with his hands.

"Donnelly!", it was Porter again...."find a bailer, you stupid pillock!"

"Stop that!", called Dunlop quietly but intently. He looked at Kevin and nodded to the stern: "Look for any more bailers in the locker." Then he turned to Porter:

"Have you checked the boat bung? – it may be unshipped."

Barely perceptibly, Porter shook his head.

"Well do it."

Kevin and Hugh scrambled across the two thwarts that lay widthways across the boat. They found another bailer and a corned beef tin containing a box. This housed a medical kit. Riley returned the kit to the locker and gave Kevin the bailer. "This'll do for me," he grunted, brandishing the empty tin. They joined the bailing group but as their first water went over the side a high-pitched yell came back at them.

"Keep bailin'!", thundered the Bosun's Mate and leaned over the side of the boat.

Then he reached towards the water and with an immense heave pulled a small, skinny figure out of the sea and in among them. The coughing, spewing seaman was "Willaston's" assistant cook, Tai Lok. He had been clinging to the looped grab-line which ran around the outside of the boat.

When it was clear that the boat was as stable and watertight as they could make it, the First Mate ordered the survivors to get out oars and row a little way from where the Willaston had by now gone under. At about thirty yards from the spot he ordered the rowing to stop. He gazed over the grave of his ship. No-one said anything. Each man was thinking his own thoughts. After a few minutes, with some urgency, Dunlop said:

"Come on......we must circle. See if we can pick up anybody else."

Submerged now, but making nearly seven knots, Markus Holzbauer's U-boat was heading for Brittany. It was a mighty distance from Hamburg, but nearer at least to Constanze and the girls. He hoped the train journey would not eat up too much of his home leave. And, good point, putting in to Lorient meant they would be spared the posed pictures with frauleins on the quay. That nauseated him – the flowers, flaxen hair, creamy complexions, frilly blouses, dirndl skirts and Dr Goebbels' cameras whirring in the background. The last time they had put into such a sideshow he had muttered to Gregor Kriebel:

"Maybe we should invite them aboard this stench-pipe – that would cool their ardour."

The crew's elation at the third and fourth sinkings had dissipated somewhat. Now all were occupied with thoughts of home.

Holzbauer was in the Officer's Mess. This "wardroom" also doubled as living quarters for Chief Engineer Kriebel, the Second Engineer and the First and Second Watch Officers. Kriebel's bunk served as the "chairs" his Commander and he employed to sit at the dining table which was screwed tightly to the floor. Across from them, Ernst Rademacher, the Second Watch Officer, a fervid Nazi, was still smiling his glowing smile:

"Four pennants on the flagstaff, Herr Kaleun - it must mean the Ritterkreuz for you!"
Holzbauer said nothing, for tin badges had no meaning for him. The Second Watch Officer, nothing daunted, continued to babble:

"My brother-in-law, in the Seekriegsleitung, says we're about to enter Die glückliche Zeit."
Holzbauer's features tightened:

"Say again."

"Die glückliche Zeit – the happy time."
The Commander rose from the table:

"Rademacher, does it ever occur to you or your brother-in-law, that the men we sent down to the black ooze were ordinary seamen, with families, like us?"
Kriebel shifted uneasily while Holzbauer and Rademacher stared at each other. It was some seconds before Rademacher looked away.

Chapter Seven

Where No Flowers Grow

The First Mate looked down at Alan Wilson. Even in the limited light it was clear he was in a serious condition.

"You look all in....how....?"

"I'll be alright, sir. If we can just brace my leg against the rocking of the boat, I'll be able to work with Mr Swain."

The other survivors lowered their heads or looked away. He was obviously badly injured and his courage moved them.

Dunlop considered:

"O.K....let's see if we can make you comfortable, then you can have a go. When it gets light we'll have a look at your leg."

Mercifully, the waters over the grave of the "Willaston" were running a little calmer enabling the lifeboat to move around the area. It was obvious that Alan Wilson knew how to handle a boat and Martin Swain followed his advice to the letter. At first, they searched without reward but suddenly the Bosun's Mate pointed:

"Summat over there, sir!"

They followed his pointing finger, to an object twenty yards abeam of them.

"Right, get over to it!"

As they changed direction, Kevin noticed Wilson grit his teeth at the up and down motions of the boat. The apprentice's features were becoming deformed with agony. For the first time now, he saw Kevin and smiled, despite his deplorable situation. Kevin gave him the "thumbs up" sign then felt stupidly inadequate for having done so.

In the following minutes, they passed corpses of their shipmates. Though the weather had improved a little, the sea was throwing them about like jetsam. Kevin's face tightened. The dead ashore were usually given the dignity of a solemn interment with loving, grieving relatives at hand. These poor souls had died alone. Now, in death, they were being flung about like dustbin trash. He recalled meeting an old salt in Sandbeck Street, close to home. Offering his condolences on the death of his father, he had shaken his head sadly:

"Poor Joe's gone to a grave where no flowers grow."

The boat neared the object Porter had pointed out. It was a life-raft, badly smashed but still floating. A figure, face down and half out of the water, was clinging to it.

"It's Matty Penman!," someone called. There was a rumble of agreement from the others. Even in the poor light they had seen a pale bald head fringed by jet black hair and immediately recognised him. It was Porter who slipped into the water, and struggled with the broad, inert man clinging to the raft.

Coughing and spluttering, Porter called back:

"I think he's alive, sir!"

"Right, let's get him aboard."

Hugh Riley and Kevin struggled to pull him into the boat and managed it at last. Hugh wrapped him in a corner of the boat cover to shield him from both the fearful cold and the waters breaking relentlessly over the boat. To recover their breath, the pair squatted down for a few moments. Kevin whispered to the motor man:

"Who's Matty Penman?"

"Fourth Engineer.....an' the unny one o' them poor sods that survived, seemingly."

"You think so? Why?"

"Look around you, lad. We're all deck bods, 'cept for him. The "Willaston" took them torpedoes in her engine room..... that's why her back broke. That U-boat captain knew what he was doin'. Come on....let's get back to the bailin'." As he toiled Kevin thought continually of Billy Elkin and was not ashamed of his emotion, remembering that the Bootle boy had died trying to earn the way to a better life for his mother and her children.

For another hour, the lifeboat went back and forth among the detritus of the sinking. Defying all possibilities, they found another two of their shipmates....both clinging to torn fragments of their ship, both still with life in them. The first of these, to the joy of the others, was hefty Harry Feltham, the D.E.M.S. gunner. He recovered consciousness quickly, as might be expected. The second man, though alive, was unconscious for several hours after his rescue. He was Tom Gratton, from Chester, Quartermaster on the fated ship.

When their search was over, the rescuers were gasping

with fatigue and cold. Exhausted, they hunched down in the boat to escape the fury of the wind and waves now that the weather was again deteriorating. At that moment the unspoken thoughts of all were in unison: the convoy had moved on, there was no sign of an escort vessel and they were completely alone, at the mercy of the weather, on an ocean as broad and long as eternity. Then suddenly these thoughts were interrupted - from the north east of them came the rumble of other explosions. Other ships were sinking, other seamen being slaughtered.

The First Mate sensed their forebodings and was anxious to distract them. Lurching precariously along the length of the boat he said:

"Right – now let's see what's in the aft locker."

With the help of Hugh Riley's cigarette lighter, which was unbelievably still functioning and laboriously shielding its flame from the buffeting wind, they rummaged about in the locker. They found a sea anchor, a small axe and a knife, a colza-oil lamp, ten flares in watertight containers and, of course, the medical kit. Dunlop grunted as he fished further into the locker:

"There's food and water in here but we'll leave it until after the First Watch. And there's something else...."

This time he produced a watertight container and opened it.

"Thanks be to God," he gasped for inside the tin were two dozen matches. Gathering up the oil lamp, medical kit and the knife he made his way forward and checked the thwarts, where he found a boat's compass. Further rummaging around the boat produced a boathook, a steering oar, a painter of stout rope and several short lengths of rope of lesser thickness. Anxious to convey some of his own new-found optimism he stood and shouted against the wind:

"Gentlemen, we've a fully rigged boat in sound

condition, plus food, flares and water. So I think, Wilson, you and Mr Swain'd better prepare to make our way home."

This was his way of thanking the apprentice for his help in boat handling but as he looked towards him the boy slipped into the bottom of the boat. Quickly, Martin Swain began to lever him up but sounded anxious:

"He's unconscious, sir. It's all sticky here....he's pouring with blood.!"

Dunlop made for the boy. Bending over him he said to Riley:

"Shelter me while I light a match."

The Scot waited for a lull in the rocking of the boat, an instant when it was steady. Then he struck the match. What the pair saw in the flickering light sickened them: the left knee had been smashed to a pulpy mass from which pieces of cartilage and bone protruded. Blood was coursing steadily through it.

Harry Feltham, who had recovered quite quickly after his rescue, scrambled towards them:

"Need a hand, sir? I'm a bit uvva first aider."

"There are some ends of rope lying about. Get them up here, will you?"

Then Dunlop glanced at the motor man:

"Light the lamp, please."

In the next few minutes, as the boat rose and fell in the heavy swell, he applied a rope tourniquet to the leg of the inert, ashen-faced young seaman.

"Let's pray this works," murmured Dunlop. "Now, where's the first-aid kit?"

Feltham opened it and the three of them looked: all it contained were three rolls of bandage, two packets of boracic lint, a small pair of scissors, a large square of linen, a tiny bottle of iodine, two finger stalls and a pot of zinc and castor oil cream.

"Stone me," said the Londoner, "I gotta betta kit than this on my motorbike."

With two or three layers of the boracic lint they formed a pad for Wilson's knee. The other survivors watched as, despite the rocking and yawing of the boat, the First Mate bandaged as tenderly as he could. He glanced at Harry Feltham.

"You take First Watch with me. In half an hour we'll slacken off the tourniquet and look at him during the night."

He asked Martin Swain to heave to and to put out the sea anchor. He turned to the others:

"It'll be some time yet to first light. To make it as comfortable as we can, we're streaming the anchor and heading up to wind. If an escort comes back this way, that'll give her a fifty-fifty chance of finding us. At daylight we'll rig the sail, fix the rowing teams and set a course. I'll make arrangements for the food and water when we can see what we've got. Now is anybody else in pain or needing attention before morning?"

Earlier, Kevin had noticed Tai Lok clutching his stomach.

"You O.K., mate?," Kevin whispered.

The little assistant cook only smiled faintly, but said nothing. Perhaps he failed to understand what was being said.

"Right," Dunlop said, "make yourselves as warm as you can and try to get some sleep."

Hugh Riley came back to squat beside Kevin.

"Get under the boat cover as far as you can," he urged.

"I'll be O.K. I'm just wondering what happened to Alan."

"They're doin' all they can for him. Just see to yourself – there's nothin' you can do."

"Harry said something about not much in the medical kit."

"Yeah....an' I wouldn't be surprised if there's regulations about that. If it's deficient it'll be down to Clive Edmonds, you can bet."

"Clive Edmonds?"

"Mr Miles's brother, an' a right waster – always lettin' Miles down."

"Even though there's a war on?"

"Mmph. Clive's got summat on his mind besides wars – wine and women mostly. Anyroad, you try and settle off. There'll be plenty of rowing to do before long."

As the others settled themselves, Donnelly noticed how nimbly experienced sailors moved – with their bodies arched, they seemed to know how to locate the best place to sleep and the best shape to adopt to minimise the misery of the weather's buffeting.

Before long he discovered that in spite of the freezing air and the flying spray, being with others under the boat cover was too stifling. He forced his head and shoulders clear. In any event, he knew he would not sleep. All he could think about was the tragic way Billy Elkin had died. The boy who was always cheerful, who had helped him so much had died, and he had done nothing to save him despite his friend's pleading. Now he watched as the First Mate and Harry Feltham bent over his other helpmate, Alan Wilson, and conferred from time to time. After about an hour of watching and thinking he heard Alan shriek with pain then afterwards moan occasionally.

When others were taking the Second Watch he saw that Ian Dunlop remained with Alan. He looked out at the horizon. A broad band of grey light had taken shape and was enlarging. Could this be the dawn? As he asked himself, his head went forward and he fell asleep.

In his sleep he saw the landmarks of Liverpool, just as

his father had seen them – the Liver Building, the Custom House, St. George's Hall. Next he saw the stadium where he had swept the steps, gathered the rubbish, cleaned the boots of the professionals and dreamed of being a star. Then he saw any number of faces – the faces of Bridie and Gerard Keating, of his mother, of "Chippy' Gallagher, of Celia Molloy. After hearing the voice of Billy Elkin he imagined he could see his face too – white with terror and twisted with pleading. Suddenly, he woke up.

The others were also waking. In spite of the overcast it was considerably lighter but although the wind slackened it still had sufficient knife in it to keep life uncomfortable.

With the others, he looked to where Alan Wilson lay. Dunlop and Swain were bent over him still. In a minute, Ian Dunlop turned to face them:

"Alan Wilson has gone. He died from loss of blood. There was nothing we could do to stop it."

The gasps of astonishment with which they met this news was followed by a deeply sad, deeply respectful silence. It said more than words could convey. Every one of them felt the loss of this energetic, competent, smiling, lovable boy. Though they said nothing some of the older hands, no strangers to deaths at sea, shook their heads nonetheless at the futility of it. Everyone now realised too that when he had volunteered to help with handling the boat he had been near his limit, through weakness and pain.

Ian Dunlop continued to look at them all and though he tried to be as dispassionate as possible, he could not entirely keep the emotion from his soft tones:

"We must now commit his body. It would be dangerous for us to crowd this end of the boat so, if you will, follow the prayer from where you are."

Led by the First Mate they said the Lord's Prayer.

With difficulty he began to intone the hymn "Abide With Me". He was immediately joined by the others and especially by Feltham, the D.E.M.S. gunner, whose fine-toned, well-pitched tenor voice made the hymn all the more poignant. Dunlop then added some deeply-felt words about the apprentice. Kevin appreciated what he heard but was then appalled to see Dunlop and Martin Swain ease the boy over the side but not before they had stripped his thick sweater from him, the sweater Bridie Keating had bought for him in Boston.

Seeing this angered Donnelly and deepened his disappointment at the brevity of the committal. Spontaneously, he leaned over the side of the boat and called out:

"Eternal rest grant unto him, O Lord, and let perpetual light shine upon him. May he rest in peace...." Some of the survivors, including Hugh Riley and Martin Swain, joined him in the "Amen".

The First Mate indicated that the sweater should be passed to Tai Lok and, for the first time, many of them saw that all the little man had on were thin trousers, a singlet and a short catering jacket. He was blue with cold and could not keep a limb still. Nodding his thanks, he took the sweater eagerly, sodden as it was. Feltham had to help him into it.

The motor man, beside Kevin, noticed his bitterness:

"What's up, lad."

To mask his emotion, Kevin glared:

"That was horrible. Alan was a good friend to me..... to everybody. I don't like to see him pushed away like garbage."

The old sailor put his hand on the boy's arm:

"Now listen.....he wasn't pushed away like garbage. That's an insultin' thing to say. Burials at sea are never very formal; they can't be. Usually, the First Mate has a stock of canvas to make a shroud. On steamships, to weight the body down they sew a few old firebars or firebricks into it. You ask "Chippy" Gallagher. Now you tell me......how could we a'done that here?"

There was a small silence. Riley then went on: "What matters is what we all felt about him an' nobody felt more than Mr Dunlop. His job now is to get us all safe home, includin' little Tai there. That's why he give 'im the sweater. Alan would've understood that."

Kevin did not reply and Riley understood well enough that finding himself in a strange, even alien, world the friendship and help of the two young men now dead had become very important to the boy. Consequently, Joe Donnelly's lad was in despair. He decided to say more:

"Yer know Kev – British masters are admired all over the world, even by the Jerries. Here we are, with the old country at rock-bottom tryin' to keep goin' with a merchant fleet that's bin run to rags. Yet for all the muddle an' all the neglect we won't admit we're goin' to get beat. The "doggedness of the British" I read about in one American paper, when we was in Boston. "Doggedness" – that what our captains've got. George Stephens had it. This lad Dunlop's got it. "Unspectacular steadfastness," this Yankee paper said. Trust this fella. He'll get you 'ome. But don't think he's got no feelins. Don't judge so quick."

Kevin bit his lip.

Although by now it was fully light the day promised to be no more than a series of squalls laced together by a freezing gloom. Ian Dunlop set about re-examining the locker under the stern seat and then turned to the airtight metal tank under the forward thwart. This revealed they had a large tin of Fray Bentos corned beef, six tins of condensed milk and several pounds of ship's biscuit. With the water breaker, a keg with a large bung, were two long-handled dippers for scooping and serving its contents. However, they were disappointed to discover the keg was barely two-thirds full.

Dunlop studied the cloth chart of the Western Ocean they had also found in their search. He sat silently, about to balance a number of factors in a mortal equation. Where should they make for? What was its distance from their current position, as he estimated it? How long would it take to get there? How much food and water would they need to keep alive for that length of time? How much of each was there in the boat? So what would be the daily ration?

When he had calculated and recalculated he looked up:

"Right the escort probably isn't coming. From the explosions we heard there'll be enough for them to do in the convoy.

His surmise was correct. The U-boat "wolf pack" had descended on the convoy sinking seven ships. One of the escorts had also gone to the bottom.

The Scot looked around then continued:

"The convoy is sailing east north east. It's making for Liverpool via Malin Head. Even if we tried to catch it, which we never could, the prevailing winds would drive us off course. So we're going to make for the Irish coast. Any comments?"

Gratton, the Quartermaster, now fully conscious, was disconcerted:

"That coast is murder, sir. Won't we be smashed up on the rocks?"

"It's a problem, surely, but I said we'd make for the Irish coast, not necessarily that we'd land there."

He waited for his point to sink in.

"Ireland isn't just an option, it's our only chance.

I think we're about one thousand miles away, perhaps less. But we're only maybe half that distance away from the air cover operating from Ulster. If we can manage to bring ourselves into the cover zone, there's every chance we'll be spotted by our planes."

Then Dunlop pointed to the mast:

"We need to set the dipping lug and put out six oars. Remember the prevailing wind is with us so if the weather doesn't worsen we're capable of doing four knots. Apart from the Assistant Cook here, we must all take a turn on the oars. We can't row all the time but I'd say, with luck, we could be within range of the R.A.F. within ten to twelve days."

Harry Feltham whistled. One or two of the others gasped. They knew that ten to twelve days was more than optimistic because each day they would get weaker. What Dunlop's estimate revealed, if they needed any clarification, was the gravity of their situation. He sensed their doubts:

"Look, we can either sit here and freeze to death, and that won't take long, or we can buckle to and get ourselves home. And remember this – we've drifted but we're still well within the shipping lanes of traffic going 'round Southern Ireland, out and return. If we're spotted and picked up before then the accuracy of my estimates won't matter. So, what's the word?"

They were silent until Hugh Riley said:

"Let's try it, sir. Do our best like."

There were some murmurs of assent.

"That's what we'll do then. Now, has anybody got injuries needing attention before we give out the rations?"

Prompted by Donnelly, Riley called out that Tai Lok needed attention. Dunlop and Feltham clambered towards him. When they examined him they were appalled. How could anyone have endured such injuries in silence?

When the "Willaston" had been torpedoed, the little Assistant Cook had been blown out of the galley on a colossal spout of steam and boiling water. His stomach was so scalded and twisted with massive burns they wondered how he could have survived the shock. Some of the burns extended to the crotch. The First Mate swallowed, then shook his head:

"All we can do for now is apply the zinc and castor oil cream and cover it with what bandage we have left."
Feltham nodded sadly. Dunlop felt foolish for undertaking such futile treatment but knew he could propose nothing better. As they ministered to him, Tai screamed for them to stop.

"Don't worry," Dunlop lied, "this is just to ease it for you till it can be properly looked at."

The First Mate was a sensitive man. He not only loathed himself for lying but also for voicing so many agonising clichés. He feared the others would find these more embarrassing than uplifting.

When he was out of Tai Lok's hearing, Harry Feltham confided to an anxious Kevin that the cream would do nothing for such frightening damage:

"It's like givin' an elephant strawberries," he muttered.

Some of the others, particularly Tom Gratton, had injuries and rope burns. They resolved to say nothing. Witnessing Tai Lok's agony they wanted him to have whatever remained in the medical kit.

When he had got back to his station Ian Dunlop looked around unobtrusively. Already the men were beginning to show signs of their ordeal:

"We'll have the first ration now. One ship's biscuit and a piece of corned beef for as long as that lasts. And half a dipper of water each with some condensed milk.

We'll have that morning and evening. There'll always be something to eat – we've stacks of ship's biscuit. Water will be the problem so we must be sparing with it. If we can catch some rainwater that'll help."

The morsels of food were being distributed. All were especially grateful for the water. Ian Dunlop signalled for his to be given to Tai Lok. When Hugh Riley offered Matty Penman his share the stocky engineer made no response. The others looked at Penman and, in spite of his size, they seemed to be seeing him for the first time. Then they realised that since they had hauled him aboard he had said absolutely nothing. Now there was a strange silence. Something about Matty mystified them. It was spooky. They all felt it.

"Come on, Matty. Here's your grub," Riley encouraged him.

Still Penman said nothing. He stared fixedly beyond the boat, broadly towards where the "Willaston" had gone down.

"Matty, you've got to eat, mate," insisted the old mariner.

Puzzled, and strangely apprehensive, everyone watched.

"What's the problem?", asked Martin Swain.

"Might be concussion," Riley replied.

"Better have a look at him," said the First Mate. He made his way towards Penman.

No matter how he was prompted, the man remained silent. He did not seem to see the food and water. He saw nothing or no-one....only the white-capped waves fixed his attention.

"I think we'll leave him for now. Probably shock."
Then, as Dunlop began to move away from him, Penman boomed:

"I want to see the doctor!"

"Me an' all mate," Tom Gratton answered.

This lifted the tension a little. Some began to laugh but it was not relaxed laughter. The First Mate went back to Penman, raising his hand to silence the laughing:

"What's the matter? Why do you want to see the doctor?"

The others were silent again, an apprehensive silence.

Matty seemed not to see Dunlop even now and boomed again into the waves:

"I want to see the doctor! He's got to get this key out of my foot!"

Dunlop signalled to Harry Feltham who joined him quickly:

"Let's have a look at your foot. Which one is it?"

Penman ignored the question even when they peeled off his wet socks which began to steam as the air dried them out. He seemed not to know that they were examining his feet and continued booming into the distance:

"I want to see the doctor! He's got to get this key out of my foot!"

His feet were inspected slowly and carefully. They also examined his arms, the rest of his body, even his head. They found nothing.

"Better leave him for now," advised Dunlop finally. Quietly, they moved away.

The survivors looked at each other, then at Matty. They began to whisper. None of them were engineers but some were experienced enough to know that Matty's cries made no sense. Dave Porter summed it up for them as he wheezed:

"Poor bugger. He's off his chump."

Presently they returned to their rations. They drank the water readily enough but most had little stomach for the food, eating only after exhortations from Dunlop and Swain. They began to set the sail afterwards and the first group of oarsmen took to their stations. Martin Swain hauled in the sea anchor and brought the boat to the heading indicated by the First Mate.

As they moved off, with the rowers pulling strongly, the wind got up again. Soon, they were thankful for its commotion and the renewed lashing of the waves, for these muffled a little the continuous, unchanging yelling of Matty Penman for a doctor and for the key to be removed from his foot. He kept up his beseeching clamour for over an hour, stopping only when he was exhausted.

Kevin and Hugh were involved in the first stint of rowing. Afterwards they slumped down, too fatigued to speak. When they had rested a little, Riley looked with concern at the youth's strained features. Reassuringly, he whispered:

"Don't worry, we're on our way now."

"I'm not worrying. To tell you the truth, I was thinking about Dad."

"What about him?"

"Well.....I was thinking about the hard graft he had to put in an' about......what he had to put up with, just to feed and clothe us. But I never heard him complain."

"Ooh.....we weren't always in fixes like this an' we weren't always in the North Atlantic. On the run to the Caribbean we used to sit on the poop deck of an evenin'..... yer know, around the dog watches.....an' 'ave many a good craic."

"What about?"

"Anythin'....about home; about you lads an' your Ma; about Kit, my wife; about football; about horses; but mostly about ships. An' your Dad was fond o' readin'. I remember once, we wuz in this place in Valparaiso an' some young snotty in the Royal Navy was takin' a rise out of Liverpool. Your Dad leaned over and said:

'So you wouldn't agree with Daniel Defoe then?'

The midshipman gives yer Dad this insultin' look an'

says:

'Who's he?'

'Oh. I thought you'da known 'im,' says Joe. 'He wrote 'Moll Flanders' an' 'The Complete English Gentleman' – pity yer didn't read that. Still, even if you left school before your exams, you're bound to remember 'Robinson Crusoe'.....an' he wrote summat else an' all.... 'no town in England, except London, can equal Liverpool for the fineness of its streets and the beauty of its buildings.'"

Riley laughed at the memory:

"The youngster went as red as a turkey-cock, settled up for his meal an' left. Aye.....he wuz a clever man was your Dad. He used to tell us things we'd have never even thought about an' 'e could open your eyes to things....."

Kevin knew full well what Riley was saying. It intensified his longing for his father's voice and his wonderful smile.

"Why do any of you go to sea at all?"

"When your Dad and me wuz your age there wasn't many other jobs goin'. It gets you I suppose.....sea life. Yer dock after a bad trip an' swear never again. Yer back home for a week an' 'fore yer know it you've signed on again."

Kevin nodded, then closed his eyes. Hugh felt sorry for the lad. He was strong an' he stuck at his job even though he couldn't get around too well. And obviously he'd had absolutely no idea what he was letting himself in for when he had signed on. Now, on his first time out he'd lost his two best mates. And he was unnerved by the row Matty Penman was kicking up, as even the most seasoned of them were. Better try to get Kevin's mind off things:

"Anyroad, you'll be 'ome soon, with that girl o' yours."

Kevin thought for a second:

"Do you know her?"

"No.....but I saw 'er with you at the Dock gate."

"At the Dock.....oh no, that was Kathy Gallagher, "Chippy's" daughter. She's just a friend."

"So there's another besides 'er?......you ger about a bit!", Riley laughed.

"No, Kathy is a friend. Well, more of a good neighbour really."

"Mm. "Chippy's" girl. He can be proud uv 'er. She looks nice enough ter fetch ducks off water."

For Kevin's sake, he decided to pursue the conversation:

"So who's this other girl then?"

"Celia Molloy. I've known her since we were little."

The youth noticed the motor man frowning.

"Molloy?.... any relation to Frank Molloy?"

"Youngest daughter."

The frown was deepening:

"Mm. An' 'ow d'yer ger on with 'im then?"

"I don't really know him but, to be honest, from what little I've had to do with him, I don't think he's very impressed with me."

"No, well he won't be, if yer don't mind me sayin' so. He's unny impressed with people he can use.....folks us can 'elp 'im get where he wants to be. He fancies 'imself as birruvva toff these days. D'yer know....if 'e met me comin' along the Dock Road e'd ignore me, an' we were apprentices together."

"He was a seaman?"

"Aye. Not much o' one. A good day's work'd stiffen 'im. That's why he started 'is chandlin' business.....not so maulin'. An' I've known 'im cut fellas dead as lent 'im the money ter get started!"

Kevin shrugged:

"Well he doesn't think I'm good enough for her, but I've just got to forget about him. Celia's opinion's what matters isn't it?"

The reassurance he was seeking didn't come. After a pause, Hugh Riley turned to him:

"Are you serious about 'er?"

"Sure."

"Well, yer entitled to do as you please – it's your life. But think about this......lads talk about marryin' a girl whereas the truth is, they marry a family. You say Molloy thinks yer not good enough for 'er. I'd say the Molloys aren't good enough for you an' that's tellin' yer straight John Bull! An' another thing while we're at it – many a man 'as struggled up the mountain lookin' for the edelweiss an' forgot about the lovely stuff growin' lower down the slopes."

Donnelly could see that old Hugh was bitter and "werked up". They both watched the limitless sea for a long time.

Suddenly came the booming entreaty yet again:

"I want to see the doctor! He's got to get this key out of my foot!"

A collective, sickened sigh came from the boat:

"Put a sock in it, Matty!", pleaded Harry Feltham.

Penman seemed to hear nothing and every few seconds repeated his cry. Usually, when the men were off watch or standing down from rowing, they slept a great deal in spite of the tempests. But Matty's cries pierced their chronic, accumulating fatigue so that sleep for anyone was beyond possibility now.

At this time the sea was calmer, but it was all relative for the slightest increase in the wind's velocity brought the sea to a new boiling. For now though, the waters were placid enough to offer little competition to the resonating cries of the poor mad engineer. Even the most seasoned, even Dunlop himself, became edgy then fearful. The effects of Matty's calls went beyond those of the storms, even of the sinking. They seemed the harbinger of a horrible death for them all.

Just as one or two were thinking that "something should be done" about Matty everything went completely quiet. He had been sitting at the starboard side of the boat, on the seat that ran fore and aft. Quickly, and still gazing fixedly to the port horizon, he stood up. They marvelled that despite the motion of the boat he managed to stand completely still. Then he began to take off his clothes.

Some called for him to stop. Others moved to restrain him. The powerful man heard and felt nothing. In minutes he was completely naked. The others, bewildered, looked at each other, then at the First Mate, who put out an arm to restrain them. Then Penman boomed:

"Yes, doctor! Yes! I'm coming for you to examine me! The key is in my foot!"

Next, like lightning, he stepped up onto the nearer thwart, ran across it and into the freezing sea. The boat rocked alarmingly as Porter, Swain and Riley lurched towards port side:

"No, no!," called Dunlop, "stay still!"

At all events their gesture was futile: Matty had been much too quick for any of them. Sick at heart, they watched and saw the bobbing bald head reappear once or twice. It was as though the Atlantic was showing them its prize before it took him under. Even after they knew that Matty had gone for good they watched for a long time.

The First Mate waited for a while, letting them struggle with the shock. Then he asked them to join in prayers for their shipmate. After the prayers and the hymn were over, Dunlop looked towards Kevin. The boy understood when he nodded. Striving to keep his voice whole, the Deck-Boy called:

"Eternal rest grant unto him, O Lord, and let perpetual light shine upon him. May he rest in peace....."

Now everyone answered "Amen."

In this lifeboat, the sectarian writ did not run. They had dead comrades to thank for that.

Chapter Eight

Ten Notches on the Gunwale

In gloom and silence they proceeded on their course for the rest of that day numbed by what had happened. They permitted themselves short, muted comments when the evening ration was being distributed. As Kevin finished chomping a ship's biscuit he drank his water from the dipper. Looking up, he saw the First Mate was making a knife cut on the side of the boat.

"What's he doing that for?."

"For every day we're in this boat he puts a notch on the gunwale. That's three he's cut," explained Hugh Riley.

Then the youth saw Ian Dunlop taking off his tunic

and putting on the sweater and jerkin Matty Penman had discarded.

"He's helped himself to Matty's things!"

"Stop fashin'. He's gotta do that."

"Why?"

"Because if a U-boat pops up they'll take him prisoner. They're nabbin' all senior officers. The Jerries reckon that's another way to cripple our convoys."

Before he covered up for the night, Donnelly sat with his head in his hands for a long time.

On the fourth day, when the morning ration had been distributed, Ian Dunlop watched the men in silence. The last of the corned beef had been distributed. Dave Porter was scouring the seams of the tin with his finger nail chasing out the last vestiges of meat and yellow fat. He found minute proportions of both and smeared them onto his biscuit to soften its dry, tasteless, monotonous texture.

Dunlop's intelligent eye noted early signs of deterioration in the survivors. Their skin seemed to be tightening, their voices were becoming distorted by thirst, they seemed a little less sure of their footing as they moved about, they spoke to each other very little and their rowing was slackening in its momentum.

He knew they were tired and becoming weaker but the problem was not completely physical. The horror of the sinking, the loss of shipmates and the later deaths of Elkin, Wilson and Penman, especially, had left them in shock and fearful of their own fate.

"O.K. listen," he said to them "we're nearer home than we were yesterday by a long chalk. So let's have another big effort to-day. And let's cheer up. Who'll get some singing going?"

They were incredulous at this but after half a minute of embarrassed silence Harry Feltham began to intone

"Roll out the barrel" followed by "The Lambeth Walk" and "Keep right on to the end of the road." His voice was very pleasant and he never struggled for the words of anything he sang. Soon he had them all singing and even Tai Lok, white-faced with pain from his scalded stomach, tried to mouth some of the words.

After half an hour or so, the singing began to falter and in a few more minutes Feltham was singing alone.

"Come on!," he exhorted them, but they could manage no more.

"Well you are a mouldy lot! Seems I'll have to do it on me tod. Alright, sir?"

Dunlop smiled and nodded. It was all the encouragement the Londoner needed. He treated them to a number of "patter songs" from the Edwardian music hall. One, "Right in the middle of the road," was Gilbertian in its pace and verbal plenitude. Feltham's rendering of it was superb. As the song ended, Porter, the Bosun's Mate, said:

"Yer should've called it 'Right in the middle of the sea!'"

There was a hint of hysteria in the laughter following this black, inept observation. The First Mate's look left Porter wishing he'd never uttered it.

By now, Feltham had moved to his next piece, a song popularised by comedian George Formby called "Chinese Laundry Blues" ("Oh, Mr Woo"). They all laughed at this and Tai Lok managed a grin, forgetting his agony for a brief spell.

More than an hour later, when Feltham had finally sung himself to silence, the First Mate nodded his thanks and there were some cheers and applause. Dunlop was grateful to Feltham. The effort had been a tour de force, calling for strength as well as skill. It had certainly helped to lighten the atmosphere a little.

After a day of comparative calm, that night was very

troubled. A northerly gale developed rapidly and the boat, beam onto it, seemed about to capsize. As the wind howled around them they struggled to lower the sail and turn the boat stern on to the fury. It made little difference, the boat still rocked violently and they had to bail like men possessed to avoid being swamped. The Arctic winds had also brought freezing cold air with them and Dave Porter and Hugh Riley found it difficult to breathe.

In the morning the gale still raged and the cold wracked their bodies. During the night Hugh Riley had tried to shield Kevin from the worst of it, whenever they were not bailing, by insisting he took more than his share of boat cover. Since this was at his own expense, in a group of ghost–like figures, the most gaunt spectre was the motor man.

Harry Feltham was still in good spirits and when the storm had moderated a little he made his way gingerly to the aft locker. Returning from it, for Tai Lok's benefit, he went into one of his droll routines:

"Hallo, me old Tai, warm enough? Parky ain't it? In fact 'it's cold enough fer two pur a bootlaces!' That's what these Scousers say – amusing fellows aren't they?"

Then he mimed the action of playing the ukelele and began a snatch of Chinese Laundry Blues:

"My vest so short, that it won't fit my little brother
And my new Sunday shirt has got a perforated
rudder
Mr Woo - - - - What shall I do?
I've got those kinda Limehouse Chinese Laundry
bl….."

Before he could finish the line, a monstrous wave hit the boat. Gigantic in size and scope it seemed certain to overturn the little craft. Miraculously, they weren't swamped but, though luck played its part, this was due to the massive efforts they made to survive. Exhausted, they gasped and vomited while their boat, a tiny speck at the mercy of that vast tormented ocean, continued to lurch and yaw.

As they recovered, Tom Gratton looked up. "Where's Harry," he asked anxiously. They gaped, then looked at each other sick with fear. The chirpy Londoner had gone. It was as though the cunning sea had stalked him and, seizing the moment he was off guard, had snatched him down to its depths. An impermeable deep gloom settled over the boat. In his stupor each one gazed at the boundless ocean. Ian Dunlop waited for an hour and only then, when he felt they were beginning to come to terms with this calamity, he led them once more in prayers for a departed shipmate.

On the morning of the sixth day, before the ration was distributed (no more than a biscuit) the First Mate spoke quietly to them now the gale had spent itself:

"This is hardly the time but there's more bad news." He paused as they all looked towards him.

"The water breaker must be leaking. It's less than a quarter full. I reckon we are about five or six days from the outer radius of aircraft cover. As from now we'll have to reduce the ration to half a dipper each day. As you know it's been impossible to catch any rain water that wasn't contaminated because of the gales. We had the last of the condensed milk yesterday. We'll just have to grin and bear it because everyday we last out is a day nearer safety."

His words produced no reaction. He had expected they would at least ask about the water breaker. They just looked away from him, dejected and apathetic. He found it hard to be hopeful now and to worsen things the cold was clearly intensifying. It must be at least ten degrees below zero and it was getting colder.

The rations were distributed. Dunlop noted that they

drank the water quickly enough but seemed to have no stomach for the biscuit. Martin Swain leaned over and whispered what the others were thinking:

"It's like eating sawdust. You could gag on the damn' thing."

The tiny water ration eased their thirst for a moment but after that it was a trial to get through the biscuits, famished though they were. Perhaps one way to make them palatable was to increase the work rate to increase their hunger. So, with Dunlop's quiet but resolute prompting, they set the sail and began to row eastward again. Now that the wind had slackened its rush and the sea had flattened somewhat they looked in all directions for signs of another vessel. There was nothing.

When they were settling down for the night, Hugh Riley murmured to Kevin:

"You'll tell your Ma we met up, won't you?"
The boy assured him on this point but was puzzled. Didn't he realise his mother knew who had spoken for him at the Wirral Line? Perhaps not, he concluded, but it seemed a strange thing for Hugh to say.

Throughout the night the cold was so bitter Kevin found it impossible to sleep. Yet again he looked back on everything that had happened since they left Liverpool and especially on the deaths of his friends Billy and Alan. He could see now that the people at home had no idea, nor would they hardly credit, the horrors men had to endure to keep the lifelines to Britain open.

The morning of the seventh day brought them close to despair for when they moved the boat cover from around them they found Hugh Riley was dead. They were profoundly shocked and saddened by the passing of this wise, friendly and competent old man, a man past retirement age who had come back to sea to "do his bit."

"Poor old lad," whispered Tom Gratton, "he froze to

death."

Dave Porter, taciturn even in his best moods and averse to paying compliments, shook his head in sorrow:

"He were a good shipmate."

The others quietly agreed. It was the only accolade these men felt worth having and they knew it would have pleased the old seaman. When they committed his body to the sea, it was clear that Kevin was still too stunned to say anything. So the First Mate led them in all the prayers including the "Eternal rest." A devout Scots Presbyterian, he spoke the words of this Catholic prayer with great respect and reverence. Afterwards he bent over Kevin and put something into his hand. "He was holding this," he whispered. Kevin saw it was a small crucifix which had obviously become detached from a set of rosary beads. When the others saw the boy wiping away his tears, they were not embarrassed.

"He were the lad's mucker," explained Tom Gratton to Martin Swain, who nodded agreement to something he already knew.

Kevin Donnelly was tortured by his own thoughts. Of all the crew on the "Willaston" he was obviously the least useful yet he had been spared. Billy, Alan, Hugh were competent seamen with jobs of their own to do but they had shown him the ropes and been his friend. Harry Feltham had been a tonic to them all and he was gone, Hugh had said Matty Penman was capable and respected - he was gone. Captain George Stephens was gone. All the others, save this handful of survivors, were gone. Yet he, a virtual passenger, was still alive. There was no sense to it.

Then he saw a succession of faces: the craggy, wise and caring face of Hugh Riley, then his father's face, then his mother's face and then the face of a girl who was also from Liverpool.

During the following two days, Ian Dunlop came to see Hugh Riley's death as a watershed. There had been almost impossible difficulties up to that point, but in spite of losing good men they had come through and were quietly confident. They had sailed a good distance, in spite of the storms, not perhaps as much as he had planned, but their chances had been at least fifty-fifty. Now he was not so sure. He had already noted the early signs of deterioration and these were now more marked.

The situation was grave mainly due to lack of water. Excessive loss of water from the tissues of the body was making it impossible for them to swallow. So they had no stomach for the hard biscuits. The reduction in their digestive juices meant that they could assimilate nothing. They had no appetite and without food they were becoming alarmingly weaker.

. After the sinking, their spirits had been as good as one could reasonably expect. From time to time they had talked of home and the food they would eat when they got there. Their hope was also reflected in the passion and good humour with which they had talked of football teams and football pools. And they had continued to josh Harry Feltham for his support of Clapton Orient. They had put their lives, experience and unfussed courage on the line.

As he watched them now though they talked very little. Parched mouths and throats didn't encourage talking, he conceded that. When they did speak the thirst was making their voices steadily more distorted and their weight loss was becoming more visible. Some had cracked and swollen lips and this spurred another thought: frostbite, if it hadn't already come, would soon be moving among them like a curse. Worst of all, if he wasn't mistaken, a terrifying shadow was creeping into the eyes of one or two and if they lost the will to live then, beyond doubt, they would all die.

He looked up the boat again. Tai Lok, in spite of his agony, was trying to smile at him. It was enough. Dunlop clenched his fists with resolution. He had to get them home. Such men as these had to be saved.

He moved down the boat and pushed out one of the oars. He called to the others on rowing duty:

"Put your backs into it lads. We're going to get there!"

When the tenth day dawned, the wind had run to nothing. Making no headway at all the boat rose and fell gently on the slight swell. The slack sail drooped from its spar. Martin Swain was keeping watch and as he looked around at the immensity of the ocean, on which they were quite alone, he swallowed with fear. No matter how hard they worked to save themselves the vast sea rendered their efforts puny.

He looked at the others. They were down to the last traces of their strength but were still sleeping only fitfully, stirring and moaning. Tom Gratton cried out in pain and mumbled something impossible to understand. Was the end near for them?

To dispel these thoughts he stirred himself. "Where there's life" and all that. Before rousing the others he cut another notch in the gunwale then turned to look at the sea again. His gaze came round to the southern horizon. In the improving light a line of small clouds was visible and they held his attention. There were about six of them, each one separated from the next by a patch of sky. It was curious but in their regularity they were like carriages on a railway train.

What was that? Astounded, his eyes widened and his jaw sagged. A dark shape had just moved across the sky-space between one cloud and another. He looked.....

and looked.......and looked. Yes!.......there it was again.

He felt his heart might burst through his rib-cage:

"Sir, sir! Due south.......there's a plane!"

In the next minutes, the boat rocked alarmingly as the men worked frantically to take out the flares from the locker. The First Mate struggled to stick the first flare onto the milled top of its container. Within seconds he was holding its effervescing, scintillating light over his head. The sea, for some distance, was bathed in its radiant glow.

"There! It's there again, sir!"

This was the Bosun's Mate, pointing towards the last intervening space in the train of clouds. If something had been there it had gone now. In case it reappeared they lit two more flares but, save for the clouds, the horizon was blank. The men sank dejectedly into the bottom of the boat. Dunlop could not let them dwell on the incident. Unless they moved on few, if any, of them would live.

"O.K. If that was one of our planes, and I'm pretty sure it was, we must be near the edge of our protection zone. So let's get under way again. It'll increase our chances and help beat the cold."

One or two looked at him imploringly. They had nothing more to give.

"I know it's tough, but we mustn't give up. We've nearly made it!"

They began to row. Kevin was sitting near to Tom Gratton and saw him blench then grit his teeth with pain as he banged his right hand against an oar lock.

"What's wrong," he asked.

The Quartermaster was dismissive:

"Nothin'. I must 'ave knocked it or summat."

They rowed for just a few minutes, developing a little rhythm and speed, when half a mile ahead a massive dark shape emerged suddenly from a bank of cloud. Then the great boom of its engines hit them. Swain raised his arms in acclamation. The shape ahead was unmistakable – it was a Sunderland flying boat.

"Sir! It's Air-Sea rescue!"

"Get the flares!.......and the lamp!"

There was a general scrambling, some falling over oars and thwarts and much cursing as they fumbled with a flare. Finally, the Bosun's Mate held it aloft while it hissed and spluttered but the colza-oil lamp would not light. They were desperate to get some sort of sign up to the aircraft and went through the remaining matches, without result.

By now the giant plane had veered to port of them and was almost out of sight. The men stood rigid, bathed in the glow of the flare. Dave Porter watched the grey speck intently and pointed the flare at it:

"He's banking, sir! He's comin' round!"

"Right!," grinned Ian Dunlop.

All eyes watched as the giant plane veered to its right, came around in an arc to its left, turned through one hundred and eighty degrees and passed over them. They could only wave and try to shout as much as their tortured throats would allow but there was no answering signal from the aircraft. This puzzled them. Tom Gratton voiced the general bewilderment:

"He must've seen us, sir!"

"Sure he did. Perhaps he was out at the limit of his range and didn't have the fuel to hang around."

He let them adjust to the situation for a few minutes then said:

"Come on, chaps. Back to the oars."

As they trundled on, no-one spoke.

By the late afternoon, they had slackened their efforts considerably. Dave Porter was bent over wheezing painfully. Tom Gratton was keeping watch. His eyes ached from scanning the horizon. Suddenly, a blob appeared there. At first he took it to be the spot that always pestered him, the "floater" in his right eye. He blinked, the blob was there again and it was no "floater".

His chest became insufferably constricted and his heart pounded. He forgot the misery of his throbbing hand and until he could make out the upperworks of a ship he said nothing. When he was certain, he called:

"Sir!......Vessel aft and approaching."

The First Mate clambered towards him. He saw the vessel but waited until it had closed half the distance between the horizon and the lifeboat. The others waited for his verdict. He concentrated to make sure, then:

"Looks like one of ours. Escort vessel!" he said.

Despite their condition, the survivors cried out and hugged each other. Quickly, self-consciously, they wiped away the tears of their delight. A little later, as the dog-watch drew near, HMS "Anthemis", a Flower-class corvette, came close. When it was obvious that no-one in the boat had the strength to row towards it, H.M.S. "Anthemis" edged nearer and let down a scrambling net to six men close to death.

Of the survivors only Ian Dunlop, Martin Swain and Kevin Donnelly were in any condition to attempt the scrambling net. Tai Lok was completely immobile, Dave Porter was seized by an acutely painful coughing fit and Tom Gratton was holding his hand in agony.

Ian Dunlop intended to wait until the others had boarded the corvette. He signalled Martin Swain and Kevin towards the net. Naval personnel watched from above as the two attempted to climb. When it was obvious they hadn't the strength to negotiate even the first rungs, two naval ratings came down the net quickly. One laid his hand on Kevin's shoulder:

"Yiz O.K., wack?," he asked.

Hearing a voice from Liverpool, the boy shielded his eyes to conceal his tears.

Chapter Nine

Mixed Fortunes

It took more than one hour to get the six survivors on board the corvette. Some were in a worse state than others but all were almost finished. The sight of H.M.S. "Anthemis" had stirred the final flicker of animation but now they were completely spent and had to be handled like helpless children. During the process of rescuing them, the stationary vessel was, of course, highly vulnerable to submarine attack. Yet the Captain would not let the process be rushed. Sensing the growing tension among his crew, who felt they were cheating the odds once too often, he looked down from the bridge and pointed to the survivors:

"They would have waited for us, you know."

When the six were safely on board, the corvette set about destroying the lifeboat. As the bullets ripped into the boat's air tanks it began to sink. The last section to go under was a gunwale with ten notches on it. H.M.S. "Anthemis" then turned in a lengthy arc and set off to the north east.

Naturally, when they were rescued, the merchant seamen had expected warmth, comfort and medical care. They quickly perceived their rescue-vessel was a hell-hole. It was crammed with men it had plucked from the sea. Including the "Clan Chieftain" and the "Willaston" nine ships from that particular convoy had been sunk by the Germans. The losses of crews had been so appalling that H.M.S. "Anthemis", happily in the vicinity, had been temporarily detached from other duties to search for survivors.

Some of those it had saved were now in the crew cabins, the officers' and petty officers' cabins, the store rooms, even the washrooms and the heads. Others filled the decks – they lay on the foredeck around the anchor winch, around the mooring bollards, they were amidships near the starboard boat davit and they cowered for shelter around a deck locker and a stowage box.

Even then the tally was incomplete for towards the stern of the vessel they were lying next to the galley coal store, the engine room vent and even the depth charge davit. It seemed that every inch of space was taken up by exhausted and cruelly injured men. Now they were six other men to be cared for.

When Ian Dunlop felt a little rested, he asked to be taken to the Captain. He was Lieutenant Commander J.D. Liddiard, a youthful, rugged New Zealander who, strangely, had been a university lecturer before joining the Royal Navy in the mid nineteen thirties. Outstanding competence and wartime pressures had seen a series of rapid promotions for Liddiard who, despite his burdens, looked fit and in control.

Though exhausted and weak, Dunlop had not lost his firm, even tones. He thanked the Captain for their rescue and expressed his admiration for the miracle being worked by "Anthemis,"

---- "in spite of the fact that there's barely room to turn around."

There was an affected cynicism in Liddiard's smile:

"You know, when this little lady was on the drawing board, they gave her a projected complement of 29. By the time she was commissioned last year that had been pushed up to 47. When the war started and it was clear we needed extra armament and equipment, plus the crew to go with them, the final count was 78. Today, including your party, Mr Dunlop, we've got 83 survivors on board. So, altogether, 161 of us are homeward bound. Welcome to the sardine can."

He noticed Dunlop looking about him:

"Pretty basic isn't she? Winston calls the corvettes the 'cheap and nasties'. We were originally designed as coastal escorts. Now we're major players in North Atlantic escort work despite the fact we're really only a deck off which you can lob depth charges."

"And in your spare time you pick up survivors."

"Right – not that we're organised for doing that. But their Lordships are under the astonishing illusion we can do it and sink U-boats too. They have no structure in place to cope with all this and don't see what's dramatically and blindingly obvious - that for this business we need a stock of spare, warm clothes; spare blankets; a well-equipped sick bay; ample drugs and pain killers and stacks of canvas for making shrouds!"

The Scot could only shake his head. This encouraged

the Captain to continue:

"A little vessel like this isn't stable enough for rescue work anyway. If we hit heavy weather before Greenock you'll see what I mean. She can roll on wet grass. And just look at that!......"

Ian followed his pointing finger to where condensation was coursing steadily down a bulkhead:

"The bloody thing's always wet, all year through!..... no forced draught ventilation, y'see. And she's been carefully designed so you can't come through from the mess-decks to the bridge without getting soaked, the galley's so far aft the grub's cold by the time it gets to you and the fo'c'sle's so bloody small you need a shoe-horn to get into it."

Then he grinned:

"Now what other exciting things can I tell you? Oh yes, the electrical system won't support gyro compasses so we've only got magnetic compasses which aren't much cop when we're being thrown about like crazy, the Asdic's obsolete and the radar system's crap – wouldn't find a bull up an alley-way."

He grinned again:

"But apart from all that – everything's unky-dory!"

They both laughed and Liddiard put up his hands in mock apology –

"Sorry you were on the end of all that, but now I've had a good grumble it's set me up for the whole of this watch!"

He looked steadily at the First Mate:

"We'll do what we can for you – be sure of that – but after my hysterical outburst you won't be surprised to learn there are no qualified medics on board. We've got one officers'-mess steward who's a self-taught first aider, that's all. The man's fantastic but what's so hard to take is that all the men we've picked up are suffering badly from exposure, some are seriously injured and some are dying. Practically all we can offer are soothing words."

"Sometimes words are a great help, Captain. And it'll be obvious, even to the dying, you're doing everything you possibly can."

The New Zealander was quite affected by these comments. To mask his feelings he spoke rapidly:

"You look absolutely shattered. We're organising some soup for you. Better not take any solids yet. I hope you'll manage the soup anyway. I'll get you taken to my cabin. There's a set of civvies in there. Take whatever'll fit you."

Dunlop protested, but Liddiard waved this aside:

"Take them! Besides, it's the only way I can look the crew in the face. They gave their clothes away days ago."

The merchant seaman put out his hand to the Captain, but could say nothing. In any event, words would have been inadequate.

Because the freezing conditions had badly affected the Willaston men it was decided to put them on the raised, railed area in front of the ship's funnel. There they would get some benefit from the irradiated heat of the vessel's Scotch boilers. Kevin Donnelly felt himself being swaddled in some coarse, stiffish material. It extended from his neck to his lower limbs. Later he discovered this was rush matting from the Captain's cabin.

"That'll keep the cold out," grinned the rating who bound him into it.

When they manhandled Tom Gratton up the ladder leading to the funnel his hand caught on a rail. He shrieked in agony.

"Yower arm gone bad ways 'as eet?," asked the mess steward first-aider in rich Birmingham tones. Tom could only grunt.

"What you'm got there?....load o'boils?......'s 'ave a

luck."

The man's jaw stiffened because of what he saw. Kevin looked across at that moment and saw the macerated pulp of Tom's hand. Fingers protruded from it like blackened twigs.

"Well.......oi'll get summat 'round it for now. They'll see to it proper when we get you to hospital," said the first-aider, feigning optimism.

Very soon coffee laced with grog was brought to the "Willaston" men. They coughed and spluttered over it but ever after would remember its taste and warmth.

Mercifully there were no threatening incidents on the homeward journey despite having to make three separate stops for burials. Whenever the weather worsened Kevin's sea sickness returned and he was obliged to sit for hours in whatever vomit he could emit.

In two and a half days they were rounding the Mull of Kintyre. As they made their way up the Kilbrannan Sound, with Arran to starboard, a wave of relief materialised which could almost be touched. Even men in indescribable pain were caught up in it. This was the time for any number of thankful prayers and not a few tears. Then they were through the Sound of Bute, past Dunoon and Gourock and safe home into Greenock. It was raining heavily as H.M.S. "Anthemis" neared her berth. When she docked the downpour ceased.

Late that night Kevin was admitted to a hospital in the northern suburbs of Glasgow. He enquired after Tai Lok, Tom Gratton and Dave Porter and was told they were at the same hospital, in other wards. Apparently, Tai and Tom needed surgery. Kevin himself was then examined and given an injection. He did not wake for forty-eight hours. When he did he was as hungry as a bear.

After a second examination he was moved to a convalescent ward where he spent five more days. Then he was seen by a doctor of the Royal Navy who told him he was discharged. As he was receiving this news Ian Dunlop walked into the ward. Kevin felt emotion and gratitude. He noticed the First Mate's pallor and weight loss. It was Dunlop who spoke first:

"How are you feeling?"

"Fine, sir."

"I'm glad you came through, O.K. Quite a first voyage for you, wasn't it?"

The youth felt awkward, fearing his emotion would become apparent.

"I'm glad you made it, sir. Thanks for what you did for us."

Dunlop shook his head sadly:

"It's getting to be part of the job these days."

"How's Mr Swain, sir?"

"Fine. He's pretty durable. Left for home this morning. Asked me to give you his good wishes."

There was a small silence.

"What are you going to do now, Donnelly?"

"Get back to Liverpool......if I can."

"If you can?"

Another silence, then:

"Well, you see sir......I've got no money. What I had went down with the ship."

"Mm. I know the problem. If we were in the armed forces this would be sorted out for us. I can let you have a couple of pounds. That'll buy you a night or two in a Seamen's Mission. Then you'll be able to get down to Shettleston. The Wirral Line has an agent there. See him about your back pay. That'll get you a railway ticket and leave a bit to spare. Do you understand?"

Kevin nodded. His problem had been resolved. He tried to express his thanks but the attempt was waved aside. Dunlop took out a pocket-book and began to scribble. He tore out a page and handed it over:

"This is the agent."

"Oh....right, sir....but where shall I see you to pay you back?"

"Forget it, and see you look after yourself, O.K.?"
Kevin was still protesting as the First Mate was getting up to leave:

"Oh....when you get home....go to see Mr Miles Edmonds at the WPL offices in Tithebarn Street."

"Mr....?"

"Miles Edmonds. He's our Managing Director. He'll want to talk to you.....about the sinking....that sort o'thing. If you can spare him half an hour, I'm sure he'd appreciate it."
Kevin's memory stirred.....the man in the Anthony Eden hat, when the ship left the Huskisson Dock; Hugh Riley had said good things about him.

"O.K., sir."

"Fine – now I must pop to see the others."
At the end of the ward, the First Mate turned and waved goodbye. Donnelly was sad to see him go. He was a gentleman, someone he felt better for having known. His visit brought back memories of other shipmates – Billy, Alan, Harry Feltham, Dave Porter. He especially missed the kind, wise motor man, Hugh Riley. Hugh came from Birkenhead. The youth resolved that when he got back he would go to see his wife and tell her what their friendship had meant to him.

Before leaving the hospital he asked to see the other three but was told it was not possible yet. Presumably Ian Dunlop had been told the same thing. Leaving the hospital the sights and sounds of Glasgow made him apprehensive. What now? He wished Hugh Riley was on hand. He would have known what to do.

After several hours of searching he found, some miles

away, the one Seamen's Mission with a bed available. He had reached it by a combination of constant enquiry, the use of local transport and a lot of painful walking. When he got there eventually he felt sick with fatigue.

The next morning, after a basic but warming breakfast, he was setting off to see the agent of the Wirral Peninsular Line. The Warden of the Mission, "Jock" Dees, a white-haired old man with kind eyes, was at the doorway. Kevin showed Ian Dunlop's slip of paper to him and asked for directions:

"Mm...........South Vaselius Street..........Shettleston. Shettleston! That's miles away. You'll have to go into the City centre – from the stop at the end of this road, then out to Shettleston."

"Oh....right," was the uncertain answer.

The old man looked concerned:

"You're not going like that, are you?"

The youngster looked down at himself:

"Well, yes....these are the only clothes I've got."

Though it had lost its pristine appearance, he was still proud of the sweater bought for him by Bridie Keating but had to concede that his ordeal in the lifeboat had ravaged the 25 dollar boots.

The Warden tutted:

"It's freezing again. You'll be back in hospital if you don't watch it. Come with me!"

In a corner of his small flat he rummaged through two drawers full of old clothes.

"These are things seamen have left behind. I keep 'em for a while then give 'em out where they'll do some good. Now try this duffle coat. It's old but it'll keep the life in you."

The coat was rather big for him and most of the other things offered were either too large or too small. However, a pair of corduroy trousers, sound if scruffy, were much more weatherproof than the flannels he was wearing. The Warden was still shaking his head:

"Yon shoes are droppin' off your feet."

They were undoubtedly battered and stained with water, but Kevin did not intend to abandon them:

"Well, they were a gift, you see – cost 25 dollars. I'd like to see if they'll repair."

Dees grunted doubtfully and next produced a pair of knee-length heavy rubber sea boots.

"These'll be about your size an' I've got the big socks to go with 'em."

When Kevin felt the warmth of the boots radiate through his feet he was grateful but he asked for his own shoes to be kept safely. They might repair he insisted. They were unsuccessful at finding any kind of coat for him until the Warden said:

"I know......wait a bit......"

He came back from behind a door with a black, pin-striped suit on a hanger.

"You see what lads leave behind. Amazing. In fact this suit belonged to a lad from Cardiff....stoker.....mad about ballroom dancing.....but he reckons it won't fit him any more so he says I can pass it on. Anyway, it's the coat that might fit you. It doesn't match what you've wearing, but what b'that? If you don't want to wear the duffle coat this'll keep the cold out."

With some contrivance they finally got the coat over Kevin's thick sweater only for the long seam under the left armpit to burst. The mishap revealed a significant length of the jacket's lining. The old man laughed:

"It looks a bit rough but you'll just have to keep your arm tucked in."

Then they both laughed.

"Thank you very much, Mr Dees. You've been a big help – I'll leave the duffle coat off for now."

Dees nodded:

"Shall I keep your bed for tonight?"

"If you will please."

The boy wanted to get home desperately but did not intend to leave Glasgow until he had visited the hospital again to see the three survivors.

An hour later he was waiting in the City centre for the transport which would take him to Shettleston. Two women stood behind him. At first he was only dimly conscious of them but then began to feel strangely uncomfortable......as if eyes were boring into the back of his neck. After a little while he turned, although reluctantly. The two women were middle-aged and the nearer one was looking at him maliciously. He turned away and the women began to whisper. Then, so he would have the benefit of her views the nearer one raised her voice to a stage whisper:

"I wouldn't mind my son having to go overseas if everyone was called up – like he was."

"That's right!", said her obsequious companion.

"Plenty of able-bodied men have avoided going. It's not right."

Kevin felt a strong urge to violence but the transport arrived. He took care to sit at some distance from the pair.

On that dank, misty morning Shettleston looked utterly miserable. Eventually, when he had found South Vaselius Street he tramped its length, past its woebegone warehouses. Finally, he came to the premises he was seeking. On the peeling paint of a narrow door there was a brass plate. It had long gone dull for want of polish but announced that behind the door was the "Head Office" of:

Jasper Corries & Co

Freight Forwarders and Ships' Agents

It seemed a frivolously pretentious overclaim.

There was no bell push and knocking produced no response. So the young Liverpudlian pressed against the door with some force. It opened and his arrival was signalled by a bell mounted over the inside of the door. This was of a type usually found in small retail shops, but whereas such bells make some effort at least at being melodious this one hissed and spat for having been disturbed.

Beyond the door, the youth found himself in a dark passage. As his eyes tried to pierce the gloom he was wondering what to do next.

"Yes?!"

The fiercely-put enquiry came from somewhere beyond the end of the passage. With his hand on the wall for safety, Kevin followed the sound. Eventually he turned into a space – not an office as such, merely a space.

Before him was a totally Dickensian tableau. Where Kevin now stood was every bit as chaotic, badly lit and grubby as the scene in "Great Expectations" when Pip visits the office in Little Britain of Mr Jaggers, the lawyer.

The only person in the space was an old, stooped man with a high domed forehead, an aged black suit and an off-white shirt with a winged collar. He sat at a sloping desk, cleaning the nib of a cheap wooden pen. Kevin's lively Celtic imagination suggested the one thing missing was a cobweb extending from the man's forehead to his desk. When he had read "Great Expectations" at school, his teacher had averred that Dickens dealt in caricatures, not characters, but here was a flesh and blood character that author would have been proud of creating.

"Well?......What d'ye want?"

In spite of the reception Kevin controlled himself:

"My name's Kevin Donnelly. I was in the crew of the "Willaston". She was torpedoed an....."

'Yes, yes. I know what happened to the "Willaston". Why have you come here?"

"Well, you see, I need the pay that's due to me....so's I can get home."

"Pay?......I've no pay to give you. Who sent you here?"

"Mr Dunlop, the First Mate, gave me this address. He said you were the agents for the Wirral Line."

"So we are....but I can't give you any pay."

Kevin was becoming impatient:

"Look – I've got to get home and I need money. The Wirral Line owes me money and I want it. What's more, I'm not leaving till I get it!"

The old man got down from his stool, came towards Kevin and hissed:

"Clear out or I'll send for the po-lice!"

"You can send for the Black Watch. I'm not budging from here till I'm paid."

Jasper Corries hesitated – whatever he paid, if the correct sum, would be re-paid. Still, parting with money at any time was a dire prospect. Then he saw a way out:

"How do I know ye've not been paid already?"

"What?!"

Ignoring Donnelly's rage he became triumphant:

"When you signed on you were given two papers – an allotment note – that's for money to be stopped from your pay and an advance note, which is a sub from your pay."

"I wasn't given any papers. There were only two things to do with my signing on – the grade card to show I was unfit for military service and a sort of - responsibility paper."

Corries was adamant:

"I've told you what always happens. I've no money for you."

The boy was fighting not to lose complete control:

"Listen, please.....the convoy was sailing and the "Willaston" was still scratching around for crew. They took me, even though I've got a manky ankle....but they said the doctor at the Port Office would have to say it was O.K. Then I had to sign a letter freeing the Wirral Line from any responsibility if I got injured because of my ankle. I suppose in all the kerfuffle the papers you're on about got overlooked. Anyway, I didn't get any money and I want it now!"

It was obvious he was telling the truth but Corries was not ready to concede:

"I'm not authorised to give you any money without written permission. An' that could take days."

"You can 'phone them, can't you? If you do they'll soon tell you I'm speaking the truth."

Pushed to the brink like this, the agent became more agitated:

"Phone?! Do you know what 'phone calls cost?"

Kevin was now beginning to despair but he still tried to control himself:

"I see. All I want is what's owed to me and you'd begrudge me a 'phone call. Is that what you're saying?"

The agent swallowed:

"Well, I'll see what I can do but all this is most irregular, most irregular. You'll have to come back later."

"Oh no. I'm going nowhere till I'm paid. Find me a chair please or give me the number and I'll speak to them. I'll ask them what sort of employers they are to leave seamen in a fix like this to deal with people like you."

Corries was cornered and he knew it. With a bitter

sigh he picked up the telephone. On busy wartime 'phone lines it took thirty minutes to get through to Liverpool. Donnelly's story was then quickly verified and the agent was authorised to pay him.

Silently, slowly, wincing occasionally as if in pain, he prepared a note for "K.D. Donnelly, temporary deck-boy." Distastefully he handed it over. Kevin looked at it. He was aghast:

"What's this?"

"Your pay!"

"Is this a joke?"

Corries leaned across Kevin and stabbed out each line in the note with an ink-stained finger –

"It's your pay! -

3 and a half weeks at £2.10s per week	£ 8.15.0d
3 and a half weeks War Risk bonus at £10 per month	£ 8.15.0d
Gross wages	£17.10.0d
Less stoppages for insurance, income tax and 'phone call	£ 4. 7.6d
Nett wages	£13. 2.6d

"£2.10 shillings a week! It ought to be more than that, surely?"

The old man spat out his reply:

"I've been told to pay you that! It's more than you should be getting - you're not even an apprentice yet – an able seaman gets less than £12 a month!"

Donnelly was not prepared to concede:

"But I can make more than this labouring in a timber yard. And what's this about 3 ½ weeks? I've been gone for six weeks!"

A gleam came into the agent's eyes. His next words

were triumphant:

"Aye. Oh aye.....but you're only paid up to the date of the sinking......and the Admiralty told the Line the date the ship went down."

Spitefully he leered at the lad.

"That's robbery!" cried Kevin

"Those are the terms of your employment and that's all you're getting!"

"But what about all these stoppages?"

"We all have to pay insurance. There's no tax code for you at the Wirral Line so I had to put you on emergency code. That's the law!"

Bitter and deflated, the boy shook his head sadly:

"And you've even charged me for the 'phone call....."

"I can't be expected to pay it! I can't be expected to pay it! It's fair.... – I asked the operator to advise time and cost on completion," Corries whined.

Kevin waved the paper:

"What am I supposed to do with this?"

"You take it 'round to get it changed. Now leave this office...clear out! You're nothing but a trouble maker!"

As the Liverpudlian went back through the grim rows of warehouses the misery of walking on his injured ankle intensified. He was thinking about the visit to Corries and still trying to control his rage when something ran between his feet. He felt himself falling then, at the last second, managed to steady himself. A screeching creature was bolting into the shadows. Before it disappeared it looked back. It was a mangy, starving cat. Its expression summarised for Kevin all the misadventures of the morning's journeying.

When he resumed his thinking and wondering he suddenly felt glad to be alone for his eyes were filling with tears. Appearing in his mind's eye were the faces of his father, Hugh Riley, Matty Penman, Harry Feltham, Billy and Alan. To make their way in the world they had been forced to take on one of its toughest jobs. The threat of death had been their constant companion so that they could qualify for a "War Risks Bonus" of £10 per month. Then death had come to them so the outlay could be justified. Moreover, if Jasper Corries were any indicator their deaths would go unheralded, unremarked even. There would be no graves to visit, no headstones to look at. It would be as if they never existed now the sea had them.

Back in his grimy office, old Corries was slumped at his desk. Anguish was eating out new lines in his face. Even though only temporarily it was too much to bear – he had sanctioned the depletion of his assets by thirteen pounds two shillings and sixpence – oh yes, someone would come before long demanding that he redeem the note and it could be weeks before he was reimbursed by the Wirral Line.

"Where do   they think I get bawbees from?", he muttered.

The last hour had been so traumatic he was forced to pour an incredibly large quantity of single malt whisky into an incredibly dirty glass and despatch it in one incredible single swallow.

Eventually Kevin Donnelly was back in the heart of Glasgow. He fingered the wages note. One good thing had emerged from his contretemps with the agent: disappointing though its value was, the note was for the whole of the wages due to him. It was not for a mere "advance," so he would be spared further toil and tension in obtaining what he had earned.

Using a small part of Ian Dunlop's loan he had a scratch lunch. He was anxious to keep as much as possible of the two pounds unspent, for he was determined to repay it by some means or other. As for the note, Corries had advised him to "take it 'round" to change it for cash. He didn't understand this and decided to ask Jock Dees about it at the Mission. What he could do now, however, was to find out the train times for Liverpool. On the following day, he intended to see Dave Porter and the others at the hospital then make for home.

While lunching he learned that the Liverpool trains left from Glasgow Central Station. He asked for directions to it and ultimately arrived at the junction of Argyle Street and Union Street. It was now just a few days before Christmas and though only mid-afternoon the light was already fading away from the City's streets. Under the railway arches of the station it was becoming quite dark. As he wandered around in search of the station entrance someone sidled up to him:

"Oi, Jimmy – have ye got a chitty for cashin'?"
He heard the question before the rumble of trains overhead drowned out whatever else the man was saying.

"What a stroke of luck. I can get my ticket and some Christmas presents before I go back to the Mission," thought Kevin.

When the man read the note he drew the boy into the shadows. After much rummaging in pocket after pocket he pressed a large amount of money into Kevin's hand.

"There y'are – I've done my best for ye," whispered the man and disappeared. Carrying the money carefully Kevin limped up the steps into the station. The only vacant spot he could find was in a teabar where he sat down among the press of people and began to count the money. He counted it once and, incredulously, began to count it again. The thirteen pounds two shillings and sixpence on the note was now reduced to nine pounds seventeen shillings and sixpence. He sat stupefied for a long time until he was asked, pointedly, by a man with a large mug of tea whether he was leaving. Dismayed and angered by the day's events he made his way to the ticket office where he discovered that a third class single ticket would cost nearly as much as a return ticket. When he had purchased it, a sizeable hole had appeared in what remained of his pay. He decided to return to the Mission there and then.

When Jock Dees learned of the day's doings from Kevin he boiled with rage:

"I wish you'd come to me with your note. I'd have sent you to a man who'da charged you sixpence in the pound....that's the standard rate, sixpence in the pound! That shark's taken a quarter of your pay! I've heard of this afore, y'know."

Kevin sighed:

"I suppose I'm paying for my learning."

"Mm, an' a dear price seemingly. 'Course that agent could've paid you out of his petty cash if he'd troubled to, then it would've cost you nothing. Still, he might have worked some flanker for all you know. He sounds as if he wouldn't give a blind man a light."

"I'd better turn in," murmured Kevin.

"Have a cuppa tea before you do. An' sit and get warm by the fire. You look as white as a sheet. My wife says you're not properly fit yet."

After the tea and the warm fire, Kevin felt better. He told the Warden he would like an early start:

"I want to see the others in the hospital, then shop for a few bits and pieces before I catch the train."
Dees nodded and they said goodnight to each other.

The following morning, as he was leaving, the Warden gave him a large brown-paper parcel.

"This is that duffle-coat. It'll fit you if it's taken in a bit. If your Mam's handy with a needle, she'll know what to do. It's got a hood on it as well."

Kevin protested but the Warden waved this aside:

"Get on with you. It'll keep the life in you. What good is it doin' moulderin' here?"

Before Donnelly's protests could continue, Dees brought out another, smaller parcel:

"This is from the wife. I think she's got a soft spot for you. She says you look lost."

"What is it?"

"It's a meat pie.......an' I hope she doesn't take to anybody else 'cause she's put nearly all our rations in it. Oh, an' there's a flask of coffee in the parcel for you........ that's my doin'."

Kevin stood at the door of the Mission, not knowing how to thank.....

"Go on.......get off with you," said the Warden. "Give our best respects to your family and look in when you're next in Glasgow." He gave Kevin a gentle push through the door.

The youth went down into the City again. He was anxious to find some gift which each of the three men would welcome. He also wished to buy two Christmas presents: one for his mother, the other for the girl whose face he saw with increasing frequency in recent weeks.

He went into the nearest department store and instantly felt he was not welcome there. It was one of those establishments secure in the knowledge that it catered for a "discriminating clientele." In his sea boots and torn jacket he cut an alien figure. The eyes of every sales assistant followed him as, after some preliminary failures, he found his way to the millinery counter. The assistant there looked with despair at a nearby colleague as he approached. She stared at him with profound condescension:

"Yes?"

"I er....I'm looking for a silk headscarf....for a young lady."

Resignedly, she plonked a box onto the counter. Gracelessly, she brought out one or two scarves for him to see.

"These are our best quality."

Anxious to make a sale, even to an undesirable, she added:

"They don't require clothing coupons at the moment."

"Mm. Nice. How much are they?"

Her heavy sigh intimated so effectively the offence she found in the question:

"Twenty five shillings."

"Oh.....I was looking for something about half that price."

"No....not for this type of scarf, I'm afraid. These are the finest Macclesfield silk."

She had darted a rebuke at him with every syllable. Ignoring this, he asked if she could suggest anything for the price he had mentioned. It was an opportunity not to be missed – exultantly the woman said:

"What about a nice handkerchief?"

She gave her nearest colleague a sidelong smirk. Kevin noted this and with a show of affability he leaned across the counter and suggested where she might lodge such an item for safe keeping. Shrieking with shock the assistant dived for the button which would summon "Security" but it was too late – Kevin was gone.

In the next hour or so he purchased two pinafores for his mother, a lady's initial ring (fifteen shillings) and an item for each of his three shipmates. Then, as fast as the discomfort of his ankle would allow, he made his way to the hospital.

First he established the whereabouts of Dave Porter. As he walked down the long corridor towards the ward, he recalled how the Bosun's Mate had berated him for his idiocy when bailing out the lifeboat. Because of what happened since, it didn't seem to matter anymore. Porter was a mate. Facing death with him had created a bond. Those without the experience would never understand its significance.

Though Porter was sitting up in bed, he looked ashen. His breathing was very laboured but he was clearly glad to see Kevin. Greetings over, the youth watched the Bosun's Mate gasping.

"Chest no better?"

"Naw. Too many fags. An' them gales knock you back."

They talked at length about the sinking of the "Willaston" and its aftermath. It provided some psychological restoration for them both.

When it was plain that Porter was tiring, Kevin said:

"I've brought you something to keep the cold out."

He held up a half-bottle of whisky. This revivified the man, who fearful of the gift's confiscation, signalled animatedly:

"Put it in the locker – quick!"

This safely accomplished, he beamed and shook Kevin's hand:

"That's very good of you, lad. An' where are you off to now?"

"To see the others – Tai and Tom Gratton."

Dave Porter's frown made the boy uneasy –

"Tai's gone, lad."

"Home?"

"No. He died yesterday. Septicaemia all through 'im. Nothin' they could do."

Again, the death of a shipmate stupefied Kevin. He could only stare. Porter shook his head. More to himself than to his visitor he muttered:

"Y'know, he had all them horrible burns an' 'e never

made a murmur."

Kevin sat down again. After a long, stunned silence he looked at the Bosun's Mate. Then he pulled something from one of his many bags and held it up:

"He had next to nothing on in the boat so I bought him this warm shirt. I was thinking – perhaps it might fit you."

"You shouldn't a done that, lad, though he would've appreciated it. It wouldn't go near me. Keep it for yerself, why don't yer?"

"But....."

"Go on.......put it back in your bag."

Kevin stirred again:

"If it's O.K. I'll go off and see Tom Gratton now."

Holding out his hand to deter this, Porter began an extended coughing bout. When it was over he wheezed:

'You'll not be seein' him either. He's back in theatre this mornin'"

"Back?"

"Yeah. He's lost his hand and part of his arm. Frost bite. I asked the Sister on this ward to find out for me. That's how I got ter know about little Tai."

"What's Tom going in again for?"

"Search me. P'raps they've got to take more off. I've tried to find out but Sister won't say anymore. Understandable, I s'pose."

He sighed:

"Anyroad, there won't be much work for a one-armed Quartermaster."

"They put him next to me on the corvette an' we got talking. He said he'd like to leave the Merchant Navy after the war and train as a cabinet maker. So I bought this for him."

The young man held up a book. It was a manual on French polishing. Dave Porter bit his lip. He coughed to hide his embarrassment. Looking away from Kevin he said:

"You're a good lad, even if you are a bit daft."

Then he began a long spate of coughing. He was clearly very fatigued; the Ward Sister was coming towards them.

"I'd better get off then. I hope all goes well."

Donnelly put out his hand. Dave Porter shook it. He smiled between his coughing and spluttering:

"Look after yourself, lad. I hope we sail together again some time."

The boy from Liverpool went down the steps of the hospital into the cold but sunlit day. As much as his ankle would allow it, there was a spring in his gait. He had been uplifted by the final words from the Bosun's Mate. Perhaps he hadn't made such a pig's ear of things after all.

Chapter Ten

Going South

Nothing could have prepared Donnelly for the chaos of Glasgow Central Station. The sixteen-sheet poster site in its precincts asking: "Is Your Journey Really Necessary?" had apparently been ignored. Soldiers, sailors, airmen, (nearly all with kit bags and many with rifles), as well as the ubiquitous red-capped military policemen, completed one part of the surging tableau. Then came the civilians, from portly businessmen, harassed mothers with screaming children, and hordes of ordinary folk going off to work, to the blazered scholars from the private academies going home for Christmas. What a log jam!

The lad from Liverpool 8, through a score of craning

necks, checked the appropriate platform for his train and limped towards it. No sooner had he joined the stream of humanity going his way than he felt himself being eased, pushed, propelled and jostled at considerable speed, towards the single narrow opening in the sliding metal screenwork where a solitary ticket collector stood guard. There was some "business" at this opening for intending passengers were bent on joining the train before former passengers alighted from it. Kevin kept the bobbing hat of the ticket collector ever in his sights so as not to lose his bearings.

He was encumbered by so many parcels – the large one containing the duffle coat, the smaller one containing Bridie Keating's gift of shoes, the shopping bag containing all the gifts he had purchased and the package containing the meat pie and the flask of coffee. He was trying to carry these last two items especially carefully but now felt sure that before long he would fall and be trampled on.

In the end, by dint of his powerful shoulders and a kind of mute resolution, he found himself on the train, mystified as to how he finally got there. A thrusting, sinuous foray through all the third-class coaches revealed there was not a seat to be had. Members of the Armed Forces and all manner of civilians also packed the passage ways between the seats, the corridors and even the spaces over the coach connections. With an apology every few seconds he pushed and shoved his way down the whole length of the train until finally he stumbled and fell into the peace and quiet of a first-class coach immediately behind the engine.

Overcome with fatigue and a throbbing ankle he slid open the door of the nearest compartment and flopped onto a seat by the window. Too tired to put his array of parcels on the luggage rack he leaned back against the linen cover of the headrest and closed his eyes.

A girl's face emerged from the imaginings so he considered what he would do when he reached Liverpool. It was quickly decided – regardless of his time of arrival he would call on her first, give her the ring and wish her a happy Christmas. By now his money was almost gone but as soon as he felt rested enough he would get some more work at the timber merchants in Grafton Street then ask her out to tea at Reece's in the City centre. What with the silver service and the waitresses in their neat outfits she would be impressed for sure.

Someone was tugging at his leg. A middle-aged man, not unlike an elegant version of Jasper Corries, was glaring down:

"This is a first-class coach young man!"

Kevin closed his eyes again. He whispered:

"The rest of the train is full."

He was too tired to look but as the compartment filled up he could hear movements, murmurings and quite a lot of rustling. His parcels were being lifted onto the luggage-rack. He opened his eyes. Now a young, pale Army officer was looking at him intently. Kevin remembered this man – when he first reached the station he had seen him on the concourse. Two women had been with him, full of care and concern. It was clear he was the one who had just stowed the parcels onto the rack.

"Thank you, sir," Kevin smiled.

When he closed his eyes again and became drowsy, more visions appeared – the courageous faces of Martin Swain and Alan Wilson, the pleading face of Billy Elkin, the wise face of Hugh Riley, the tragic face of Matty Penman, the grinning face of Harry Feltham and then the faces of the others.....Dave Porter, Tom Gratton, Tai Lok, the imperturbable face of Ian Dunlop, whose cool competence had brought some of them safely home from the sea. Lastly he saw the face of his own father and the warm regard to be read there. The roll-call complete, the boy fell into a heavy sleep.

Now that he was safely detached from them, others in the compartment began to discuss him in low tones. His sea boots and torn jacket marked him out as a trespasser. A middle-aged woman, full of disdain, suggested they send for the guard.

"I don't see what harm he's doing," said the young officer, "no-one's looking for a seat."

"But they might be!", the woman insisted.

The officer sighed:

"If you're going to do that you might at least wait until he wakes up. He looks all in."

A strained silence followed. In the corridor Armed Forces personnel and other third-class passengers unable to find anywhere else to stand pressed against the windows and door of the compartment. Those first-class passengers who already felt hard-done-by now considered themselves in a state of siege.

When Kevin woke, he sensed the hostility of many around him. So he was really not surprised when the door slid open and a railway-guard confronted him. Even so, the man seemed reluctant about his mission, whatever it was. Donnelly guessed the man had been sent for so decided to take the initiative. He smiled:

"When do we get to Preston?"

This provided the guard with an opportunity. Suddenly, he found his courage:

"We're not stopping at Preston!"

"But it said so on the timetable – change at Preston for Liverpool."

"Well now it's change at Crewe for Liverpool."

"Why?"

"Because these things happen – there's a war on, haven't you heard?"

Kevin bit hard into the soft tissue of his mouth. Still he wrestled to control his anger. He grinned:

"War? Is there? I missed that. Must've been reading the 'Dandy'."

This strengthened the guard's thin resolution:

"Let me see your ticket, please."

The guard took the ticket. He half-turned towards the other passengers so they might share his triumph:

"This is third class. You're not supposed to be in here."

"But there aren't any seats in third class."

"Makes no difference. You're not supposed to be in here."

"It makes a lot of difference to me because I've paid for a seat and I'm entitled to it."

Appalled by Kevin's obstinacy, the disdainful middle-aged woman leaned forward:

"You're not supposed to be in here!"

Quickly, the guard followed up her shrieking:

"If you don't move I'll have you put off at Carstairs."

The Liverpool youngster decided to dispense with diplomacy. He turned to the woman first:

"Listen love – I know you've paid a bit more for your ticket but that doesn't make me a lower form of life. I've seen you, and most of these others, look at me as though I should be put down. I don't want to talk about it really but I've just been on an interesting journey – to America. The Jerries got upset about us coming back with food for you lot so they sunk my ship. Ten of us got into a lifeboat but at the last count there were only five of us left to say what happened. 'course I shouldn't complain – I didn't lose a limb or go crackers like some I know but I'm as weak as a kitten. So since I've paid for a seat I'm having a seat."

He saved his final words for the guard:

"Anybody who comes to put me off'll have to carry me off."

To see and hear more clearly what was going on the passengers in the corridor had pressed nearer the door. As they glimpsed the sickly young seaman slumped near the window their mood became ugly. They began to offer snippets of advice to the guard:

"Leave him alone," was one suggestion, "Bugger off!", another. Stripped of any moral authority and muttering to himself, the guard left the compartment and pushed his way down the impossibly crowded corridor.

Kevin began to feel very hungry. He reached up to the luggage rack and brought down the small bag which contained the meat pie and the thermos flask. The pie smelled wonderful. Mrs Morag Dees, the Warden's wife, had packed the space within its crisp crust with lean, tender beef. As Kevin ate, its rich aroma filled the compartment. The sight and smell of this impromptu meal was too much for the disdainful, middle-aged woman whose eyes stood out in horror. Fiercely, she darted appalled looks about her, hoping to discover someone who shared her revulsion. No-one looked up.

"Well!", was all she could snap.

As Kevin poured his coffee the young army officer leaned towards him. He was pointing an elegant, polished steel hip-flask towards the coffee:

"Would you like something in that?"

The boy nodded his thanks and as the officer leaned forward Kevin noticed a large patch on his forehead from which the skull bone was missing. It was an indentation over which the flesh appeared to be too tightly stretched. It extended from above his left eye into his hairline and was obviously a war wound. Kevin realised why the two women on the station concourse had been so riven with anxiety.

As he drank the warming liquid with relish, Donnelly looked across the compartment and into the corridor. A soldier, sitting on a kitbag, winked and gave him the "thumbs up" sign.

From then on, the journey proceeded smoothly but hardly fast enough for its Toxteth passenger. Carstairs, Carlisle, Penrith, Tebay, Oxenholme, Carnforth, Lancaster – at each station there was a slowing down, then a stopping, then a waiting, then a closing of doors, then a whistle, then another waiting and only then a barely perceptible new movement of the train. All of this increased his impatience so that even the hills and fells of the Scottish lowlands and the rugged beauty of Cumberland and Westmorland gave Kevin no respite from his restless, nagging longing to be home.

They went through Preston at speed, on a line well away from the platform and it was obvious from the cries and consternation further down the corridor that other passengers had been surprised by the fact that there was to be no stopping at the town with the magnificent church spires. Unable to sustain his attention to the passing scene any longer, Kevin went to sleep again.

He was wakened by a general commotion, the young army officer saying goodbye to him and telling him this was "Crewe", the important interchange station. Some other passengers were making for the compartment door and the mass of humanity in the corridor began to shuffle forward. Kevin stood up to say goodbye to the officer then sat down again. He had decided to wait until there was a better opportunity to move.

Turning back towards the window he was surprised to see someone on the platform glaring at him. At first he was conscious only of a hateful face. Now he could see it belonged to a soldier. Unbelievably, the man drew back his head slightly then, with a fierce forward movement, spat at the window with all his strength. A stream of saliva moved steadily down the glass. Donnelly decided to move. Ever since H.M.S. "Anthemis" had docked at Greenock, someone, in some way, had shown their contempt for him. No-one had gone this far.

When he stepped onto the platform, struggling again with his many parcels, he looked around desperately for advice. Suddenly, a porter was passing him at great speed:

"Liverpool?", the youth called anxiously.

Before he disappeared into a press of besieging travellers the porter waved his arm towards the distant, west side of the station:

"End of the footbridge! Leaving now!"

The boy bent down towards the platform and then, his panoply of parcels gathered together, he began limping towards the broad steps leading up to the footbridge.

"Hey.........I'll take them!", someone was shouting.

Hurriedly, he looked back. It was the soldier who had spat at the window. He was bounding down the platform. As his bags were being grabbed Kevin stood bewildered.

"Come on!", cried the soldier, his feet already on the first broad step......"You'll miss it!"

Though the soldier was carrying his own kit, as well as Donnelly's parcels, he moved very quickly. Astonishingly, as they crossed the footbridge they came abreast of two well-dressed middle-aged women, one of whom was the disdainful vixen who had involuntarily accompanied Kevin on the journey from Glasgow. Her companion had obviously met her off the train. As he passed the pair he heard the disdainful woman say:

"Look – there's the tramp who forced himself into our carriage!"

"How dreadful for you," were the comforting words of the other woman.

What a scene there would have been if Kevin had not been so preoccupied with catching his train! Propelled by his fury, a burning, acidic reflux was coming up into his throat – but now the soldier was talking. In breathless utterances as they ran he was apologising for "losin' me rag". He hadn't been aware of Kevin's "duff leg". He had seen him "squatted in first class" and taken him for "some posh bloke who'd wangled a deferment." He had no time for "scroungers", he'd "bin at Dunkirk" and "lost three good mates."

They arrived at the stationary local train and confirmed its destination. Kevin was in luck – it should have left for Liverpool Lime Street by now. The soldier opened the door to an empty carriage, leapt inside and put Donnelly's parcels onto the luggage rack. He looked guilty but was trying desperately to be affable. Recovering his breath, he asked:

"What's your work then?"

"Merchant Navy. Just put in at Greenock."

Now the soldier's guilt increased so much his face darkened with anguish:

"Listen, cock – I'm sorry. I shouldn't a' done what I did. I shouldn't......but since Dunkirk.....I can't get me head right......I just come out o' Army hospital.....bin under a trick-cyclist. He was as piggin' daft as I am."

He was looking imploringly at Kevin:

"D'yer see, cock?"

"It's O.K. I understand."

Impulsively, the soldier began to fish in his pockets. He pressed something into Kevin's hands:

"This is all I got mate. You look after yourself...... O.K.? I gotta go now......Merry Christmas."

As he ran back up the broad steps he turned and waved. Kevin looked down into his hand where there was a small green packet of five Wills Woodbine Cigarettes.

He got into the empty carriage and sat down. Recalling the soldier's remarks about the Army psychiatrist he began to laugh. The laughter became more urgent. Its tone climbed higher and higher then suddenly, he began to cry. As he wept, the train pulled away from the platform.

Very slowly they left the urban mish-mash of Crewe-at-war. After a while the placid, imperturbable greenness of the Cheshire countryside soothed him and helped him compose himself.

He was alone in the carriage for the whole of that slow journey. He let the events unfold in his mind exactly as they had happened. First there was the leaving of Liverpool and his realisation of all that was entailed in getting under way. He recalled asking Hugh Riley about all the heightened activity when the pilot had boarded the "Willaston" – who was the "pilot" anyway? what did he do?

In his patient, careful way old Hugh had described how dangerous the seemingly simple task of moving down river really was, with the Mersey crowded with ships at anchor and unseen sunken wrecks. He had outlined the danger consequent to "Jerry" dropping explosive mines in the channel, which was why the Royal Navy had to sweep it every day, but that even then some mine might have escaped their attentions. Such hazards could only be overcome by the knowledge and skill of the pilot who these days would often have to operate in the reduced lighting of the "black-out". As always, Hugh Riley had left him much wiser but well aware of his own naivety, his ignorance of the lore of ships, the sea and the river.

Then his thoughts moved on – to the convoy outward, to Boston and the Keatings, then to the homeward leg, the sinking, the lifeboat, the deaths, the rescue, Glasgow – with its good and bad experiences, the journey to Crewe, the disdainful, middle-aged woman who had obviously not believed his story, or chosen not to believe it, and then – the soldier. Kevin had lived through all of it, lived to think about all of it.

He understood so much more now. He understood why men like Martin Swain barked and rasped as he did for, in the end, the readiness and cleanliness and efficiency of the ship depended on her officers. Their job was to develop in the crew that disciplined response to danger that might save lives and save ships. Their salvation was in their own hands. When peril confronted them they could hardly ring Head Office for instructions.

And he had seen the human side of these men-in-charge too. It had been written on the face of Ian Dunlop as he held Alan Wilson in his arms. The sickening sorrow of this young sailor's loss, the misery of losing the ship and so many shipmates. The pain and exhaustion and guilt of survival. Alan's face in death came back to him, like the holy picture in his mother's Missal – Michelangelo's Pieta – Christ taken down from the Cross.

What of the crew?   - men who had developed a detachment from danger in order to carry out their duties that more effectively, who wasted no time or anger on the "Jerries" and who could only do what they knew best, sail the seas in spite of all that those seas and the "subs" could do to them. And what of the crew he didn't know?.....the Welsh, the Scots, the Indians and the others in the engine room.....twenty of them, all lost without trace.

He realised that when he had left Liverpool he was really only a boy, full of boy's hopes, a boy's self absorption. Now he was going home staggered at the immensity of all that had happened. Had what had happened made him a man? Was he a man now?....could one become a man in six weeks?......could a boy have maturity thrust upon him? He wasn't sure, but if he was a man it was because of other men......quiet, noble, unfussed men who had shown him how men must work and live and, if need be, die. And manhood didn't come with birthdays: Alan Wilson had been a man.

He began to feel physically uncomfortable. First he eased his right side off the seat. Next he eased his left side off the seat. It was no use: to get respite he would have to stand and so he was glad that the carriage was empty. The seat was covered with a moquette fabric. This was patterned with small squares. Within each square was a raised mound of moquette. The mounds had now been warmed by the train's heating system and they had dug their warmth into his flesh. It was flesh that just a short time ago had been slopping around for ten days on a lifeboat seat which was always full of salt water. Consequently, from the small of his back to halfway down his thighs, Kevin's flesh was a livid red mass as sore as any boil. He had not even been embarrassed when the young Scottish nurse had applied the soothing cream as he lay face down on the hospital bed – because all he wanted was relief from the suffering. So now he was standing in the railway carriage because the alternative was a hundred mounds of moquette, a hundred little islands of agony.

Eventually the train puffed its way into Runcorn. In the developing dusk he looked down to the wide estuary of the Mersey. Of all the good men in the "Willaston" he was the only one coming home to Liverpool. He swallowed hard. The fading of the day could not obscure the pinpoint of light on the crest of each wave in the river. Within this scintillating tapestry the face of a girl emerged quite clearly.

For the last section of the journey the train decided to go even slower. Slower and slower as it neared the great City. From Allerton onwards its speed was no more than a crawl. In the face of his mounting excitement he became so disorientated by this that when the train stopped suddenly and he glimpsed the edge of a platform through the gloom of the black-out he gathered all his parcels quickly, opened the door and rushed from the train. But it was only Edge Hill and he had to scramble back again.

At last, however, they were making their way through the huge stone cutting that led into Lime Street Station. He had time to look at the great cathedral-like cutting for, going through it, the train stopped and stopped and stopped again. In spite of the dark he persuaded himself he could just see some of the chisel-marks left by the stone-cutters. No doubt like the men of the "Willaston" they had also died in obscurity.

The train had barely stopped for the final time when he left it and began to limp down the platform towards the concourse, oblivious of the crowds surging around him. Thanks be to God. He was home and soon it would be Christmas.

When he passed through the ticket barrier and was at the edge of the concourse he suddenly felt giddy. Perhaps it was the excitement of coming home, perhaps the arduous journey had sapped his fragile strength. Whatever it was he felt decidedly wretched. Looking across the station he saw a teabar with one or two servicemen around it. He didn't want to delay his return to Toxteth but unless he was able to steady himself he would never get there anyway. Hoping that a warm drink would help he made for the teabar, slowly, cautiously.

He asked for a cup of tea. The woman serving at the bar gave him an unfriendly stare and shook her head. A man appeared behind her:

"Sorry mate, members of H.M. Forces only."

"But I feel a bit unsteady, I just wanted....."

"Oi!....hoppit!....this is only for people in uniform!"
An officious member of some organisation or other was waving him away. Lacking the strength to argue he turned around and made for the exit adjacent to the North Western Hotel. All around him he felt a tension in the air – people were testy and preoccupied.

Moving slowly down the slope at the exit he looked across St. George's Plateau to the grandeur of St. George's Hall and St. John's Gardens. Now he understood the reason for the tension – on the far side of the road lay a vast assortment of blitz paraphernalia – fire engines, large snaking fire hoses, ladders, turntables and a WVS mobile canteen. Weaving in and out of this obstacle course were members of the Fire Service, the Auxiliary Fire Service, the Police Service and the Civil Defence. With a sinking heart he guessed that St. George's Hall had been hit. His father would have been outraged.

The giddiness returned and he leaned against the corner of the North Western Hotel hoping so very much that before long his head would clear.

"Kevin?......is that you?"
There was no doubt about the enquirer – in any part of the world, the voice of Martin Tynan would have given him away. When Kevin turned slowly to face him, however, he did not expect to see his towering frame in R.A.F. uniform.

The Toxteth Celtic centre-half leaned forward, took in Kevin's predicament and smiled:

"You bin on the ale?"
As much as the black-out would allow, Tynan peered at his friend, then registered his disbelief:

"What fire did you pinch the suit from, mate?"
Not waiting for an answer and looking closer he said:

"No, it isn't a suit. More yer elegant casuals. Hey!.... what the hell 'ave you bin up to, you sloppy bugger?"

In the next few minutes Kevin told him briefly about the Atlantic convoy, the sinking of his ship and the journey from Glasgow. Martin slipped a hand under Kevin's shoulder:

"Come on, mate – let's get you home!"

They went to the tram stop.

"Are the trams runnin'?" Tynan asked a special constable.

"Where are you heading?"

"Park Road."

"Yeah – you should be O.K."

As he spoke, a tram was coming down Lime Street towards them. They boarded it and landed into the animated conversations of the passengers. "Jerry" had come two nights ago and had returned last night, bombing Bootle, Birkenhead, Seaforth, Wallasey and the City itself from seven in the evening to four in the morning. Anfield had "had it bad", "hundreds of houses" had gone. Warehouses had been set on fire and, in addition to St. George's Hall, the young men learned of other locations where there had been damage – the Mill Road Infirmary, the Gaiety "picture place", St. Anthony's School, Crescent Church and St. Alphonsus' Church. Exchange Station was closed – so Kevin now knew why he had been diverted home via Crewe. The pair had only to listen in order to learn.

As the tram made its way along Renshaw Street, the conductor came towards them. When Martin said "Park Road", the man asked Kevin for his fare. Despite Martin's interventions Kevin insisted on paying his own fare and took a ticket in return. When the RAF man offered his fare, this was waved aside. Tynan looked at the conductor doubtfully but this did not seem to impinge so he said:

"How come he has to pay and I don't?"

The conductor did not answer. This irritated Martin

Tynan who pushed his fare forward and declared:

"If he has to pay, I pay!"

The conversations on the bombings had stopped suddenly and everyone was looking towards the boys. In order to resolve the situation as quickly as possible the conductor muttered:

"You're in uniform."

Martin was now extremely angry. He looked at the other passengers:

"I'm bein' trained as a pay-clerk so I ride free."

Pointing to Kevin he added:

"But he's bin sailin' the ocean blue, up to his neck in shit an' feathers – so he has to pay. Can yer wack that?" Notwithstanding the mixed metaphor, the other passengers understood the import of Martin's question. Kevin's appearance only served to confirm to them that he had "been through it". They began to remonstrate but the conductor was ahead of public opinion. He came to the boys again, asked Kevin for his ticket and returned his fare. As they moved along Great George Street the lad, embarrassed, gazed out at the black, intervening space persuading himself he could see the escalating grandeur of the Anglican Cathedral.

St. James's Place, Park Place, Park Road – he really was home. Her face appeared again. He would go to see her – now, as he had promised himself. He wanted to go to his own home of course, to see his mother, to reassure her. But he had to see the girl first, to make her a present of the ring, to wish her a happy Christmas, to fix a further meeting if she was willing. In his blackest moments he had planned all this – there was to be no change of mind.

In spite of Kevin's arguments, Martin Tynan stepped from the tram with him:

"But this is out of your way!"

"I'll see you to the door – make sure you're O.K."
The big man took all the packages and set off, helping Kevin along. In five minutes or so, they stood before the door:

"Are you sure you're O.K.?"
Kevin nodded.

"I'm only on a '48', but I'll slip up to see you before I go back."
Then Martin was gone.

Kevin looked at the door. His hands were clammy, his mouth dry. He hesitated. This was war-time. Supposing she had taken up with another bloke......seriously.

As soon as he knocked he could hear voices. After a pause, the door opened and her mother stood there. He smiled:

"Hallo, Mrs Gallagher. Is Kathleen in?"
The woman hesitated. Then, into the blacked-out, sloping street she whispered, catching her breath:

"Is it.....Kevin?"
Answering her own question, she put her hand to her mouth then stepped out into the street and held him tightly. Kissing him on the cheek, her voice breaking, she said:

"Come in, lad."
Kevin felt himself being gently pushed down the narrow hallway which led to the living room. He had difficulty entering the room crowded as it was with the immense gathering of the Gallagher family. Right down to the smallest elf-like wakeful child, they were all there. When they saw him they stopped speaking.

Wiping their eyes, the two eldest of the Gallagher sisters moved behind Kathleen. As surreptitiously as they could, they pushed her forward. She stood in the centre of the room facing him, shocked by his appearance. In spite of the palpable sadness in the room he smiled at her:

"Hallo."

She lowered her eyes and could not raise them again.

The silence returned. At last Mary Gallagher came forward and put her arm about him:

"Kevin, son......she can't tell you.....but it's your mother.....she's died."

Having got out the news, she began to weep.

Kevin said nothing. He looked first at Kathleen, then at her mother:

"Died?"

"Chippy" Gallagher rose from his rocking-chair and shouldered his way through his family. Mary Gallagher stood aside as he put his hand on Kevin's shoulder:

"Air raid, son. Night before last. Your Ma had gone to see her cousin up Vauxhall way. He's given it to the North Docks – the food warehouses in Dublin Street, the Grain House at Waterloo an'......"

Mary, anxious they should get to the point, cut in:

"Your Aunt Molly's had some bad news. Seemingly, her husband's bin killed in North Africa."

Remembering his "Uncle Sandy", Kevin could only shake his head.

Then Mary Gallagher again:

"You know how feelin' your Mam was. She put her hat an' coat on and went up there straight away."

"Anyroad," added Chippy, "Jerry had come over just after six but from about eight o'clock it got worse. There's some railway arches in Bentinck Street. They're not a proper shelter but folks use 'em, yer see. He flattened 'em. Police came this mornin' ter say they'd recovered your Ma's body'......they've haven't found Mol, yet."

He squeezed Kevin's shoulder and unobtrusively moved to one side.

Kevin Donnelly still could not speak. He looked

earnestly into Kathleen Gallagher's eyes. Suddenly, she cupped his hands in her own, kissed them and pressed them to her face. It was an act of the most tender love which everyone in the room would always remember. Then she began to cry and shaking her head to and fro she gasped:

"Oh, Kevin......you look so poorly."

When he held her tightly, he felt her tears run down his cheek.

Chapter Eleven

That Other Battle

I

*"I may be right, I may be wrong
But I am perfectly willing to swear.
That as you turned and smiled at me
A nightingale sang in Berkeley Square"*

He was walking past Bessemer Street on his way to
Midnight Mass. Someone had left their front door open
and the sound of the song reached him. It had been one
of the "hits" of nineteen forty. Another was "Whispering
Grass" and he remembered some months ago laughing

at Liam, the youngest of the Gallagher children, who had sung it to himself and then asked: "Mam, how can grass whisper?" Not satisfied with the uncertain reply, he had shrugged:

"Well, it's a daft song anyroad. I wish I'd never learnt it."

It was providential that such little shafts of light from the world around him entered Kevin's consciousness – for he was stupefied by grief and shock and it was as if his mind was trying to heal itself by letting in such inconsequential fragments.

Kathleen Gallagher sat beside him during the Mass, having arrived breathless. She explained in low tones that she had been helping to "get everything ready for the kids". During the Mass, whenever the words of a hymn or an invocation of the priest were breaching Kevin's control, her devotion to him prompted her to slide her fingers into his and grip them very tightly.

As they left the Church, the priest and his curate spent a long time expressing their respect for his mother's spirituality and their heartfelt condolences to him. The congregation, waiting to exchange Christmas greetings with their pastors, stood silently and patiently while they talked to the boy. The youngsters were then joined by Sam Hilditch, the trainer of Toxteth Celtic, and Martin Tynan. They were relatively inarticulate but the quality of their silence was enough for Kevin. Both implored him to "look after" himself, Hilditch adding: "An' get that foot seen to!"

Christmas came and went like a phantom. The Gallaghers insisted that he attend their Christmas table as the honoured guest. Food rationing had been introduced in Britain by now so it was the first of many Christmases marked by the absence of turkey and plum pudding. Yet the skill and ingenuity of many a Merseyside mother,

Mary Gallagher included, were equal to the problem. A cow's heart and a few pieces of rabbit were substitutes for the turkey and, in the absence of fruit and suet, a Christmas pudding was contrived with such ingredients as cold tea, swede, grated carrot, mock cream, cornflour, vanilla essence and a small quantity of previously hoarded sugar. Despite his desolation, Kevin Donnelly could not remember enjoying a better meal.

Immediately after Christmas, he was asked by the police to identify his mother's body. When he returned to Beresford Road he found his brother Vincent had arrived on compassionate leave. In spite of all he had witnessed during the return journey across the Atlantic, the younger brother was visibly upset by his visit to the mortuary. All he would answer to Vincent's anxious enquiries was:

"It was a bad job."

He was never to say anything more than that.

The boys were of great comfort and support to each other during these days and the body of Liz Donnelly was released to them at the end of the short period they needed to arrange her funeral.

They honoured her although, with her cold tenderness and aloof love, she had often been an enigma to them. Yet they knew that behind her dismissive attitudes, her tenderness and love were real and deep. She was not a misery but she was undoubtedly predisposed to disappointment, as if convinced that this was all the world offered. Yet they loved her without limit knowing that her peculiar brand of motherly love had left an indelible mark for good on their lives. It was noticeable that many of her neighbours and fellow-parishioners followed the cortege the not inconsiderable distance to Toxteth Park Cemetery. After the interment many of them nodded when one neighbour concluded her condolences by adding:

"She was such a clean woman."

On the night before he returned to his Regiment, Vincent sat with his brother in the house on Beresford Road. They were listening to the wireless. The evening news bulletin contained President Roosevelt's promise that the United States would serve as "an arsenal for the democracies." Kevin switched off the set and sighed:

"Perhaps this New Year will see things pick up a bit for us."

Vincent did not reply. After a silence he touched on what they were both thinking:

"I shall miss her, you know, Kev."

"Yeah. Me an' all, but....."

"But what?"

"Well....I just wish she'd given us a bit of praise now and then, told us she was proud of us. She never said anything to you about your drawings, but the art master pinned 'em up all over the school. Look at all the cups and medals we've won footballin' – she never said 'well done', just chinned about the dirty kit she'd got to wash. Now we're never going to get any pats on the back."

"Listen Kev.....you couldn't have had a better mother, you....."

"I know that!"

"She just wasn't the sort for praising you – but it didn't mean she didn't feel things. Try an' see it from her side a little bit. Dad would disappear for six, nine months at a time an' she had to be mother and father an' all – shoppin', cleanin', layin' out the money, keepin' the two of us in hand."

Kevin laughed:

"An' we were right scallies at times, weren't we? Remember when you, me an' Martin Tynan sat on ole Cooney's fruit and veg cart and the poor ole donkey went up in the air?"

"Yeah, an she took our part about that an' plenty

of other scrapes. She was always on the go – mendin'
fuses, takin' us for haircuts, getting the coal in, makin'
sure the tradesmen didn't work any flankers on her and
keepin' this place as clean as a new pin. D'yer know – I
come from school one wash day and a cinder or summat
must've flew out o' the boiler-'ole and got wedged under
the back-kitchen door. It had bin scrapin' and screechin'
an' she couldn't shift it – so she took the bloody door off
its hinges! It's true....when I come in she was waltzing
around with this door – an' she wasn't the height of two
pennorth o' copper! Look at all the work she did up at
the Church an' the way she prayed us through all our
illnesses and the tests we had at school. I've known her
sit up all night sewin' so's we were properly turned out
for the Sacred Heart procession."
By now Vincent was at full spate:
     "Listen, kidder – think of all the food she's put on this
table, even when Dad couldn't get a ship. Have you ever
gone short of anythin'?.......even since the war started?....
no....an' why's that?....because whenever there was a
queue – for anythin' – Ma'd be in it. I don't have to be
here to know that. I'll bet she's spent hours queuein' this
past year and she'd've gone on queuein' if she thought it
was for summat that'd do you good."
He paused, then:
     "Remember, as well, how she was with Dad."
     "How do you mean?"
     "She worshipped him. I tell ya – when I was on picket
duty some weeks back, somebody'd left one o' them
'penny dreadfuls' in the Guard Room – 'Exotic Romances'
– summat like that. It was squash but there was a coupla
things in one of the short stories an' I thought they hit the
spot as far as Ma's concerned. This story was all about
upper-crust people an' the fella, he's all teeth an' trousers
y'know an' he thinks his girl's stringin' him along, so he

says:

'Penny, dear – true adoration is clothed in action.'
Can you imagine folks talking to one another like that?"

"Not in Toxteth."

Vincent looked across at him:

"No, but you get it, don't yer?.......actions speak louder than words. An' that's how Ma was with Dad – and with us as well."

"Yeah. So what was the other thing in the story?"

"Well this Penelope's as giddy as a beetle and the fella's Ma, Lady Louise, decides to put her straight. She says there are two kinds of love a woman can have for a man – improper love an' proper love. She says improper love is when she doesn't love the man for what he is, but loves him in the hope of turnin' 'im into some sort of fantasy guy she's dreamed up. She's bent on changin' 'im – an' that road leads to misery. But if she loves 'im for what he is – proper love – then they've got every chance of makin' out.

An' that's how Ma was with Dad. Did you ever know a time when she stopped him doin' what he wanted to do? She might moan but even when there was next to nothin' comin' in, she still made sure he bought his books. An' whenever he come back it was to kids that were cared for and a house like a palace. There is another thing – where did Ma, an' all the women like 'er, find the guts to send their husbands and sons to summat as hellish as the sea? They waited on 'em hand and foot and cared for 'em all their lives an' then they had to let 'em go. I hope there'll be a medal for wives an' mothers at the end of this lot – but I doubt it. An' as for Liz Donnelly – our mother – if Dad had lived all through the war, he'd never 'ave got a 'Dear John' letter tellin' him she couldn't stand it any more or she'd found another fella."

He sighed a long sigh:

"She was a lady, Kevin. An' if she isn't in Heaven I don't want to go there."

Kevin put a little more coal on the fire and sat back in his chair. Vincent encouraged him to talk about his Atlantic experience. His brother did not find this easy. Only after some prompting and questioning did Vincent obtain any picture of the horror and the courage Kevin had witnessed. Even then the picture lacked substance and precision so that Vincent regretted asking him about it in the first place.

Rather than being ready to talk, Kevin seemed anxious to rub it out of his memory. Or was that true? Vincent wasn't sure. Certainly the boy's life would always be marked by the thoughts of what went on out there, but was there something else? Vincent decided that in some tiny crevice of Kevin's mind there was something – hard to say what – but it was there – nothing so certain. Still, better leave it, the lad needed rest from it all. He allowed himself a final comment on the subject:

"Anyway, our kid – if you never do anymore, nobody can say you haven't done your wack."

Kevin said nothing. When Vincent spoke again he'd changed tack:

"I'm really glad you're getting together with Kathy from next door, She's a good girl. Let her look after you for a bit, build you up. An' get your foot fixed before it gets any worse. Find a job, but take things a bit easier. Don't overdo it. You know your problem, Kev?.....You think too much about things. You want to put the world right and you'll never manage it 'cause it's in such a bloody mess."

"What about you, Vin? How d'you think you'll get on?"

"I'll keep my head down and concentrate on stayin' in one piece."

"No you won't. You didn't volunteer for that."

"Listen, it's goin' to be a long war. Jerry's got better guns, better kit and men that are better trained. An' however much that mad sod in Berlin grabs, he'll never be satisfied. So millions'll die. Millions....."

"You think so?"

"I know so. All we can do now is try an' catch up. An' if we're too long about it, it's Goodnight Vienna."

"You still won't keep your head down. I've never known you run away from anything."

The older one leaned forward:

"Our mob was helpin' some of the lads that had come back from Dunkirk. One fella on the quay had lost his leg. He was cryin'. The sergeant-major said:

'What's this lad? Cryin'? What are you cryin' for, soldier? No need to cry.....You're a hero now.....in six months time you'll be a bloody nuisance!'
Summat to ponder there, bro. So if I get tempted to go for a medal I'll just think of all the spivs an all the wide boys snuggled down 'ere in old England and that should kill the urge stone dead."

They both laughed. Being with Vincent that evening had made Kevin laugh for the first time since the death of Billy Elkin. It was bitterly cold next morning when Vincent hugged his brother and left for Lime Street.

Kevin returned to the fireside then. He thought at length about Vincent's words on his mother, owning that they were all true and that he had been too ready to bridle about her nature. Since coming back to Toxteth he had slept a lot, making up the deficit accumulated since he went to sea. Again, helped by the fire, he began to doze but, about to slide into a deeper sleep, he rallied: someone was knocking at the door.

A tall man stood there, with a document case under his arm:

"Mr Donnelly? Kevin Donnelly?"

The youth nodded. The man smiled:

"Good morning. I'm Arthur Mulliner, the Office Manager at WPL."

He touched his document case:

"I have some business at the Toxteth Dock this morning and since I'm so near to you, Mr Miles Edmonds, our Managing Director, asked me to call. How are you feeling?"

"Not too bad, thanks."

"Mr Edmonds was wondering if you are all right and if you feel up to it, he'd like you to pop in to see him – just for a chat. He's absolutely devastated by the sinking, we all are. He knows you're the only one to get back here and he'd like to hear whatever you can tell him about it – but only if you're well enough."

"Yes. In fact, I promised Mr Dunlop I'd contact the Line. It's just that I haven't got 'round to it yet."

"Oh, that's perfectly understandable – absolutely – don't worry about that. Well what about tomorrow afternoon – at 4 o'clock?"

Again Kevin nodded. Arthur Mulliner smiled, raised his hat, said "thank you" and walked away briskly.

Kevin thought: "Seems a funny do. What can I tell him? I wasn't exactly Commodore of the convoy. Still, I will go – and I'll let him know a thing or two."

The following day in a comfortable office near Tithebarn Street's junction with Hackin's Hey, Kevin sat facing Miles Edmonds. The relaxed, friendly-faced old man, who had visited the "Willaston" on the day she left Liverpool for the last time, was making concerned enquiries about the boy's well-being. Then he asked him to relate the details of the sinking and its aftermath.

Kevin did not dwell long on this though he did emphasise the courage and skill of Ian Dunlop and the fortitude of his fellow survivors. In fact, he reserved most of his energy for a description of his visit to WPL's agent, Mr Jasper Corries. Angrily, he outlined his treatment at the hands of a man who seemed bent on reducing the world and all its works to a cash nexus.

Like all Merseysiders, when inflamed by injustice, he was able to find a pointed, fitting comment. His final words about the visit were these:

"I sailed with your Line because I'd heard you were a good company. But that man does you no good – in fact, he does you a lot of harm. I don't know about 'Jasper' – it ought to be 'Grasper'!"

Miles Edwards had listened without interrupting. He leaned across his desk:

"You have had an appalling experience for which I am deeply sorry. I can tell you - that man is no longer associated with this Company. If you do go to sea again, I hope you'll give us another chance. I can promise you things will be much better."

To Kevin's surprise he said he had learned of his mother's death and wished to offer his sincere sympathy. He accompanied Kevin to the door and shook his hand warmly, adding:

"I appreciate the work you did for the Company and I've put this in writing. Mr Mulliner has the letter."

Kevin looked into Miles Edmonds' eyes and managed a smile.

Arthur Mulliner had obviously been waiting for him and they walked to the vestibule together.

"Did your talk go well?"

"Yes, I think so. I'm glad you've got rid of that toe-rag in Glasgow."

"Mm. He got his just deserts. He'd been responsible for food supplies when our vessels were sailing from Scotland. We discovered he'd been invoicing us for vegetables at top prices and giving us stuff ready for the pig-bin."

Donnelly shook his head sadly:

"But how does a Line like yours saddle itself with somebody like that?"

Mulliner lowered his voice:

"I'm afraid that's Mr Clive's doing - you know, the brother. I think it's safe to say that Corries was appointed when they were well down the whisky bottle.....but I never said that.....understand?"

The man shook Kevin's hand:

"Here's your letter, expressing our thanks. And I can tell you this - there's a job with us whenever you want it."

The lad dodged into the Kardomah café in Castle Street. He was anxious to read the letter. He sat transfixed – within its folds he found a number of large, crisp, white £5 notes – five altogether. He had never seen a 'fiver' before – what a beautiful thing it was. Just feeling the crinkly bank paper there in his hand made him feel like a millionaire. Twenty five pounds! Was there that much money in Liverpool? In the whole world? There was – and he had it. Then he read the letter again and again. Its tone and sincerity affirmed what a gentleman Miles Edmonds really was.

It was dark when he left the Kardomah and the black-out was likely to make getting home even more difficult. It did not deter him – he reached Liverpool 8 in record time and knocked vigorously on the Gallagher's door. It was Kathleen herself who answered him. She looked quizzical but sensed his excitement:

"Hello, love. What is it?"

"Have you had your tea yet, Kath?"

"No – we were just....."

"Well apologise to your Ma for me and put your coat

on. We're dining out!"

And that's how it was that, much sooner than he had ever anticipated he was able to keep the promise he had made to himself – to take Kathleen Gallagher to Reece's Restaurant off Church Street.

It was not a fabulous meal. Wartime austerity did not allow for that. They each had a poached egg on toast and after that, the smartly dressed waitress brought a two-tiered stand full of fancy cakes. Kathleen chose a chocolate éclair and, as befitted his status as host, Kevin scoffed two items – a custard tart and an Eccles cake. And, of course, the tea came in a silver teapot. They drank from bone china cups and giggled surreptitiously when the waitress called Kevin "sir" and Kathleen "madam". Kathleen gaped when, having settled the bill, her consort handed the waitress a sixpenny tip. They left the restaurant on air. It had been a meal for the gods, for as much as anything they had dined off the atmosphere.

He took her to the cinema in London Road, which was showing Noel Coward's "In Which We Serve". Like the rest of the audience Kathleen was moved by it so that, at the interval, when Kevin returned with the usherette's most expensive ice-creams, she whispered in his ear:

"I'm proud of you."

"Why?"

"Well – it's there, in the film, what you went through."

"But I'm not in the Royal Navy."

"Yes, but you did brave things – same difference."

"I didn't do anything brave. All I did was get in people's way."

To terminate the exchange she punched him in the ribs.

Going home on the tram he decided to answer her unspoken enquiry. He described the meeting with Miles

Edmonds and included details of the letter and the money.

"Oh he's so good – Dad has always said it."

"Mm – well apart from anything else I can now pay my wack on Ma's funeral expenses. Vin had to pick up the bill there."

At her door she took his hands in her own again and pressed them to her cheek. She looked up at him:

"I love you Kevin Donnelly."

He returned her look and she said:

"Actually, you're supposed to say it first but if I wait for you to open your mouth, the war'll be over."

"No, no. Be fair Kath, and give me a chance. You see, I love you as well."

"Well, that's alright then, isn't it?"

They kissed each other tenderly, said their "good nights" and opened their doors simultaneously. Then they closed them, slowly.

Things were certainly happening for the next morning he received a letter from the Royal Southern Hospital. It was signed on behalf of "Mr Patrick Fielding" and specified that he should attend for a 10am appointment on the following Tuesday – less than a week away. The doctor in the Shipping Pool at the Pier Head had done what he said he would: arranged for him to see an orthopaedic specialist when he returned to Liverpool.

Kathleen was overjoyed:

"Oh, Kev – it'll soon be put right now. I know what pain you've been having, even though you try to hide it. And when you're fit I'll be dragging you to Upper Parliament Street, you see if I don't."

"How do you mean?"

"To the Rialto – the Rialto Ballroom! It's got a lovely spring floor – you just glide across it – oh, sweetheart, I can't wait. I'm really made up for you."

He looked quizzical:

"Steady on – I've just got to get it sorted out first."

Sam Hilditch was also pleased:

"You'll get back on the team sheet in no time. An' you haven't got far to go either to get it fixed. The Southern's near to my local on Hill Street."

On the Tuesday, Kevin reported at the hospital by 9.30am. It availed him little for the out-patients department was already full to bursting point. Long after the time of his appointment his name was finally called and he was directed to another packed room. Learning that the room was for patients awaiting X-ray examination, he remonstrated with an overworked radiographer who sighed and said:

"I know the letter says 'Mr Fielding', but his clinic isn't until Friday and he wants an X-ray of your ankle first."

After the false alarm, he and Kathleen waited in limbo for another three days until, on the Friday, he found himself facing an immaculately dressed man who, in spite of his comparative and surprising youth, also appeared harassed and overworked. As he looked at the X-rays on the illuminated wall-panel, Patrick Fielding's first question was:

"Why didn't you have it examined sooner than this?"

"I thought it was just a sprain – and it would clear up in time."

"A sprain? This isn't a sprain. A sprain is just an overstretching of the ligaments. This is much worse."

"Oh.....well....what is it then, doctor?"

"A comminuted fracture of the lateral malleolus..... an ankle fracture. How long has it been since you injured it?"

"About two months," Kevin lied, knowing that it was

at least twice that long.

"I think it's much longer than two months and it makes me wonder how in heaven's name you've managed to walk on it for so long."

He sat opposite Kevin and looked at him steadily:

"What's happened is this - a small fragment of bone has come away and been trapped between the fibula and the talus. That results in wear of the articular cartilage. In your case, this has already caused an arthritic condition. I suspected it when you limped in here, obviously in pain."

He paused.

"You now have traumatic arthritis and it has developed despite the comparatively short interval since the injury because.....and I'm sorry to be frank here.... because of your own neglect when a proper diagnosis, removal of the bone fragment and a proper period of immobilisation were absolutely necessary. So I'm afraid, Mr Donnelly, you're going to have to live with the pain and the limp from now on."

A dumbfounded Kevin, despite his dry mouth, managed to ask:

"Wouldn't an operation put it right?"

"No. At an earlier stage I would have suggested operative removal of the small fragment and revision of the malunited fracture. However, your pain is from the arthritis and that will not recover. I'm afraid that an operation would only make matters worse. We can take some measures now to support the ankle – for the "push-off" stage of your walking, and we'll be writing to you further about that......I'm sorry."

A few minutes later, Kevin stood at the junction of Hill Street and Caryl Street being buffeted by a freezing westerly wind. He limped over to the corner shop, opposite, for an item now familiar – a glazed paperstrip containing five Aspirin tablets.

"Kevin!"

He turned. It was Sam Hilditch, who lived in nearby Caryl Gardens and had obviously been hovering around waiting for news. When he was told of the specialist's verdict he found it unbelievable:

"But.....it can't be!"

However, as he listened to Kevin's outline of his hospital visit he accommodated by degrees to the fact that what "can't be" actually was so. That evening, in "The Little Woodman" public house on Hill Street, he shared his grievous news with an understanding, sympathetic audience. Finally he sighed:

"It's all so bloody stupid. He coulda bin another Frankie Soo."

Kathleen Gallagher's receipt of the news had results that could scarcely have been forecast. On returning from work she knocked at Kevin's door to be confronted by a youth who had meditated all day on his unhappy situation and grown steadily more morose. She declined the invitation to cross his doorstep. The mores of that time and the prescriptions of faith and culture dissuaded her. It was well known they were a courting couple so she must do nothing to "give scandal". Whether this added to Kevin's irritation is a moot point. Certainly he was in no mood to give her more than a brief summary of his misfortune.

In her anguish she pleaded and protested – there had to be a better outcome than this. Kevin snapped at her:

"No! That's it! Do I need a hammer and chisel to knock it in? Nobody can do anything about it!"

"Don't bite my head off, Kevin.....I can't help it."

"I just don't want to discuss it anymore......O.K.?"

She decided not to match his wrath but smiled

tenderly:

"Never mind......let's forget it.....and go down to the Dingle tonight."

"What?"

"The Dingle.....The Gaumont..... 'The Grapes of Wrath'......Henry Fonda. You said you wanted to see it....."

"I don't want to see it. I don't want to go out.....and I can't forget it! I'm a gimp....a cripple.....for the rest of my life."

"Oh, stop it!.....it's just a bit of a limp...."

"Right!......O.K......nothing to bother about. How would you know?! Do you have to put up with it? Do you have to stand the pain? The kids around here were quiet for a bit, now they've started up again – 'Here comes Hoppy Donnelly'.....do you have to contend with that?"

Passers-by, hearing the raised voices, were staring. Kathleen began to fish out her handkerchief. At that point he surrendered completely to self-pity:

"Anyway I've been thinking about things. I want to be on my own from now on. It's probably the best thing. In fact, it's only fair, so you can start seeing someone else."

"But that's ridiculous!"

"I know.... the whole bloody thing's ridiculous but that's how it's going to be!"

"You're being silly!"

"Right. Well if I'm silly, you just go on up to the Rialto and flash your figure at some bloke who isn't silly!"

"Oh.....," she cried out and slapped him hard across his cheek. Weeping, she fled through her front door. His cheek burning, the boy slammed his own door, on the inquisitive passers-by, on the world.

The next morning, sick at heart and as unobtrusively as possible, Donnelly made for Lower Parliament Street.

He wished to see Jack Owens, the manager of the timber merchants, where he had worked as a casual labourer. He was looking for a full-time job.

"You can start right now," was Owens' reply, explaining how he had lost men to the "call-up" just when he was being "pulled out o' the place" with orders for timber to repair bomb damage, to build army camps and aerodromes and for any number of other projects.

Kevin had a tender conscience. He found it necessary to explain about his arthritic ankle. Owens was bemused:

"Is it worse than it was before?"

"No."

"Well it never stopped you working before so it's up to you, lad – if you're happy. I'm happy."

He was told what pay was available for a standard week of fifty hours. There would also be "plenty of overtime" if he wanted it. The pay was no fortune but would enable him to pay the weekly rent of 4 shillings and 2 pence for the house on Beresford Road and the cost of his grocery order from the "Co-op". This would leave about twenty five shillings per week for other bills, plus clothes, shoes, and his "pocket". Beyond this basic calculation Kevin did not wish to venture. He nodded his agreement to the terms and within fifteen minutes was handling heavy lengths of timber.

His next few weeks were spent in virtual solitude. Nearly all his conversations were with workmates. However, his relationship with the Gallagher family was somewhat strange and rather touching. Though he had no contact with Kathleen, her mother acted as though no quarrel had occurred. After his mother's funeral he had given Mary Gallagher, at her request, a key to his house and his ration book.

He trusted her completely and was thus saved from

all the tiresome detail of the weekly ration – four ounces of bacon per head, two ounces of tea, 4 ounces of margarine, 2 ounces of butter, 8 ounces of sugar and the mysteries of the egg allocation. She also monitored the 'points' he required for biscuits, peas, soups etc. Each week Kevin wrote out his order and Patrick, eleven years old and the eldest of the four Gallagher boys, took it to the "Co-op". Patrick looked forward to the task, not only for the sum he earned for running Kevin's errands but because he never tired of watching the shop assistant pull on the overhead wire which connected the shop counters to the cashier's kiosk in the gallery above. Away would fly the metal cup containing the bill and Kevin's money and back it would zoom with his change.

Every week Mary washed Kevin's laundry. Unless he told her he was working late she also lit his fire each day. So he became used to returning to a warm room, a weekly change of bedding, clean linen and on Friday nights the grocery order in the beautifully constructed brown paper "Co-op" parcel identical to the ones he had carried home himself as a boy. In all of those weeks, the fractured relationship with Kathleen was never mentioned by anyone.

Then something happened to re-shape the way things were developing. First, a "background" explanation is necessary. In those days, many of the poor could not even afford the penny required for a newspaper. Latter-day social historians may doubt this statement, though it is true. Usually at least one family in the street could afford the paper and would buy it. Nearby families would send a child to ask for a loan of the paper if the buyer and his family had read it. So by the end of the evening, one paper would have been read by quite a few families. The borrowers would have saved themselves the significant sum of sixpence per week plus the cost of the Sunday newspaper as an added bonus.

Since his retirement the paper-buying role had been acquired by "Chippy" Gallagher. So Kevin was not totally surprised when, on St. Patrick's Day (March 17th), he answered a knock on the door and found "Chippy" there holding up a newspaper. The little man tapped it:

"Seen this?"

Kevin invited him in. "Chippy" watched while he read the news. In the space of one week, and in separate actions, British destroyers had been responsible for the elimination of three great U-boat aces from the Battle of the Atlantic. Otto Kretschmer had been captured. Joachim Shepke and Gunther Prien had perished. All three had taken a tremendous toll of British shipping and Prien, a hero to the whole of the German fleet, had carried out the daring raid on Scapa Flow where he sank the mighty battleship "Royal Oak".

Donnelly smiled grimly:

"Nice to have some good news, for a change."

"Yeah. You never know – things might turn 'round out there."

"Chippy" seemed in no hurry to leave and nodded when offered a cup of tea.

"Not such good news from the other side of the river," Kevin mused.

On the evening of March the twelfth the Luftwaffe had dropped flares over the whole area of Merseyside. The bombs began to fall and continued to do so until 3a.m. on the thirteenth. The docks were the primary target particularly on the Cheshire side of the river and considerable damage was done to houses in both Birkenhead and Wallasey. The Birkenhead General Hospital had to be evacuated and water, gas and electricity services were disrupted in Wallasey. Later, on the thirteenth, the raiders returned and again the main damage occurred in the Cheshire boroughs. Many people were killed or injured. "Chippy" responded to Kevin:

"I hope our lads'll keep givin' it 'em back. The R.A.F.'s the unny weapon we can do it with!"

Quite suddenly, he changed tack:

"What's this to-do about with you an' our Kath?"

"I'm sorry – I shouldn't have spoken to her like I did."

"No, you shouldn't. She's really upset. She's got it in 'er head you think she's cheap. An' that's not right, Kevin. Kathleen's a good girl."

"I know that, Mr Gallagher. It's just that I'd had some bad news about my ankle – I thought it wasn't fair for her to be saddled with a cripple when she could be out dancing with other chaps. I know she's fond of dancing – I suppose I was jealous of her dancing with somebody else so I said what I did, about her flashing her figure."

"Yer know Kevin, you're no dud. Most times you've got your head screwed on the right road, but sometimes you talk like yer not the full quid. What's all this about bein' a cripple? You've got a bit of a limp, you'll have to learn to live with that. If you want to see a cripple, I'll show you one. Do you know Frank Martindale?"

"No......(?)"

"He lives in Cairns Street, behind Princes Avenue. His family come from the West Indies originally but they've been in Liverpool longer than us. Frank was a good seaman and tried to make a career of it. He was studyin' for his Second Mate's Certificate so that'll tell you. He was hit in the back with a crane hook that was swingin' about. At the end of a long traverse a crane hook packs quite a wallop. Anyroad – it was in New York – the hook hits him, he goes over the ship's rail and onto the quay. It's a wonder he's alive - as it is, the whole of his right side is useless an' he's stuck at home for the rest of his days livin' on next to nothin' although it wasn't his fault. That's a cripple for you an' a nicer, more deserving lad yer couldn't wish to meet."

Kevin felt ashamed and could say nothing. "Chippy" was making for the door:

"Oh, an' by the way – Frank's cousin, who comes from Granby Street, was in the engine room of the "Willaston", so as you'll realise, he went down with her."

"Chippy" turned then:

"You must do what you think best, lad – but I'll tell you this – dancin' or no dancin', if Kath can't have you she won't have anybody."

II

On the following Friday evening, Kevin knocked at the Gallagher's door. He asked to see Kathleen. She appeared, fixing him with a solemn look.

"I thought I'd go over on the ferry tomorrow morning – to see Hugh Riley's wife. I should've gone long before this. The raids have reminded me. I've got her address from WPL. I was wondering if you'd like to come with me.....(?)"

She was still looking at him levelly, her eyes saying nothing. Then, slowly, she nodded her head.

"I'll call for you at nine o'clock, if that's O.K."

Again, she nodded silently.

In Birkenhead they wandered down the ravaged streets, past the demolitions and the smell came again Kevin remembered from similar damage in Liverpool, compounded of pulverised brick, plaster, soot and the sour vapours produced by water sprayed on burning wood. They were still largely silent with each other but smiled when they passed a house in the midst of much devastation where a woman was fastidiously rearranging the lace curtains at the one set of windows which were still whole.

When they arrived at the Riley's address they stopped in shock. Half the house was gone and, above the mounds of debris, trusses poked out of the damaged roof like so many sore fingers. Kevin felt Kathleen's hand curl around his arm as they stood there.

"Are you looking for Kate?", someone asked.

"Hm. Mrs Kitty Riley," said Kevin, to make sure.

"Yes. She's up at the Rest Centre."

"Is she.....hurt?"

"No.....she's helping out!"

Neighbours and Civil Defence Workers then directed them on their way.

Kitty Riley was very pleased to learn that they had come especially to see her. She seemed a composed woman but dabbed her eyes when Kevin explained he had been Hugh's shipmate. Kathleen held her hands as, faltering now, she told them of Hugh's great love of ships and the sea, concluding:

"And then, when the war came and he heard all about the sinkings, he said 'Kit, I can't sit here poking the fire when men are out there getting killed. I couldn't eat a morsel of what's been fetched for us.' I knew it was no use arguing with him. I knew he'd have to go."

Kevin then told her of the great esteem in which Hugh had been held by his shipmates. He also explained carefully why he himself, on his first voyage, had been left so decidedly in Hugh's debt. Then he brought out the stump of a crucifix:

"He had this in his hand when he died."

Kitty broke down and Kathleen held her.

Some of the helpers in the Rest Centre brought tea to them. They were all still excited about the incident in

Lancaster Road, Wallasey. It had occurred on the morning of Sunday, March the sixteenth. Three rescue workers heard what they thought were the faint mewings of a cat within a pile of debris. When they called for silence they heard the noise again. It was, unmistakably, the cry of a baby. The men worked carefully but quickly. They brought out a girl, just a few months old, from where she had lain, half-choked with dust, since the early hours of March the twelfth – three and a half days before. Both the baby's parents were dead but she was handed into the care of grateful, maternal grandparents.

When Kathleen and Kevin were finishing their tea, Kitty noticed the ring on Kathleen's finger – the initial ring he had bought in Glasgow for fifteen shillings. Kitty smiled:

"I think I've seen one like that before."

She held up her left hand. Next to her wedding band was an identical ring.

"My name's Catherine, but he always called me Kit. He said he hoped it would do until we could afford a proper engagement ring but I told him it didn't matter."

At the door of the Centre she smiled at them:

"I'm ever so pleased you came to see me and tell me about Hugh. What a lovely looking young couple you are. Just you take care of one another."

On the ferry returning to the Pier Head, Kevin looked at Kathleen's ring. He took her left hand:

"It's a nice enough ring – trouble is, it's on the wrong finger."

He moved it from the middle finger to the third finger. Despite the light in Kathleen's eyes she feigned a rebuke:

"You're supposed to ask me first – and be kneeling down!"

"I can hardly kneel down here but I tell you what I

can do –"
As he kissed her with great enthusiasm, fellow passengers were so impressed they called for an encore.

During the short walk from the Overhead Railway station to Beresford Road several things were decided: there would be a June wedding, Vincent Donnelly would be asked to be best man. He would also be asked to agree to the use of his late parents' house as the matrimonial home and Kevin would return to his voluntary work with the Civil Defence. Kathleen was unsure on this last point but agreed when he reminded her of the incident in Lancaster Road, Wallasey and the rescue of the baby girl for, as he said, without the Civil Defence workers there would have been no rescue.

The news from the couple was greeted with great joy, especially by Veronica Gallagher, the eldest daughter, who was triumphant:

"I knew they'd come back engaged!"

On the first day of the following week, and after arrangements made by Sam Hilditch, Kevin was able to resume his voluntary work as an Air Raid Warden. Two days later he was asked to return to the Royal Southern hospital so that, as promised by Mr Patrick Fielding, a fitting could be prepared to alleviate the pain and stress of his ankle. With the fitting eventually in place, his mobility and his outlook improved significantly.

From then on, to the first of May, the Luftwaffe was busy enough over Merseyside for the nightly pattern of wartime life to continue. Parents and children returned from work and school to prepare for the shelters. Sandwiches, tea, blankets, hot water bottles, books, magazines and favourite toys were all assembled for the trek. The shelters were to be found in back gardens, streets and the basements of churches, schools and countless other buildings. Buckets of sand were replenished, stirrup-pumps made ready and, thanks to German high explosives and incendiaries, enough "incidents" took place for the folk of Liverpool 8 and every other district not to forget they were under attack. The smell of gas, the smell of earth, the taste of soot and the amalgam of other odours loosed by the "blitzkrieg" gave the very air they breathed power to signal their peril.

Kevin, ever vigilant, with his cries of "put that light out!" to those unable to grasp that the black-out improved their safety, was not always popular. However, before long, citizens would come to realise what they owed to Kevin and his colleagues. In the mornings, sleepless adults and children often discovered their favourite route to work or school was blocked by an unexploded bomb. Something else to frustrate them.

Then on Thursday, the first of May 1941, Merseysiders began to understand that whatever had gone before was no more than preparation for a serious and sustained onslaught. The official reports of what occurred between that May Day and Thursday the eighth of May constitute a dossier of death and destruction which took place on both sides of the Mersey. In later years, historians would speculate that prior to his attack on the U.S.S.R. in June, Adolf Hitler sought to shatter Britain's defensive and offensive capacity by obstructing her supplies. He sought to do this by destroying her ships at sea and laying waste her Western ports, including the key ones at the mouth of the Mersey. In effect, he would then be able to put Britain "on the back burner" until he had finished off Russia, which he considered a mere detail, finally reverting to Britain to apply the coup-de-grâce.

In terms of casualties, the night of the first/second May was not a heavy one but damage through both fire and high explosive was widespread. The Low Hill area and Cazneau Street were badly affected. The rain of incendiaries did their worst damage to the Crawfords' Biscuit Works in Binns Road and the nitre sheds at the West Brunswick Dock. Near to the Donnelly home, bombs were dropped in Fisher Street off Grafton Street with many trapped and injured. High explosives were also dropped in Jamaica Street, near Parliament Street. Kevin Donnelly thus had some intimation of what was in store, for the body of Moses Jolliffe was recovered in Jamaica Street while in Fisher Street a foot was found but there was no body to accompany it to the mortuary.

Just before midnight on Friday, May the second, wave after wave of enemy bombers approached the area. Over several hours they attacked relentlessly causing heavy casualties and considerable damage. The Mersey Docks and Harbour Board buildings, the Corn Exchange in Brunswick Street and the South Castle Street district came in for relentless pounding. There was damage in Pitt Street and St. Michael's Church was wrecked. In Linnet Lane a house billeting soldiers was hit, killing five of them. Church House, headquarters of the Church of England diocese, was gutted and all diocesan records were lost. This raid had almost doubled in intensity from that of the previous night. Serious fires raged at the South Queen's, Coburg and Wapping Docks, at Sparling Street, Bridgwater Street, the former White Star building in James' Street and the headquarters of the Gas Company in Duke Street.

On the night of Saturday, the third of May, Kevin Donnelly and some of his Civil Defence colleagues were deployed to the centre of the City for this was when it sustained its most devastating raid. In a night of destruction and terror three hundred tons of high explosive rained down upon it. Outside of London and in relation to its size Merseyside became the most bombed area in Britain. Again, in relation to its size, Bootle sustained more damage and casualties than anywhere else in Britain.

Moreover with several hundred fires requiring pumps the Fire Services were judged to have had the heaviest task in relation to the area affected than any other Fire Service had to face during the massive raids of 1940-41. On this night, gas, water, and electric mains were seriously affected and the Central Telephone Exchange was cut off. The area bounded by Lord Street, Paradise Street and Canning Place, which Kevin had come to know so well through walks with his father, was devastated.

Wolstenholme Square; Leyton Paper Mills, Henry Street; the Tatler Cinema, Church Street; the Salvage Corps, Hatton Garden; the Head Post Office; Littlewoods Building, Hanover Street; the Government Buildings in Crosshall Street; the Museum and Library in William Brown Street; the Magistrates' Court, the Custom House, Central Railway Station and India Buildings were also seriously damaged. Bluecoat Chambers, Liverpool's oldest building, was virtually destroyed.

Large fires caused damage at Princes Dock, Riverside Station, Dukes Dock, Canning Dock, Salthouse Dock, the East Wapping Basin and Stewart's Warehouse. The S.S. Clan McInness came in for similar treatment. During his nights' efforts and from subsequent reports, Kevin Donnelly concluded, if not in quite these terms, that the economic, administrative and cultural life of the area, along with its inhabitants, were being pitched into some giant holocaust.

With the rest of the population he was sickened by the terrible episode at the Mill Road Infirmary. Here, a very heavy bomb fell into the back courtyard. Three large hospital buildings were completely destroyed. The rest of the hospital was damaged as were houses in its vicinity. Many people, including patients, were trapped in the debris. Then, to make matters more horrific, fire began to consume the ambulances and cars parked in the courtyard. Among those beneath the debris were a patient on an operating table and a nurse in attendance. Miraculously – a miracle brought about by several hours of exhausting work – a volunteer rescue party saved them both.

At the final tally, seventeen members of the hospital staff, fifteen ambulance drivers and thirty patients lost their lives. Seventy people were seriously injured and three hundred and eighty patients had to be transferred to other hospitals.

The other "incidents" from that fearful night have passed into the history of the City. The first concerns a munitions train standing at Clubmoor in the Breck Road railway siding. This received a direct hit. In spite of flying debris and widespread raging fire a group of railway employees volunteered to help avert tragedy. They worked furiously to uncouple thirty-two wagons each of which contained at least ten tons of explosives. After hours of toil and at tremendous risk to their lives, they managed to uncouple the wagons and shunt them into a siding.

The second "incident" goes under the cryptic title of "the Malakand". Early on Sunday, fourth of May, people in the Liverpool area believed that an earthquake was under way, such was a massive detonation, unlike anything they had previously heard. In the Huskisson Dock, the Brocklebank freighter SS "Malakand", loaded with a thousand tons of high explosive bombs, had finally blown up. This was after hours of desperate effort by crew and firefighters who had struggled to save her despite repeated attacks by enemy bombers.

The explosion was so immense that some of the "Makaland's" plates were found two and a half miles away. Part of a four-ton winch from the vessel was found in

Stanley Park. The Overhead Railway, which lost several of its spans during the blitz, was showered with Lever Bros. soap from her cargo. The damage done in and around the dock was colossal. Dock sheds vanished into thin air as did the great concrete quays – all that remained was the sand on which they had originally been constructed. Either by the explosion itself or by flying debris, nineteen smaller vessels in the Dock were also sunk.

On the following night, the fourth/fifth of May, the Belgian Seamen's Hostel in Great George Street was hit by high explosives. Houses were demolished in Catherine Street, Fairy Street, Mountjoy Street and Magnum Street. The clinic in Northumberland Street was seriously damaged and St. Silvester's School and the Rotunda Theatre were destroyed by fire. Again, the Borough of Bootle suffered badly: a significant amount of its domestic and industrial property was wrecked.

The night of Monday, fifth May saw Kevin and his colleagues extremely active for there were fires in the Brunswick and Queen's Docks. In addition to the many incendiaries in the Docks area, the Germans pressed their attacks with great determination in the location of Bold Street, Berry Street and Colquitt Street transforming it to a sea of flame. In the havoc, St. Luke's Church was burned out and Goodlass Wall's paint factory was gutted. The Gas Company's building in Duke Street was destroyed and the Anglican Cathedral was hit in the roof of a transept by a small high explosive bomb. It suffered little structural damage but many stained glass windows were blown out.

The London Road/Islington area also came in for the Luftwaffe's attention. The T.J. Hughes' store was damaged as was St. Silas's Church in Pembroke Place. Two wards were damaged at the Royal Infirmary, one seriously. Nearer the river, some damage was done to the landing stage at the Pier Head, while warehouses in Lancelot's Hey, the Salvation Army Hostel in Park Lane and buildings in Canning Place also suffered. The Nurses Home at the Children's Hospital and houses in Bedford Street and Abercromby Square were also included in the night's list of "incidents".

Kevin and Sam Hilditch would always remember the night of Thursday, May sixth/seventh as the one when their Civil Defence team was stretched to its limit. Heavy raiding and heavy damage were again elements in the formula with high explosives to begin the destruction followed quickly by torrents of incendiaries. In their area, Wilson's Flour Mills in Park Road were burning fiercely. A pipeline was fractured at the Dingle Oil Jetty and fires appeared to be consuming several of the Southern Docks.

What remained of the Custom House, so dear to Kevin's memory, was extensively damaged by fire. The tramways office in Hatton Garden succumbed to the flames and it was necessary to evacuate the patients from the Heart Hospital. The James Street area was also laid waste. Throughout, the anti-aircraft defences and the night fighters fought to stem the onslaught and the stupendous efforts of both the professional and auxiliary firemen prevented even worse calamity. As it was, buildings were destroyed in many areas, including Abercromby Square where St. Katherine's Church was desolated. Beneath the buildings there were many trapped citizens. High explosives on that vital artery, the Liverpool Overhead Railway, damaged the "permanent" way.

The night of the seventh/eighth of May was the final episode in the "May blitz", as the locals came to know it. It was the same story – of heavy damage throughout the City. In the Scotland Road area, many dwellings were destroyed. Serious damage was also done to the churches, schools and air raid shelters. In Water Street, the Tower Building was extensively damaged when a high explosive bomb fell through its light well. In Sir Thomas Street the Morris and Jones' food warehouse was gutted and in nearby Whitechapel people were trapped beneath the Shakespeare Hotel. At the Dock Office of the Mersey Docks and Harbour Board the ceiling had been shored up for strength with several heavy beams, When a bomb exploded outside, the arrangement collapsed in a mass of plaster and dust. It was like lowering the final curtain on eight days of bloodshed, misery and terror.

In the days that followed Kevin learned that on the Liverpool side of the river nearly one hundred thousand houses were destroyed or damaged. In Bootle, where the fires were simply enormous, eighty per cent of the houses had been hit or set on fire. Twelve brave members of the Women's Voluntary Service had been preparing meals there for the homeless and were themselves killed. Three quarters of Bootle's Rest Centre accommodation was also destroyed.

He witnessed every type of suitable building – Churches, Church Halls, Cinemas and Schools - being adapted as Emergency Rest Centres. He saw military personnel erecting marquees and providing field kitchens. He heard that ten thousand blankets were being rushed into the area. The news from the other side of the river was that seven thousand five hundred people were being evacuated from Wallasey. In Birkenhead, where the famous Argyle Theatre was gutted, twenty five thousand houses had been damaged.

He was very moved to see that as well as the Food Relief Convoys now arriving there were vehicles marked "Food Flying Squad – USA to Britain". It reminded him so much of the warmth and generosity of Boston's Bridie and Gerard Keating.

When he returned to Beresford Road, Kathleen and Mary Gallagher brought out their large tin bath and set it before his fire. While he peeled off the clothes he had worn for a week and eased his exhausted frame into the bliss of the hot water, the women were preparing his bed. They had taken the largest of the oven shelves from Liz Donnelly's gleaming kitchen range, swathed it in towels and pushed it between the sheets so they would be properly aired. Then they went back home to prepare him a hot meal. Two hours later he was sleeping the sleep of the just and next morning "on the dot" he reported for work at the timber yard.

As he toiled with Jack Owens and his depleted band of helpers to bring the yard to order from chaos, Donnelly, his strength returning, talked rapidly:

"He won't lick us you know. Thousands of people have been evacuated from the City but they're coming back every day to keep the place going. The only thing left of the Corn Exchange is the front entrance so they're trading on the street. I was in town and I saw these queues of people – all sorts – men, women, children, nans and grandads. They were waiting for lorries that take them into Huyton Woods to sleep. There's no pushing, everything's in good order. It's bloody sad but it's wonderful to see."

And, of course, he was right for by the end of May the great Merseyside gateway to the West was operating near the peak of its former efficiency. Despite the fact that fifty-one thousand were homeless in Liverpool the will of its people and the assistance of nearby towns enabled the stricken area to recover its breath and return to its wartime role with even greater urgency and commitment than before.

The power of this recovery is perhaps symptomised by the fact that although forty eight craft were sunk during the May Blitz, the Mersey Docks and the Harbour Board was able to salvage and return to service nearly half of them.

When he was next with the Gallaghers, "Chippy" directed his attention to some editorial in the "Liverpool Echo". It read:

"The long sustained blitzkrieg on Merseyside has inspired the fire-fighters, fire-watchers and wardens to a truly magnificent vigilance and alertness and they hurled themselves into action in hundreds of places with enthusiastic efficiency and utter disregard of personal safety."

Kevin said nothing but thought a great deal. And he was reminded of these comments when he learned later that apart from the grievous damage to his City's fabric and its treasure, two thousand six hundred of its people had been killed and a similar number had been seriously injured. Perhaps he and his colleagues had done something to prevent an even worse outcome.

III

The City was not self-conscious about its blemished face. For some time to come tension and apprehension would still be there but not desperately so. It had won its own particular phase of the Battle but now events had to move forward. So, buildings in danger of collapse were demolished; blocked streets became unblocked; massive heaps of bricks, plaster, stone and glass were hauled away. The City's ravaged timber, from its great beams and roof trusses to its slender laths, was taken from sight. The raids had made its gaunt citizens even more gaunt for it continued to be a world of missed sleep, corned beef sandwiches, tea with condensed milk and cut-down old clothes. Yet no dock in the system ever lost its momentum through shortage of labour. If morale was the soul of victory, Merseyside was going to win.

When "Chippy" and Kevin were allowed to go down into the City they saw for themselves what had become of it. If the expletives are deleted, "Chippy" said little. Kevin could also gape and express his gladness that his father would never witness the great breaking up and tearing down that had occurred. And, even in this black interlude, something happened that appealed to their Liverpudlian sense of the comic.

Near to the ruins of the Central Railway Station a kiosk was open for business. A queue had formed, though many of its members had no inkling of what they were queuing for. When Kevin learned that the prize was a packet of Victory –V lozenges (colloquially known as "VVs") he joined it. Most of his "points" for confectionery went to the Gallagher children but in that week's Co-op parcel he had used what few remained for a quarter pound of mint imperials – a present for Kathleen. But he thought the gift a bit "skimpy" so he would "body" it up a little with the cough sweets – an increasingly common stratagem because "VVs" required no "points".

He was joined in the queue by Billy O'Hare who also hailed from Toxteth and was employed as a ship's scraper. People always allowed Billy ample room in queues, his clothing having become suffused with the odour of his trade and even traces of its output.

"What's the queue for, Kev?", he asked as he arrived.

"VVs."

Billy considered, then he coughed:

"I'll wait – they can't be any worse than these I'm smokin'."

Kathleen Gallagher was living with that mixture of

excitement and trepidation that is the lot of brides-to-be. On the one hand, she was to be the wife of a boy she had always adored. On the other, how could she possibly look lovely for him in this age of "make-do-and-mend", this time in which people were being exhorted to make their own clothes using pattern books and recycled materials? The wedding date was now less than a month away and the City was still tending its wounds so, for Kathleen, that eternal dilemma of "what am I going to wear?" reached a new high intensity.

In the end, and as it usually does, everything worked out well. The energy and vigilance of Mary Gallagher and her daughters were rewarded. They discovered that the Women's Voluntary Service (WVS), one of Britain's unsung and most meritorious organisations, would lend out a wedding dress of "standard" size. It was in white velvet and the veil originally used by elder sister Veronica added to its elegance. A 'Drene' shampoo and a pair of tongs were all that was required to transform Kathleen's mass of already beautiful auburn hair into a vision of splendour. "Chippy" took her to the altar bursting with pride and Kevin, transfixed by her radiance, was overjoyed to be there if only to make up the numbers.

As the couple left the church, the use of confetti being illegal due to wartime restrictions, the wedding guests signalled their joy for the couple by bombarding them with hundreds of small white paper discs which the resourceful Kathleen had collected from the paper-punches at the bank in Water Street.

The wedding-breakfast, and the reception which followed, provided more examples of ingenuity's triumph over austerity. A splendid wedding-cake was produced using ingredients as mundane as haricot beans, vinegar, nutmeg, carrots, margarine and dried egg. The well-known generosity of Merseysiders contributed to the reception menu because relatives and friends had saved up items from their own rations in order to help - though for those pastries intriguingly called "maids of honour" Mary Gallagher confided to her closest friends that, when the cooking fat was exhausted, she had fallen back on liquid paraffin.

Unhappily, Kathleen was not able to realise her dream of "going away" in a superb two-piece suit. However she was able to purchase two prettily-patterned "Economy Frocks, average size." Slightly "taken in" with her dextrous use of the needle they were very attractive. The trousseau was completed by a pill-box hat topped by two wedges of material shaped like butterfly wings and set into it at forty five degree angles. It resembled nothing so much as a fairy cake but Kathleen wore it at a coquettish slant which undoubtedly gave her what in those days was called "zing". Seeing her, a little boy from further down Beresford Road called "what a corker!" It was the ultimate accolade.

Vincent Donnelly, whose battalion was undergoing divisional training in Northumberland, had been granted a thirty-six hour pass to be his brother's best man. When he kissed his sister-in-law and hugged his brother he was more visibly moved than anyone in the assembly. The happy couple left for a two-day honeymoon in Southport, a decided improvement on the honeymoons achieved after many wartime weddings.

In the three months that followed, they settled down with each other in Beresford Road. Kevin went to the timber yard each working day, Kathleen to the bank. Although Liz Donnelly had kept the house neat and in good order the youngsters wished to put their own stamp on the property to establish the fact that it was now their home. They decided that their living room must be re-decorated.

Kevin repainted its doors, windows and skirting boards with the only gloss paint available, coloured chocolate brown. There was no wallpaper for sale, so like everyone else, he took his bucket to the paint shop for his allocated quantity of distemper, chosen by Kathleen and coloured pink. He was also able to acquire a smaller quantity of distemper in tortoiseshell grey. When the pink distemper had been applied to the walls he shaped a sponge in his fingers and stippled the walls with the grey distemper. The shape of the stipple he contrived was not unlike a bird in flight and he carried out the stippling with great precision down its columns and along its rows. Kathleen was proud of him. All the Gallagher family and quite a few neighbours came to see the result. They echoed her sentiments.

He also obtained whitewash and refurbished the brickwork in the yard area behind the house. Kathleen became adept at making "pegged" rugs. These were fashioned from strips of old clothing and other textiles which were fed into hessian or washed sacking using a clothes peg for a tool. In time, she covered every space in the house where there were bare boards or flooring in need of renewal. As she became more skilled at the task she was able to achieve quite detailed coloured patterns.

When she worked at these articles Kevin watched her. Only a short time ago she had been a somewhat "giddy" teenager, her head full of film stars and the twopenny magazines telling stories of glamour and romance. Now she was fast becoming a skilled and energetic housewife, working at a full-time job and turning out to it smartly, if inexpensively, dressed. Her only concession to "expense" was the leg tan she bought when possible. Silk stockings were unavailable. The recently invented nylon was hardly to be found either. Lisle stockings were available but generally loathed, especially among younger women. The leg tan was applied in liquid form. Sometimes to complete the illusion a helper would draw a black line up the back of each leg to simulate the stocking seam. Kevin thought it prudent that Kathleen would have no truck with this for it seemed to him that many of the helpers who drew the "seams" had rarely drawn anything else.

The year moved on. Towards the end of June, Hitler attacked Russia and soon the Red Army was in retreat. On September sixteenth "Chippy" was waiting for Kevin's return home. He brandished his newspaper – the United States had declared its increased support for the Allies. All fast eastbound convoys (of the HX type) would be taken over from the Canadian Navy at a point south of Newfoundland and given formal protection by US Navy destroyers to the Mid Ocean Meeting Point (MOMP) where they would be handed over to British Western Approaches Command.

"We'll get there in the end!", promised Chippy.

At the end of the month there was further good news: Kathleen announced she was pregnant. On December seventh the United States joined the Allies when Japan attacked her naval forces at Pearl Harbour. Despite the grim news on Christmas Day that Hong Kong had fallen to the Japanese, like all families in Britain, the Gallaghers and the young Donnellys tried to bring some enjoyment to the Christmas season, hoping that the new baby would herald better times.

Throughout the early months of nineteen forty two and despite the hazards of the Winter Kathleen continued her work at the bank. Like thousands of other families the young couple became keen filmgoers. "Citizen Kane" and the acting of Orson Welles made a great impact on Kevin while Walt Disney's "Dumbo" was Kathleen's favourite perhaps because it stirred her developing maternal instincts. The David Lewis Garrison Theatre, as it became known in those war years, was also a handily located venue for their entertainment. The wireless was extremely popular with the couple. Kevin always listened attentively to "The Brains Trust." "Sincerely Yours", with Vera Lynn, established itself with both of them. It was difficult to find anywhere that Vera's "White Cliffs of Dover" was not being played and sung.

In late February came their first crisis. Kevin was toiling in the timber yard when a white-faced Frank Owens came over to him.

"Your wife's been taken to Sefton General," he explained.

Donnelly stood rooted to the spot. Owens waved:

"Well, go on – get up there!"

Not thinking about the possibility of local transport Kevin began to run and continued running – out of Grafton Street, into Parliament Street, past St. James' Place, on to the rise of Upper Parliament Street, past its junction with Princes Road and the Rialto Ballroom, up the long stretch to Lodge Lane and into Smithdown Road. He said a prayer for his mother as he passed Toxteth Park Cemetery and minutes later burst into Sefton General Hospital exhausted and in great pain from his throbbing ankle.

"She's had a show," explained the sister in the natal unit. Seeing he was mystified she added:

"She's lost some blood and must be kept quiet and resting."

Kathleen ceased working from that point and carried the baby to its full term. In late June of nineteen forty two, to extensive acclaim and intensive admiration, Maureen Elizabeth Donnelly made her first appearance. She had immense blue eyes and clear indications of her mother's wondrous auburn hair. Even at this the earliest stage, the women of the family were willing to forecast that, in her time, she would "break a few hearts." There was intense debate about the baby's name which Kevin brought to a halt:

"We must call her Maureen."

"Why?" they chorused.

"Because she's got Kath's eyes and Kath looks like Maureen O'Hara."

There seemed no point in arguing further.

In the months that followed Kathleen, Kevin and Maureen settled down as a family. When their baby was born neither of the parents was yet twenty years old. Instinctively, however, they knew the married state was for them. They had surrendered their "freedom" willingly, knowing they were with their life's partner. Kathleen blossomed as wife and mother. Membership of a large family had prepared her for the roles. Kevin enjoyed being husband and father. He loved both of the women in his life and pushed the perambulator with pride. Readily, he became skilled at doing his quota of changing, bathing and powdering the little one. He could also be counted upon to do his share of walking around the bedroom during her wakeful hours.

So they looked, and felt, like a family – as stable as any family could be. Until, that is, things began to change. At their mother's funeral Vincent Donnelly had sensed that something lurked in a tiny crevice of his brother's mind, something he could not express, something perhaps of which he lacked full knowledge. Then, despite all the preoccupation of marriage and fatherhood, what was lurking in Kevin's subconscious began to plague him. For her part Kathleen noted that what was initially a delay in answering her questions became substantial withdrawal from conversation. His silences became harder to endure: obviously, something was "on his mind".

When his solemn stillness became impossible for her

she made the first move:

"What's the matter, Kevin?"

The way the question was put signalled she expected a proper answer. He looked at her for a second or so......

"I want to go back to sea."

When she asked the question she had been holding Maureen. Now she put the sleeping child into the little cot "Chippy" Gallagher had made for her and sat down facing him. It was the answer she had been dreading and she was determined to drive the idea from his mind.

"The sea? Are you mad?"

"No, not mad.....but I've just got to get back, Kath."

"Why?"

He hesitated. How could he explain that unless he went back the past would always haunt him, always make him feel ridden with guilt?

"Can you remember when we went to see Kitty Riley? She told us Hugh had said he couldn't sit poking the fire while other men were risking their lives for him. That's how I feel."

"But you've played your part! You've been torpedoed......you came back more dead than alive..... and look at the work you did in the Blitz!"

"Kathy......Hugh, Billy, Alan and the others....they didn't just help me with my job. Billy saved my life. Hugh looked after me and kept me alive in the boat. If Alan hadn't steered us away from the sinking, probably none of us would have lived. Now they're dead......and I'm here. D'you know how that feels? Guilt is choking me. I smell of guilt. It's as though I had a pact with them – and I've got to keep it or I shall always drag guilt around with me, like a dead weight."

"Pact.....what about the pact you've got with us..... Maureen and me.....don't we count?"

"Of course you count!......but what's the best way I

can look after you both?....staying here in a safe job?....
or being out there, helping to bring back the things you
both need? Having a wife and child is a good reason for
getting back into the war, not sliding out of it. If you've got
something precious to defend, you defend it....you don't
leave it to other people. All sorts of blokes are helping us
– not just people from around here and the rest of the
country – men from Belgium, Holland and other places.
Your Dad's told me that every other day a Norwegian
merchant ship's being sunk. The Norwegians have lost
their own country but they're trying to save us. How can
I sit here in comfort and do nothing?"

Full of anguish she looked at him pleadingly:

"I don't know about all that. I only know about us."

She searched his eyes:

"Is it me you're tired of? Aren't you satisfied with
what I do?"

"I'll never get fed up with you, Kathleen.....or the baby.
You should know that. Everything you do is perfect."

However, he couldn't tell her that her care and competence
were working against her in fact....that the meals she
prepared and the comfort she wove around him only
increased his guilt, in an insane way only intensified his
need to get away. She sensed she was losing the dispute
so what had been argumentative anxiety now turned to
bitter anger. She wanted to lash him with her invective.
She told him that what he proposed was not noble but
self-indulgent and self-destructive. To satisfy his vanity
he was prepared to sacrifice the happiness and security
of those he claimed to love. At the climax of her tirade she
was so desperate a sneer came into her tones that even
she found distasteful. Wasn't he overestimating his own
importance....what could he do.....a cr......

"A cripple, Kath?......it's O.K.....you can say it."

Hating herself for having gone too far, for wounding

him, she held out her arms but he did not respond. Instead he talked in a gentle, dignified way that touched her heart:

"A cripple can do lots of things, Kath. A cripple can learn how to push around heavy baulks of timber. A cripple can run sometimes – all the way from his work up to Sefton General Hospital because of what he feels for a woman. With a bit of luck, a cripple can become a good seaman."

He stood over her. Unselfconsciously he ran his fingers through her glorious hair. Quietly he said:

"I promised Frank Owens I'd go back tonight and put in a few more hours. It must be very hard for you to understand but if I don't go to sea again I'll never be any good for you, for baby or for myself. Whatever little I can do in this war, cripple or not, I'm going to do it."

He left the house then, closing the door so silently she barely knew he had gone.

Kathleen Donnelly went to the cot, touched the perfect skin of Maureen's plump cheek, and returned to her chair. Then she sobbed as though her heart would break.

Epilogue

DEAR READER,

        That completes the story as I originally imagined it. At the beginning of the book I expressed the hope you would find it interesting and worth your while..... I do trust that was so. Of course, the way the story ends raises the question "what happened next?" Mentally I have worked out what I think did happen and here I am happy to share my thoughts with you. To cover the subsequent fortunes of every character would require another book so below I have outlined for you what happened to just two families, one on each side of the conflict.

I

Men are not supposed to remember such details but Markus Holbauer had instant recall of everything that touched on his courtship of Constanze Delp. Her cousin Franz, a fellow naval cadet, had arranged tickets for Markus and himself to hear her song recital at the Frankfurt Music School. Markus had found her beauty breathtaking and when he heard that voice – of such unusual charm, with its tone so full yet so soft and bewitching, he knew that there was no escape for him. Her control, enunciation and phrasing served only to seal his fate.

He had pleaded with Franz to arrange a meeting and his wily friend had brought him to Mainz, her home city, then left them together in its mountain of a Cathedral. She had spoken so eloquently of its twelfth century Gothic windows and early thirteenth century sculptures, its Renaissance tombs and its Baroque choir stalls he felt he was being led by an angel on a journey through the history of art.

He had bombarded her with letters and showered her with presents and was astounded that her reaction to these things had been wholly positive. There was nothing for it, he must bring her to Hamburg to meet his parents and just one day after her arrival he had walked her away from the Binnenalster towards the elegant Jungfernsteig boulevard, so favoured by lovers. There he had asked her to marry him. She had accepted his proposal but entered one caveat:

"I cannot be the perfect naval officer's wife, Markus. If there is a war I cannot exult in the death of others, enemies or not."

He said he understood and everything was settled.

That was eight years ago, in 1935, eight years in which his love for her had only deepened. How prescient she had been to see war as a possibility in those seemingly far-off days. Now, in July 1943, here he was successful in what the world gives, Herr Korvettenkapitan Markus Holzbauer, Iron Cross First Class, successful commander, who in the face of impossible odds had kept his U-boat intact and his original crew safe and sound.

And what had marriage brought to the former Constanze Delp? The ardent love of a man who would always treasure her, assuredly, and the precious gift of two lovely daughters. Yet the price paid had been a heavy one – the loss, it would now seem, of her career in music; the responsibility, shouldered alone, for two children and two aged in-laws; and confinement in a dingy house in the dingy suburb of Hammerbrook.

Nor was that the worst of it. For he was convinced that the Geheime Staatespolizei still watched and waited. His last leave had brought them no nearer to discovering what had happened to Shlomo Telsner and his family. Their enquiries had met with obfuscation and indifference. Only his rank and his decorations had saved them from menace, for the time being at least.

He was not a man of extremes, so he hated extremists. How, he asked himself, could Germany, among the world's best educated nations and the first to achieve universal adult literacy, so far suspend its critical faculties as to allow a gang of murderous crackpots to take control of it?

Now the War was not going well for the Fatherland. He sensed that here in the North Atlantic "Die glückliche Zeit" – "the happy time", so called, was drawing to a close. More Allied resources were being committed to the Battle. Their newly formed attack groups were being successful in hunting and sinking more U-boats. Improved Asdic, Radar and High Frequency Direction Finding systems were delivering results as was the fearful "hedgehog" pattern of depth charging. The development of longer range Allied aircraft and, perhaps most important, the massive capability of U.S. shipbuilding, were moving the balance of advantage away from Germany.

Holzbauer ascended to the bridge. The U-boat had surfaced in the dark grey dawn to recharge her batteries. As it was getting lighter by the minute they ought to be speeding things up. The Commander was hot under the collar after yet another argument with Rademacher, the Nazi. Holzbauer was proud of the way the crew had responded to the danger and discomfort of their lives at sea. They were brave, unquestionably, but more than that, their hazardous, uncomfortable existence had fused them into a close comradely band. Like him, these men found the embarrassing intensity of Rademacher hard to stomach.

He had clearly appointed himself as the Fuhrer's representative on board and never ceased to exhort them with the observations of his brother-in-law in the Seekriegsleitung (German naval staff), whose latest news was that some Allied seamen were being picked up after their second and even third sinking. Whether it would therefore be better to machine-gun survivors seemed a logical question.

Holzbauer had been furious:

"No-one on this boat will ever machine gun survivors!"

"But Herr Commander, who said 'moderation in war is imbecility' but the British admiral, Lord Fisher?"

"I'm sure, Rademacher, he did not have machine-gunning helpless men in mind! The argument is closed!"

Why did he allow the man to infuriate him so?

Rademacher was clearly a fanatic. And what was more......

"Herr Commander!! Fine starboard quarter! Destroyer!!"

The cries came from the utterly reliable First Watch Officer. Holzbauer took a second or so to turn, confirm the identification through his binoculars and give the order to dive. The sleek, grey, powerful vessel was coming at them with great speed.

Twenty four hours later the corvette H.M.S. "Anthemis" was making her way through the same area, with two naval ratings closed up as look-outs.

"Hey, there's a jelly-fish!", said one of them, pointing.

"Stupid sod – they wouldn't come this far up!"

"I tell you – it's like one o'them Portuguese Men o'War. There's its body an' all the squiggly bits underneath."

The second man peered:

"Them's somebody's tripes! One of our destroyers went through here yesterday, sunk a U-boat."

"How do you know it's part of body?"

"Huh!.... you should see what depth charges do to a body...it bursts, man. Look there's part of the stomach and the intestines. Hey!..... there's the Kraut's hat.... The captain."

"Stone me!..... why do you say he was the captain?"

"He's the only one of the crew with a white cap cover."

"The slimy bastard!" the first man exclaimed, spitting into the sea. The gesture was futile as well as obnoxious for HMS "Anthemis" had moved on and what remained of Markus Holzbauer was already bobbing in its wake.

The phenomenon of the RAF's firestorm occurred in Hamburg thirty six hours afterwards. The fires in Hammerbrook began to join up and, as the mass of hot air rose from the giant inferno, cold air was sucked into the flames at a speed great enough to uproot thick trees. Flanked by flames twenty metres long, a woman struggled with her children to get to water, any water. If they stood in the water they might survive. She lurched through the melting asphalt and when the road became firmer she slipped on the fat oozing from the incinerating bodies. She was falling.....falling..... "Markus!..... Markus!....... Lieb................."

Helga Wetzel was a Trummelfrau (rubble woman). She and the others must clear the narrow streets so the fire engines could enter otherwise, if the raiders returned, there would be another catastrophe. It was two days since the firestorm and still the City stank of roasted flesh. The foul kitchen smell reached down, down into her stomach so that from time to time she was forced to vomit. But she needed to master the problem because she must see Lothar, the district leader of the Labour Service, before the end of his shift. She knew he was pleased with her work and would give her some bread and a little liver sausage, which she would take to the cellar where she had left her children.

Yet what was this? Three pieces of clinker with white threads, which she knew to be striations of calcined bone. One clinker was about sixty centimetres long, then a smaller one, then a tiny one. Hm...... Helga shrugged and with a swish of her brush and a clang of her shovel she clattered Constanze, Antonia and Katje Holzbauer into her pram-wheeled dustbin.

II

Kevin Donnelly survived the war. His next journey out of Liverpool was on the MV "Burton", a WPL vessel under the command of Ian Dunlop. He stayed with the company until 1966 when, following the death of Mr Clive Edmonds, its assets were sold and it was wound up. He remained at sea all his working life after deciding to make a career of it in the most determined fashion. Within two years he had obtained the Ministry of Transport's Certification as Efficient Deck Hand. Within another two years he obtained a further Certificate attesting to his classification as Able Seaman. In a further four years he obtained his Second Mate's Certificate.

He used his off-watch hours to prepare for the examinations and followed this up with intensive study when he was ashore. In order to preserve as much of his time at home for Kathleen and the children (more about them later), he allocated the late evenings and the small hours to study, often falling asleep over his books and being wakened by the rattle of milk bottles. When he first began his studies, "Chippy" Gallagher introduced him to Frank Martindale, the seaman who had been badly crippled following his accident in New York. Frank, having ploughed the lone furrow of private study himself, was able to give Kevin valuable advice particularly during revision periods. By virtue of his experience at sea and his own conscientious preparation for Certification he proved an excellent mentor. Kevin could sense that being called on to help in this way had given Frank valuable purpose in his own life. He took great pleasure in Kevin's news that he had obtained his Second Mate's Certificate and reinforced the young man's intention to press on further. In a further two years Donnelly was awarded his First Mate's Certificate and after yet another two he achieved the status of Master Mariner. By then it was 1955 and he was almost thirty four years old.

His friendship with Frank Martindale continued and Kevin felt it deeply when that gentle, wise man, with whom he had spent so many happy and rewarding hours in Cairns Street, died in 1962. Frank had deserved so much more of life. To say that Kevin missed him is to understate his loss significantly for Frank had become a mentor not only in examination preparation but in how one should live. Kevin found his friend's courage and generosity of spirit in the face of appalling misfortune a constant inspiration. Knowing Frank enabled Kevin to see his own infirmity as more than bearable.

It was a great joy to Donnelly when, in 1961, he was appointed by the Wirral Peninsular Line to command his own vessel. He remained a captain for a further twenty six years, retiring in 1987. During that time he stayed in full employment and sailed continuously in British vessels. "Hoppy" Donnelly as he affectionately became known across the trade routes of the world, was universally respected for his competence and character.

He lamented the indifference of the nation towards the war record of the men who had sailed under the Red Ensign. As in the First World War, they had saved Britain from extinction and this time nearly thirty thousand of them had given their lives in the process. Their reward was to see the almost total run-down of Britain's merchant fleet in the post-war period. At the beginning of the twentieth century almost half of the world's goods were carried in British merchantmen. By the year 2000 two-thirds of Britain's own trade was being shipped in foreign vessels, usually under a flag of convenience. At the time of the Falklands and the Gulf Wars she had been ignominiously forced to charter foreign ships in order to make up the small support fleets of each Task Force. Despite the contrary view taken by nearly all other maritime countries, Britain doggedly refused to give any economic or political protection to the merchant fleet. Such was the humiliating reward for the loss, in the Second World War, of a greater proportion of her personnel than had been sustained by any of her Armed Forces.

Whenever he felt bitter about this he recalled the words of Miles Edmonds. In 1966 when WPL was being wound up it had provided a farewell dinner for its employees to which Kevin and Kathleen had been invited, Among the stirring words the Chairman used to describe Britain's lost merchant seamen were these:

"Few, apart from their nearest and dearest, and those of us who knew them so well, venerate their memory. Yet these were quiet men of uncommon courage. If ever you pause to give thanks for your peace and prosperity, think of them sometimes. They laid the foundations for the life you enjoy."

In the years to come, whenever he remembered what Miles Edwards had said that evening, it would trigger the total recall of a conversation with Ian Dunlop. This took place during the last voyage before Dunlop's retirement, when Donnelly had the privilege of serving as his First Mate.

They had become friends as well as colleagues. Kevin had talked of his difficulty in sharing with Kathleen the ins-and-outs of his job and particularly his wartime experiences. She saw so little of him yet had to endure his silences. He much regretted this but could find no remedy.

Dunlop had looked at him:

"Don't worry. We all have the same problem. But how do you tell a woman about the time a stoker was screaming with a rivet in his eye? Or explain about when you pulled off a seaman's glove, saw the black stump and knew his fingers had come with it? You grabbed a shipmate from the sea and he was alive, but with no legs. These things don't sit well in conversations when you've put the kids to bed.

Some experiences are beyond words. I could never convey to a living soul what I felt in the roots of me when a wonderful boy like Alan Wilson died as I held him.

Anyway, perhaps we have a duty not to tell them. Why should we tell them? Isn't it enough that the nightmares still plague us? Why disturb them with the degradation and the misery? Don't they deserve some rest from their own worries?....everything from blocked drains to the baby's lazy eye.

And don't underestimate your wife. She knows and sees everything, including what you don't tell her. Sometimes I think Elspeth has worked her way inside my skin and is suffering with me, though not a word has passed between us."

Three children were born to Kevin and Kathleen. Maureen Elizabeth became a medical doctor and chose to serve the patients of one of Liverpool's poorest districts, with the unfussed dedication she had learned from her hardworking, conscientious parents. Michael Joseph became a very successful businessman, founding a firm of systems analysts serving the computer industry. He was always bound to succeed combining, in Kevin's estimation, Joe Donnelly's charm with Liz Donnelly's capacity for hard work.

Their third, and youngest, child was Gerard. He was born in 1946 after a difficult pregnancy and a birth exhausting for mother and baby. He grew up a weak child with breathing difficulties. There were times in his early years when Kevin, on shore leave, would be sitting in the living room and hear Gerard upstairs struggling to breathe. Kathleen knew that the innocent, desperate sounds went to Kevin's heart like a knife. For she also knew full well the depth of Kevin's love for the children, love that tested his calling as a seaman, that made him profoundly sad whenever he left them.

Among the children's great joys in their early years were the visits of their Uncle Vincent. He had been Mentioned in Despatches for an action in the Normandy Campaign and liking the life decided to remain in the Army after 1945.

It was always an occasion of great rejoicing when he came back to Liverpool on leave and schooled the trio in both foot and arms drill. They also took great pleasure in his outrageous lies. For example, one day Michael was examining Vincent's medal ribbons in minute detail. The conversation went as follows:

"How many medals have you got altogether, Uncle Vin?"

"Ooh...difficult to say.....about nineteen I suppose."

"And what was your best medal?"

"Oh, that's easy....it's the one I got for saving 29 men from certain death."

Michael's next wide-eyed question:

"How did you do that???"

"I shot the cook!"

When Vincent had completed his regular engagement he was discharged with the substantive rank of Regimental Sergeant Major (Warrant Officer Class II). He married a widow, Gwen Hughes, whom he had met during the war while she was serving in the ATS. Even as young adults, the Donnelly children were always delighted to visit the house on the hill overlooking Colwyn Bay for more of Vincent's incorrigible clowning.

Kathleen Donnelly was not demonstratively pious but she had an unswerving fidelity to the tenets of her religious faith. She saw Gerard's sickness as a cross she had to bear. So when Maureen asked her one day:

"Mum, why does God let Gerard be so poorly?"

it came quite naturally for her to say:

"Because Gerard is very special to God. He has chosen him to show us how to bear our pains and not complain."

She did not know at that stage how special Gerard really was. This became clear on his seventeenth birthday when he announced he wished to become a priest. Kathleen and Kevin were fearful: would the boy's frail health match up to the pressures and the solitude of the role? Yet, Kathleen reasoned, perhaps they needn't worry – the seminary was just a few miles away and afterwards he would be at a parish in the Archdiocese where they would never be far from him.

They had to abandon such wishful thinking when Gerard announced that he knew it was his vocation to be a missionary priest. He would serve the servants of God in those unhealthy, unreachable places where so many of the world's poor are left to scratch out their existence. The protestations finally abated and Father Gerard Donnelly took up his post in the most remote of remote places on the South American continent. And that was where, just after his thirty-eighth birthday, he was murdered.

He had defended his parishioners' rights to their land which was being wrested from them by bandits for working for the drugs trade. He had paid for this with his life. Kathleen was adamant – they had to see for themselves where he had ministered to his people and they had to bring his body home. When they got there and witnessed the reverence and awe with which the grave was tended they realised that he could not be moved for the Toxteth blood which had dripped from the machetes had made the ground holy. He was already home.

The Mass in celebration of his life was thronged. The family who loved him, the bishops and priests he had inspired and the playmates with whom he could never keep up all gave thanks for his having come among them. And from then on, for those that had eyes to see,

Kathleen Donnelly's life was changed. The inner light that animates all of us grew dim in her. So it was not really that surprising when, four years later, they took the feisty, still beautiful, Liverpool girl who had learned to be a mother and a father and laid her to rest in Toxteth Park Cemetery.

Now well into his eighties, Kevin Donnelly lives on. As their family expanded, the couple went to live in Aigburth, close to the Serpentine. These days Kevin has a flat in a nearby development built on the site of a former girls' grammar school.

Using a stick these days, he walks each day to the river front in Grassendale Park returning home by way of Cressington Park and Salisbury Road. He takes special delight in meeting the young mothers with their children and so makes sure he has coins and confectionery to hand. Sometimes, however, he can be seen staring intently down river and then the mothers take care to shepherd their children quietly past him. What is he straining to look at?..... the approaches to the North Atlantic? a clearing in a fetid South American jungle? or a well-kept grave in Toxteth Park Cemetery?..... quite possibly, all three.

III

Dear Reader,

If you will indulge me for a few more seconds I can tell you what happened to one other character from our story.

In the first Chapter, we met Laurie Mather, the supremely gifted footballer who really wanted to be an accountant. As things turned out, he became neither professional footballer nor accountant. In 1943, the fateful year of the Hamburg firestorm, he died of starvation and repeated beatings in a Japanese prison camp.

Guide to futher reading

When I was familiarising myself with the background to the novel I found the following works helpful and I acknowledge my indebtedness to their authors. I commend these titles to anyone wishing to know more about a story that deserves to be told and retold.

Buchheim, Lothar- Günther
"Das Boot" (The Boat)
London: Cassell & Co, 1999 edn.

Edwards, Bernard
"The Quiet Heroes"
Barnsley, S. Yorks: Leo Cooper, 2003.

Lane, Tony
"The Merchant Seamen's War"
Liverpool: The Bluecoat Press, 1990.

Monserrat, Nicholas
"The Cruel Sea"
London: Penguin Books, 1956 edn. (reprinted 2002)

Woodman, Richard
"The Real Cruel Sea"
London: John Murray (Publishers), 2004
see also this author's "Arctic Convoys" published by John Murray, 1994.

"The Battle of the Atlantic", An Anthology of Personal Memories
Liverpool: Picton Press 1993
provides excellent first-hand memories of the Battle, while the following two works also give extremely vivid accounts of the lot of merchant seamen:

(i) "My name is Frank"
     Woking: Unwin Bros, 1941

(ii) Pearce-Jones, Guy
     "Two Survived"
     London: Hamish Hamilton, 1941

Obviously, both of these titles are now out of print, but can be accessed via the Archives Section of the Merseyside Maritime Museum.

Merseyside's Blitz of May 1941 is graphically described in the following publications:

Liverpool Daily Post and Echo Ltd (Authorised Reprint published by Scouse Press, Liverpool, 1983)
"Bombers Over Merseyside"
and the following Liverpool Echo Special Editions:
"Blitzed! The people's war," published July 3, 2000
and "The May Blitz", published April 30, 2001.

I hope you find these details helpful and I thank you again for reading "Those in Peril".

John Frain
Liverpool, 2005